# THE LAKEVIEW MANOR MURDERS

## Jim Wheeler

**Speculative Scatter Studio**

*To Mary*
*You told me I could do this. I want everyone to know that this one time you were right.*


*To Vietnam Veterans everywhere.*

# THE LAKEVIEW MANOR MURDERS

# PRESENT DAY

There are times when I feel like an old man whose better days are long gone. Today is one of those days. Now over seventy years old and semi-retired, I spend my free time sipping on Jack Daniels, reading Early American literature, and watching old movies. I will, however, take on an occasional case if it doesn't require any strenuous physical effort. So, when an attractive young woman wanted to hire this old warhorse of a detective to take on some tough guy who refused to leave her alone, I reluctantly sent her to a younger colleague. Forty years ago, I would have jumped at the chance to set the big boy straight, but those days have long since passed. In fact, considering the way I approached dirtbags like that, and along with my time in Vietnam, most people are surprised I managed to live this long.

Ironically, this is the month of August, and impressively hot just as it was back in 1979 when I met another young woman, an exquisite and mystifying beauty who hired me to clear her boyfriend of murder. Though many years ago, much of that case will never be forgotten. Still, I think I'll pull out the journal from that year just to refresh my memory.

Let's see . . . 1979. Ah, here it is . . . Yes, and the first page I turn to recounts my first encounter with the employees of the infamous Lakeview Manor Motel and Lounge.

1

# THURSDAY

## August 16, 1979

The first thing I noticed about the Lakeview Manor Motel & Lounge was that there was nothing to notice. Protected by an overgrown cluster of formidable evergreens that stood like sentries, the colonial inn and twenty individual cabins more closely resembled a military garrison than a welcoming lodge and restaurant. But the trees weren't sentries, nor were they formidable, because they did nothing to prevent the murder of Johnny Hodges.

Though nearly six in the evening, the parking lot was virtually empty, hardly a surprise considering I passed the entrance two times before spotting the wooden signpost partially obscured by neglected shrubbery. My curiosity then reached its peak when I drove down the secluded and extended driveway that concealed the mysterious establishment from the busy highway and the unsuspecting public. And even though few would consider me a cautious person, I decided to take it slow on my first murder case, parking my modified '67 Camaro in a slot facing the highway.

With no sign for a manager's office, I could choose to enter either the lounge or the dining room. Since a peanut butter and jelly sandwich was my only meal that day, I left the steaming August heat behind and walked up the steps of the rustic porch for a bite to eat.

At first glance, the frigid dining room resembled every mess hall I'd ever seen. Widespread and neatly arranged tables stood in rigid lines with salt and pepper shakers so perfectly placed that I lifted a pair to see if they were glued down, and even though public smoking had yet to be prohibited, no evidence of nicotine soiled the acoustic ceiling tiles or bare white walls. In fact, there was no detectable odor, sound, or even a breath of air to be felt, only the distant hum of an efficient air conditioner. All this, along with the shiny unscratched hardwood floors, seemed to be more than enough evidence to showcase a room held in reserve for a special occasion that had yet to arrive.

There were three other doors in the room, one that led to the kitchen, matching swinging doors to the lounge that resembled those that you'd see in a Western movie, and an emergency exit on the opposite side. The sign by the entrance said to seat yourself, so I took a table in the corner with my back against the wall and as far away from the lounge entrance as possible. Then I laughed at my paranoia, and waited . . .

And waited . . .

And waited.

My instincts told me to dislike the waitress when, and if, she decided to make an appearance, until finally, a large robust woman barged through the swinging louvered doors. Storming across the floor, stomping her feet along the way, she threw the menu onto the table and whipped out a pad from her apron like Annie Oakley drawing her gun at a Wild West show.

I smiled, hoping that a pleasant exchange might change her demeanor, then asked, "How's the food, Tex?"

"Best damn steaks in the state of Maryland."

The noticeable irritation in her raspy baritone made

it clear that the cowboy reference flew right over her head and, even worse, that my winning smile had no effect on her aggressive attitude. Our encounter worsened even further after I opened the menu and expressed an understandably honest, immediate, and obvious shock which brought about an antagonistic scowl accompanied by an impatiently tapping foot.

"You get what you pay for," she snapped.

Very true on many occasions, but taking note of the unused surroundings, I doubted that this dinner could possibly be worth such outrageous prices, and even though my client gave me the green light to spend any amount of money I deemed necessary to clear her boyfriend of the murder he didn't commit, it would have been unprofessional to take advantage, so I ordered a New York strip with a baked potato and salad.

Tex was a better bartender than a waitress. I had enough time to down three rail whiskeys before she brought the bread, and as it turned out, the booze provided an appropriate foundation for the most pathetic meal I ever had the misfortune to sample. The lettuce looked more blue than green, so I didn't try the salad, the potato came directly from the field without a visit to the oven, and the steak . . . The steak tasted like it might have come from either a part of the cow's hoof or a chunk from its hide. I swallowed as much as tolerable without gagging but finished only the bread which was less than a day away from stale.

Obvious that the pitiful food and substandard service purposely deterred business, it became abundantly clear that the Lakeview Manor's kitchen had no intention of earning a five-star review in the Happy Motorist Travel Guide. Until then, I had only known what my client told me, claiming that the Manor was simply a motel-restaurant-lounge where a high-class escort business operated. I immediately deleted restaurant from the description because the likelihood of the Manor earning a profit dishing out dinners of such poor quality challenged any sense of reason.

Kathy Radney was my client and one of the escorts that the recently deceased Johnny Hodges managed in the service he operated from the Manor. She insisted that most of the business was legitimate, but considering its hidden location, along with the indigestible quality of the food, her insistence only fueled my growing skepticism, especially after she finally admitted that some of her fellow escorts played around with their job descriptions.

I asked myself how the manager's death might affect the operation. Was he a shrewd businessman, or a shady hustler? A legitimate business could conceivably survive without him, but an illegal enterprise with hidden funds and privileged connections might fall with the death of the controlling force —that is unless another player stood behind Hodges waiting for a chance to take over. An obvious motive for murder and something to consider. I wondered if there might be a couple possibilities on the other side of the louvered doors that led to the lounge.

When my incompetent waitress finally returned with the check, I discreetly mentioned Johnny's name. She brushed me off with a vague grunt, then quickly retreated. But before I had a chance to think of a different approach, two impressive giants burst through the swinging doors even more quickly than Tex— and they weren't interested in my critique of the dinner.

"What's your problem?"

"I don't have a problem."

"You do now."

I was glad that I waited until after I ate—and before I paid the check—to have this problem. A professional ass-kicking is much less enjoyable on an empty stomach. A good dinner—or, in this case, any dinner, most of which was bread—softens the blows. And since the room was empty, no witnesses could testify how my tardy dinner guests tried their very best to persuade the outstanding feast to exit the same way it entered. Nevertheless, the food stayed down as the two heavyweights brutally pounded my body until they were satisfied with their work, adding the finishing touch by tossing me out of the dining room and onto the scorching parking lot.

"And don't come back."

Earlier that day, while fixing a peanut butter and jelly sandwich for lunch, I assumed that the gentle knock at the door of my office/apartment came from my neighbor's precocious eight-year-old son who loved to talk about old movies. Infatuated with Garson and Tierney, I couldn't wait to hear which one of their films he wanted to discuss. But when I opened the door, there stood a tall attractive young woman.

"Are you Jim Smith?"

"Yes."

"Jim Smith the private investigator?"

Since my name and occupation were clearly stenciled on the door, her insistence puzzled me.

"Yes, I'm Jim Smith. Please come in."

I motioned for the prospective client to take a seat in the chair by my desk, just a few steps from the door. The slight aroma of perfume sweetened the air as she passed. But before taking a seat, the young beauty turned to face me, then as tears filled her eyes, she broke down and collapsed on the chair. My heart immediately turned to mush. What hardship could possibly upset this exquisite creature? Did she lose her beloved cat? Could her basement be flooded because the water department inadvertently destroyed a vein near her home and refused to accept the blame? Or could her husband or boyfriend be running around, which would surely be the shock of the century? What man in his right mind would cheat on this beauty?

Through my few years of experience, I learned to throw together a quick, but usually accurate assessment of a client's character and intentions, but until that day, no woman had affected me so strongly. In her early twenties, and not particularly beautiful with classic features, this young woman more closely resembled a work of art that might hang in a museum, her appearance so striking that I would have chased down her cat, sucked the water from her basement, and beat the crap out of her husband or boyfriend just for being an idiot—all without asking for a dime. From the beginning, her inexplicable charm hypnotized me.

Sitting as comfortably as the worn chair allowed, elegant and erect like a model, tears streamed down her lovely face. Neatly dressed in black slacks and a white blouse, nothing tasteless or flashy, and with no pretentious jewelry, the stunning beauty personified anything, and everything, any man could desire. Visibly shaken over some trouble that required immediate attention, with her head bowed as if in prayer, she remained in that perfect posture. I walked over, gave her a tissue, and sat on the edge of my desk, leaning toward her.

"I'm here to help," speaking slowly in hopes of calming her down, "Whatever you need. Take your time and tell me the problem . . . Whenever you're ready."

I took a seat at my desk and patiently waited until she finally looked up and spoke, "A friend recommended you. He said you help veterans, especially those who served in Vietnam."

"I help anyone I can. Now, how can I help you?"

"It's my boyfriend." She paused, choked back a sniffle, then continued, "Well, he's probably not my boyfriend anymore . . . He's been arrested . . . for murder."

7

"Did you say murder?"

"Yes."

The midday light peeking through the blinds of my office window created a black and white atmosphere like a film noir movie from the forties. I became Humphrey Bogart meeting Mary Astor, another enigmatic beauty with a secret and a purpose in the classic Hammett mystery dealing with a priceless statue. But the character of Sam Spade was a seasoned detective, until then most of my experience had been limited to helping people with routine matters.

A case with the urgency and significance of murder was the break I needed. Not that I wanted someone to die for my benefit, but while everyday problems paid the bills and fed me, domestic issues like grass cutting, snow removal, and trash pickup provided very little challenge. Six years had passed since changing my major in college, deciding not to write about the wrongs that affected my life and those around me, but to confront the issues face to face. Fortunately, although unintentionally, I did build a reputation helping veterans get the benefits they deserved, and my more difficult cases brought about many uncomfortable confrontations with the government agencies that abused or ignored their obligations.

I wondered why the young woman came to me. Other than hearing about my history of helping veterans, she had no logical reason to hire me. The thought crossed my mind to recommend one of the more experienced investigators in the area, but only for a moment. After all, I got into the business to make a difference, and this attractive woman definitely needed help. I waited until she finally calmed down just enough for me to ask about her boyfriend's arrest.

"What's your name?"

"Kathy Radney."

"Okay, Kathy, I'm sure this will be difficult, but I want you to tell me exactly what happened, starting from the beginning."

Kathy wiped away the tears, then began by describing the escort service that operated from the Lakeview Manor Motel. As soon as she mentioned her workplace, I recalled the accused murderer's name, and that of the deceased, because a few days earlier the morning paper covered the murder and the subsequent police investigation. It seemed that Kathy's boyfriend, Chris Palmer, knew where she worked but heard from a friend that the business might be something more than an innocent escort service catering to an affluent clientele. That night Palmer went to the Manor to see for himself. A heated argument with Johnny Hodges broke out, and Kathy's boyfriend received the same rough treatment I would experience later that day. Sometime during the early morning hours—the coroner estimated his death at around 3 a.m. give or take a half hour—Hodges was shot in the head while sleeping in one of the motel's cabins. The police found out about the altercation and promptly arrested the boyfriend who had no alibi.

"He didn't do it, Mr. Smith. Chris is so gentle."

"If he's so gentle, why did he come to your place of business? He should have realized that confronting you at the Manor might cause a problem of some kind. He could have waited until he saw you later."

"I don't know why he came out to the Manor, and I'm sure he never wanted to cause any trouble. Chris knew that I worked as a hostess and sometimes as an escort, but before that night, he never told me about any suspicions he may have had." She paused, looked down at her tightly clenched hands, then raised her eyes to meet mine. "But when Johnny noticed Chris talking to me, he came over, and that's when something happened that I can't explain. I'm not sure why, but Johnny grabbed Chris. Chris looked at Johnny for just a moment before he tried to pull free. They struggled, but not for long because the bouncers came over and threw Chris out."

9

She leaned toward me with a pleading expression, "Please, Mr. Smith, isn't there something you can do?"

That simple gesture meant to issue a sincere plea accomplished just the opposite. Fascination gave way to doubt. A distant voice in my head told me that something didn't seem right. I thought about Bogart and Astor, recalling their first meeting when Astor's character struggled to make eye contact with the detective. Kathy, on the other hand, stared deeply into my eyes, hardly blinking though damp with tears. And yet, like the heroine in the classic movie concerning the jewel-encrusted falcon, this girl knew something more. I needed to maneuver through the developing smokescreen to find out what it was.

"Kathy, there must be more. You told me that Chris didn't suspect anything, but then he showed up to see for himself. It's hard to believe that your boyfriend didn't say something earlier about any suspicions he may have had. Are you sure he trusted you? I read about your boss's murder in the paper, and the state's attorney's office seems to think of this as an open and shut case. Now, if I'm going to help you and your boyfriend, you must be totally honest with me. What else is there?"

My prospective client sat silently still while I patiently waited. Finally, she looked up and stared at me with an uncomfortable expression, "The business does have a reputation."

"The kind that Chris suspected?"

She didn't answer. It had to be as he, and now I, believed it to be.

I asked the question that needed confirmation, "Kathy, is this reputation justified, or is it an exaggeration?"

Slowly, she answered, "I have heard . . . No, I *know* that some of the girls give their clients special treatment for extra money, but that is strictly their business, and if Johnny knew, he never encouraged it. I'm sure of this because he never asked me to do anything more than escort my clients to business functions or to the theater, and that's all. It's the truth, you must believe me."

Once again, mystery clashed with the now familiar prayerful pose. Was I being sucked in? And what about her boyfriend? Was Chris Palmer a sucker or an innocent pawn? I peered into those spellbinding eyes, teary with emotion, staring back at me. I'd seen working girls before, especially overseas; they all carried themselves in a way that advertised their line of work. This smartly dressed woman struck me as one more likely to hold an influential position in any of the firms whose executives she supposedly escorted. But could Ms. Radney possibly be a high-dollar call girl? I'd rather have complete confidence in my clients, but in this case, it didn't matter.

"I believe you, Kathy."

She smiled, "Thank you, Mr. Smith."

Okay, did I actually believe her, or was it because the case involved murder? I immediately dismissed the question from my mind.

"Now the hard part. If your boyfriend didn't kill your boss, who did?"

"Why are you asking me?"

"You knew him, and you know the people who worked for, and around him. From what you told me, and from what I can see, you were one of his more popular girls. Am I right?"

Kathy smiled and nodded.

"I thought so. Now, because of your popularity, you may know more than you think. Did Hodges have any enemies? Anyone who runs a business, especially one with something of a reputation, must have an enemy or two."

"I suppose there were a few people who didn't like Johnny, but not enough to kill him."

"Okay, has anything happened lately, something out of the ordinary, or even a little strange?"

"Well, there were always the rumors. And then there was the FBI."

"The FBI. That's certainly unusual; when did they come around?"

I rummaged through my desk, looked for, then took out a legal pad. The search took a little less than a minute, but Kathy waited as if she knew what I needed, beginning only after I found a pencil and looked up.

"It went on for about a week, no longer," she continued. "They finished just before Johnny was killed. Three agents questioned the girls, especially the two Asian girls Johnny hired last spring. Then they questioned the bartenders, the waitresses, and the bouncers, but they leaned the hardest on Johnny and Mr. Barlowe. I remember that because Mr. Barlowe was really upset with Johnny because the agents treated them like criminals."

"Who's Barlowe?"

"That's Frank Barlowe; he's the manager of the Manor."

Kathy paused as I wrote down his name, then she continued by giving me all the details we had already covered. I recorded my notes as she spoke, each word clear and distinct, as if she was afraid I might miss something.

"Like I said, the agents were incredibly tough on Johnny and Mr. Barlowe. They treated them like criminals."

"But when the agents questioned you, didn't you have some idea why they were there, or didn't they tell you what it was that they were investigating?"

"No, but why would they tell me anything?"

"Well, the vice squad would investigate any alleged prostitution concerning the rumors, but the Asian girls you mentioned might have been illegal which would have brought out the feds, or possibly immigration officials. Didn't their questions give you any indication that the new girls might be the reason for their investigation?"

"No. I'm sorry, Mr. Smith, I don't even remember the questions. Like I said before, they leaned really hard on Johnny and Mr. Barlowe."

"Yeah, I know. You already said that."

I found myself gazing at the mystifying girl, struggling to focus on her account of the business at the Manor and the murder itself. Those stunning eyes simply stared back, a touch glassy like a scolded puppy who had just chewed his owner's favorite slipper. And yet her demeanor didn't seem the slightest bit ruffled. Even in the early afternoon heat of my office, cooled only by the small rotating fan on my desk, Kathy hadn't broken a sweat. I began to have doubts. Did she rehearse this story, or was she coached and told what to say?

"Kathy, the FBI wouldn't waste their time on an investigation unless it was in their jurisdiction."

Kathy cocked her head with a puzzled expression, "I'm not sure I understand what you mean."

Her indifference strained my patience.

"Come on, Kathy, you work for a business that supplies escorts, and who knows what else for money. Now, even though you've told me different, I suspect that your boss, and also this Barlowe character, encouraged the girls to give clients the special treatment you mentioned and then take their cut. Not only that, but it also appears that your boss acquired some Asian girls from an international pool of some kind, a business move that more than likely prompted the visit from federal agents. That's the part I find curious. Now, didn't you see anything suspicious? Or didn't you ever see Hodges or Barlowe treat any of the customers differently?"

"No, I didn't. Honest."

Clearly on the defensive, yet only the slightest bit agitated, she continued to maintain her innocence.

"Johnny never wanted any of us to do anything that might hurt the service. His instructions were always to accompany our clients to business functions or to the theater. While it's true that some of the other girls may have crossed the line, I never did. I swear!"

Then, after that emphatic declaration, she hung her head.

Kathy's story was hard to believe. After many skirmishes with government agencies, especially federal agencies, it became clear to me that they waste very little of their valuable time and effort on some impulsive or uncertain investigation. I stalled, curious to see how Kathy would react to even more hesitation. I looked down at my notes and scratched my head. Not a minute passed before another eruption of tears sprang out.

"I knew it. I shouldn't have come here. I knew you wouldn't believe me."

She jumped up from the chair, and with the grace of a ballet dancer, turned an elegant pirouette and headed for the door.

"Get back here," I yelled.

She stopped, paused a moment, then spun around to face me with a defiant glare. I couldn't let her go.

"Please . . . Sit back down."

She obeyed, but back in the manner of the scolded puppy.

"Kathy, I'm not going to judge you, so don't try to defend yourself, it's only a waste of time."

I gave her another tissue that I might offer a grieving wife crying over her unfaithful husband, the compassionate act that precedes a referral to one of my competitors better qualified to deal with the emotions that accompany domestic struggles. But Kathy had cast a spell on me that was not only dictated by her appearance. Some unique and unseen charm compelled me to take her case.

"Okay, that's enough for now. How can I reach you?"

"Does this mean that you're going to help Chris?"

I smiled, "That's what it means."

"You can reach me at my new job," she said proudly. "It's a dress shop in the mall not far from the Manor. Here's the number."

"Can't I call you at home?"

"Yes, but I'm seldom there; I'll give you that number anyway, but try me at the store first."

Not often at home seemed strange to me, but I took both numbers before discussing my fee. A minute later, almost as in a dream, the enchantress was gone; all that remained was the scent of her perfume and the memory of those hypnotic eyes. But in the time that it took to pour a Jack Daniels over ice, and as her haunting image faded, one overwhelming thought replaced Kathy's mystical charm: I was convinced—for no other reason than intuition—that an innocent man was suffering in jail.

And yet, Kathy's story seemed so questionable that I wondered what reasoning persuaded me to swallow it hook, line, and almost sinker. The testimony she gave, especially concerning the uncertain reputation of the escort service, seemed so contrived, or at least rehearsed, that I wondered if the beauty had revealed all she knew. My bewildering client repeated a couple phrases word for word, an indication of rehearsal from being coached. But what motive could there be for hiring me if pretense was her game? During that first interview, I sensed a certain amount of dishonesty—something I will not tolerate in a client—so I pumped up my fee to match that of my competitors. That decision wasn't based on greed, but rather a test of Kathy's true intention, a test easily passed when she paid my advance in cash doled out in hundred-dollar bills—just as Mary Astor had given Bogart.

I laughed at myself, took a heavy swallow of Jack and a bite of my peanut butter and jelly sandwich. A pretty face was clouding my usual better judgment—and not for the first time. That overwhelming compulsion to protect, defend, and ultimately rescue any damsel in distress, told me to ignore all the alarms and suspicions I felt concerning my new client's story.

And of course: Murder! No need for any of the gentle persuasion I reluctantly used when dealing with politicians and bureaucrats who overlooked their obligations. For this case, I would interview and interrogate suspects who may have killed someone. I could actually see myself in the role of Sam Spade.

But Kathy's charm and a chance to crack a murder case wasn't my only consideration. Women confused me. It didn't matter if they were pretty or plain, tall or short, heavy or slight, my parents taught me to protect and respect all women. As a result, I could easily be taken in. Since most of my clients at that time were men, the issue affected very few of my cases, so I hoped that this encounter with such an enigmatic client might provide valuable experience for my business, and possibly in my personal life as well. Not that I considered having an affair with my client—an unprofessional act to say the least—but a little playful sparring might provide something of an education along with some free entertainment.

Nevertheless, there would be no entertainment of any kind until I addressed the serious issue that demanded my attention. I downed the last drop of Jack and headed for the county jail.

◆ ◆ ◆

Ed Polhaus was the duty sergeant at the county jail, a

cop I'd known since he arrested me when I was searching for a missing teenage girl, an incident we both still laugh about, but a misunderstanding that wasn't so funny at the time. As soon as he saw me, Ed came out from behind the desk and shook my hand as if we'd been friends for longer than just a few years.

"How you doin', Jimbo?"

"I'm doing fine. How about you, Sarge, is everything okay? I don't usually see you in uniform sitting behind a desk. I also noticed a little bit of a limp when you walked over here. What did you do . . . slip on a bar of soap?"

He laughed, "Took a shot in the leg about a week ago; it wasn't serious, but they put me on light duty for the month. I'd rather be on the street, but rules are rules. So, what brings you up here . . . got a client?"

"Yes sir, Chris Palmer."

Ed gave me a sympathetic look and slowly shook his head. "Sorry, my friend, but I think you picked a loser this time. That poor kid doesn't have much going his way. He won't open his mouth, not a word to anybody, not even to his parents . . . has his mother in tears every time they visit, and they've been here every day."

"Haven't seen the girlfriend?"

"Didn't even know he had one. Maybe she came when I was on break. I could check the log if you want."

"No, don't bother. I'll check in with her later. I'm sure she has her reasons. All right to go in?"

"Sure." Ed pushed the buzzer to let me pass, then added, "It's good to see somebody stepping up to help that kid, and I'm glad it's you. Seems like a nice guy who got mixed up with the wrong crowd . . . just the kind you know how to handle." He laughed again, "You have to admit that you do get along with the wrong crowd better than most, Jimbo."

I laughed, too, but it wouldn't have been funny if I knew then what would happen later that day with the wrong crowd at the Manor.

Any other visitor would have been thoroughly searched, but Sergeant Polhaus allowed me to pass without emptying my pockets. I walked down the corridor to the visitors' room, sat on a bench and waited. It wasn't an eternity, not as long as the wait for service at the Manor would be, but there was more than enough time to read the graffiti penciled and scratched into the tables and benches, some of it humorous, some desperate, but sadly, most a scathing indictment on our modern society.

Finally, the cellblock door opened and the prisoner was escorted into the room. The jail attendant, another officer I knew, just looked at me and shrugged his shoulders.

"Here he is, Jimbo. Good luck. And you're going to need it."

Chris was tall, about six-three, wearing baggy prison overalls that failed to hide a muscular build. His features were almost child-like, the reason Sergeant Polhaus referred to him as a kid even though he had to be about my age, somewhere around thirty. The babyface, a direct contradiction to his physique, didn't make Chis an inbred murderer, but thanks to some criminal sociologist's classification, the state's attorney would ignore his boyish features and compute his physical capability and all the other evidence into a pretty good case for a conviction.

The prisoner took no more than three steps into the room when he stopped and stood at attention like a military recruit. Standing about six feet away from me, stiff as a buck private, impassively staring at the emptiness in front of him, his appearance and demeanor caught me off guard. Hardly breathing, hands at his side, the prisoner refused to look at me. Chris Palmer could have been anything from a monk to an axe murderer. And yet, his tired and puffy eyes told me more than I needed to know. Somehow, the events at the Manor, and his subsequent arrest, had turned my client into a soul with no emotion.

"Hello, Chris, are they treating you okay?"

No answer. He either disliked my asinine question, or he disliked me personally. Since we had never met, I hoped it was the question.

"Take a seat, I'm here to help you."

Still no response, only an infrequent slow blink of his tired eyes that made him look like he could fall asleep at any moment.

"I'm sorry, Chris, I know how tough this must be for you. My name is Jim Smith. I'm a private investigator. Your girlfriend hired me; she seems to think I can get you out of this mess."

Sincerity produced the same effect, even after mentioning Kathy. Chris's position and appearance never changed. I stood to face him, trying to make eye contact.

"Kathy believes you're innocent and, from all she told me, so do I. It would help if you could answer a few questions."

As I tried to prompt any kind of reaction, the accused killer's demeanor remained the same. The young veteran must have surrendered to what he believed to be an inevitable outcome, and even worse, he didn't care. How could I get through to him? But though not a word passed between us, his pathetic appearance revealed one undeniable fact to me if to no one else: Chris Palmer did not kill Johnny Hodges.

It was then that I decided to make the trip to the Lakeview Manor Motel.

◆ ◆ ◆

So there I lay, bruised and bloody, finally gaining my senses on the parking lot of the infamous Lakeview Manor

Motel. An obstinate ambition to find justice for Chris Palmer put me there. My client didn't deserve to be in jail for a crime he didn't commit, and I didn't deserve that beating for trying to help.

I got up and stumbled to my car. Police Sergeant Ben Quincannon—my best friend since we met in Vietnam ten years earlier—convinced me that, after establishing the habit of aggravating as many people as I do, carrying a gun would be a good idea. Though reluctant at first, we compromised, and I rigged a secret compartment under the dashboard, large enough to hold the snub-nosed .38 we agreed on.

I took the gun from its hiding place and shoved it into the waistband at the middle of my back. It felt awkward. One would think that after serving three years in the army, carrying a firearm would seem natural to me, but the truth is that I dislike guns, preferring instead a good old-fashioned donnybrook— but a fair contest, not two against one, especially when they don't even give you a chance to stand up. Until that day, the .38 remained securely tucked away, but as Ben predicted, the day had arrived when drastic measures needed to be taken. The pain validated his prophecy. That much punishment was unnecessary and unjustified. I didn't expect such an extreme reaction to an innocent question about the deceased. A stern warning would have been enough to send most people away.

But I'm not most people.

Though fully aware that it was probably a wasted effort, I went back to the dining room. As expected, my new enemies had retreated, but I needed a little extra time to calm down after the working over they gave me. For the first time in my career as an investigator, I was carrying a gun—not the time to lose control.

I cautiously approached the swinging doors that were so much like those from a Western saloon and peered over the top. Two steps led down to a dimly lit room, the likes of which I had never seen. Four rows of small black high-top tables with two chairs each filled the room and were the only furnishings. Hanging paintings, best described as nineteenth-century porn, decorated the dark blue walls. To the left of the room was the manager's office; the door was closed. There were no windows and no dance floor or stage for a band, but stretching from the exit on my right to the opposite wall stood a bar that was about forty feet long, also painted black as the night. Even the ceiling tiles were black.

The obvious conclusion struck me. That's why the entrance from the busy highway was so well hidden, and that's why the motel had no outside or separate office to check in for a room like most. The dark atmosphere. The obscene wall art. The Lakeview Manor was no motel, and it was surely no restaurant nor the home for some innocent escort service.

The Lakeview Manor was, without question, a brothel.

At the far end of the bar sat my two enemies I now assumed to be the bouncers Kathy mentioned and across from them, behind the bar, stood a tall slender bartender. I swung open the doors and started down the steps. The incompetent waitress who served me the garbage they called dinner had been sitting at the near end of the bar, but as soon as she saw me, quickly ran out, leaving her smoking cigarette behind.

"Hey, Cliff," the bartender said, "Look who's back . . . This guy must have a bigger problem than we thought."

The big man laughed, "Yep, time to get back to work."

Slowly, like in old Dodge City on Saturday night, I walked toward the two men.

"I don't know why you guys are afraid of a couple questions," I said, now only a couple feet away. "I'm just a struggling reporter trying to make a living."

"Fuck you and fuck your living,"

The profane attempt at intimidation came from the bartender who seemed confident that I was about to take another fall. After that, time slowed to a frame-by-frame cowboy movie showdown as the big man the bartender referred to as Cliff stood to face me. He closed in, drew back his fist while the other, almost reluctantly, stepped away from his stool. It was during those few seconds that I recalled all the undeserved beatings I took as a youngster before learning that hurting some son-of-a-bitch who was trying to hurt me felt better than turning the other cheek. It wasn't until my junior year in high school that I won my first fight, splitting a senior's nose and sending him running to the nurse. Like the two bouncers at the Manor, the senior was twice my size, which he thought gave him the advantage. As it turned out, these two musclemen were physical clones of my first victim: all power, only a little speed, and with no technique at all.

Cliff attacked. I snatched the big man's fist, threw my knee hard into his groin, crushed his nose with my forehead, then shoved him down to the ground where he landed in the fetal position. With time to spare, I circled the other, elbowed his kidney, and sent him off to sleepy land with the butt of my gun which I then leveled at the bartender who hadn't enough time to raise the sawed-off shotgun hanging at his side.

"Put the gun on the bar." He complied. "That's good. You should keep that in a higher place if you expect to use it."

Even scrawnier and shorter than I thought, the bartender stood no taller than five-eight or nine and weighed a hundred pounds at most. The sub-floor behind the bar made him look that much bigger. He had a huge nose that looked out of place on such a skinny face, vacant blue eyes, and a pockmarked complexion. Not as frightened as he should be with my .38 pressed against his forehead, the skinny man grinned as he feverishly chewed on a large wad of gum that smelled like spearmint while his foot tapped a violent rhythm, his body swaying from side to side.

"What's your name?"

"None of your fucking business."

That irritating smug smile made me want to pistol whip him right there, but I needed information more. Keeping the bouncers in sight, I slowly switched the .38 to my left hand, took the shotgun with my right, and leaned it against the side of the bar beside me. The bartender stared at me, though at times he would glance over at the two men lying on the floor, one clearly knocked out, while the other endured his pain in a fetal position, holding one hand on his bloody nose and the other on his throbbing testicles. Without knowing Cliff's pain tolerance, whatever needed to be done had to be done quickly.

With the next glance at his friends, I grabbed the bartender by the throat with my free hand, jerking his body toward me, lifting him off the floor, and shoving the gun barrel hard against his temple. His breathing quickened, but he never stopped chewing. I put my nose as close to his as possible without looking cross-eyed. His smirk disappeared.

"I'll ask you just one more time: What's your name?"

"Fuck you."

I bit his nose, drawing blood. "Wrong answer. What's your name?"

"Brewer . . . Brewer, you mother fucker." He shook his head, sending specks of blood flying, along with the wad of gum that landed on the bar. "Man, you're in big trouble. You don't know who you're fuckin' with."

"Yeah, you and your friends keep telling me I have a problem, but for now the problem is all yours, and it's pressed against your head. I want answers, and I want them now. You can start by telling me if you were working the night Johnny Hodges was killed."

"Yeah, I was behind the bar when the kid attacked Johnny."

"How serious did it get?"

"How serious did what get?"

God, he was scrawny; my thumb and fingers almost met at the back of his neck. Even lighter than I thought, it took very little effort to yank the bony bartender over the bar and onto the floor. Turning him so the other two would be in my line of sight, I straddled his body, gave him a love tap with my gun, then shoved the muzzle into his mouth. Good timing because Cliff, still bleeding from his broken nose, was struggling to get up, "You son-of-a-bitch."

"Don't think about it, cowboy, or I'll blow you away right after I deal with this scumbag." The big man stopped his attempt to stand so I turned my attention back to the bartender gasping through my chokehold on his throat.

"Let's get this straight, Mr. Brewer, I ask the questions and you provide the answers. When I pull out the gun, those answers had better follow. Now, did Johnny Hodges attack Chris Palmer the night he was killed?"

I pulled out the gun, chipping a tooth along the way with the tip of the barrel. He struggled for a breath.

"No, that kid grabbed Johnny, but Cliff and Pinkie jumped in before the chump could do any damage." He reached for his mouth, "You bastard! Look what you did to my tooth!"

"Don't worry about your tooth; I'm sure you have a dental plan."

Then I did a double take.

"Pinkie?"

"Yeah, Pinkie."

"Okay, you're doing better, keep talking."

"What else do you want me to say? I told you. Cliff and Pinkie threw him out. He screamed that he'd be back."

"What about Hodges?"

"Business as usual. Johnny was an ice cube; nothing ever got to him. After we closed, he went to his cabin, and I took him his bottle."

"Did you always do that?"

"Do what?"

"Take him a bottle, idiot."

"Yeah."

"Was he alone?"

"Yeah, by then all the girls were gone, but he never took anyone with him anyway."

"What about the FBI?"

"What about 'em?"

I squeezed my grip around his neck and looked over at Cliff who still hadn't moved but was intently looking my way as he wiped the blood from his nose. I needed to hurry.

"You can't be this stupid."

"Le'go," he garbled. I eased my grip. "They just snooped around, like you, you bastard."

"What questions did they ask?"

"Just some bullshit."

"And what bullshit answer did you give them?"

"Nothin' man, I ain't no rat."

"Who owns this place?"

"How the fuck do I know."

I banged his head against the bar.

"Some fucking conglomerate, man. I'm gonna kill you, mother fucker."

"Like you killed your boss?" I doubted that he could be that stupid but asked anyway.

"Hell no, look at this place. I'll be lucky if I keep my job."

I released his neck and smiled at the bartender and his friends. It was time to go. I walked around the tables, away from the two men on the floor, and backed slowly toward the exit, but just before making it out the door came the same predictable warning: "Don't come back, mother fucker." It was Brewer's hoarse voice. "You don't know who you're fucking with."

"Hey, man, you definitely need to do something about that nasty language."

I hurried to my car, got in and closed the door. Before replacing the .38 in its hiding place, I noticed it was empty. There was never a need to load it before that night. So, while driving away, between shifts, I loaded the cylinder. A stupid mistake that had more to do with luck—the next time fortune may not be on my side. Little did I know that the next time would happen sooner than I thought.

# FRIDAY

## *August 17, 1979*

I've suffered from insomnia since my parents died the summer after my high school graduation. While an advantage in Vietnam, I assumed the condition would go away after my discharge from the Army, but it never has, even to this day. Power naps help, but three or four intermittent hours of sleep a night are normal for me. During that humid night in August of 1979, those few hours would have been a blessing, and yet I slept thirty minutes at most as my body ached from Cliff's and Pinkie's pounding.

The bouncers' assault concentrated on my midsection, though they did leave me with a busted lip and a decent sized lump on my head, the result of an awkward landing on the Manor's asphalt parking lot after they launched me off the porch. Thank God there were only three steps or the damage could have been worse. Still, no matter how bad I feel on any given morning, there is one daily habit that I seldom miss: my three-mile run.

Friday was hotter than the day before. After jogging only two miles, and skipping the usual intermediate wind sprints, I went home, took a cold shower, scrambled a couple eggs, and tried to restore some measure of energy. An uneasy stress joined forces with the physical pain. While eating breakfast, I wondered if Kathy chose the right man for this job, thinking that my client might have been better off retaining a more experienced investigator. Be that as it may, she made the choice . . . I decided to go on.

My instinctive belief in Chris Palmer's innocence needed tangible evidence to convince the police to reconsider their investigation. After all, Kathy Radney had given me little to go on, Chris Palmer wasn't talking, and the visit to the Manor didn't produce the result I thought it might. There had to be another lead to follow that wouldn't come from my client or Chris.

Before I left the jail following my unproductive meeting with the accused, Sergeant Polhaus gave me Chris's parents' phone number. Seeing them could prove to be a waste of my time and theirs, but I hoped they could give me some insight into Chris's character that would explain his attitude. Also, it was just possible that they might provide some credible—and less painful—leads to follow.

Mrs. Palmer gave me directions to a working-class neighborhood in a section of Baltimore County not far from the Manor where neatly trimmed lawns and colorful flowers decorated the houses in spite of the oppressive heat. Built just after World War II, the houses were older than you might find in that part of the county, their stucco exteriors predating the exodus of the working class from the city along with the majority of the factory and shipbuilding jobs lost to foreign and political interests.

After his son's arrest, Mr. Palmer, a college professor, took a leave of absence, interrupting the philosophy class he taught during the summer semester. And even though the emotional stress must have weighed heavy on his mind, Tom Palmer nonetheless tried to make small talk as the three of us sat on the porch drinking coffee.

"What do you think about electing a female president, Mr. Smith?" Mr. Palmer asked. "Now that England voted in that Thatcher woman as prime minister, Mrs. Palmer thinks it's a good idea."

"I think I'll claim the fifth, sir."

"In that case, you are either a very smart young man, or a politician. Which is it?"

We all laughed even though the Palmers couldn't have known the absurdity of the question: I have never been accused of being a politician.

"Well," he added, "I told Nancy that all the females in America would vote for any woman for no other reason than she's a woman without giving the issues a second thought. As for me, I'd vote for the man from Mars if I thought he . . ." then, with a playful glance toward his wife, "*or she* would straighten out this irresponsible government. Oh, and another thing—"

"Thomas," his wife interrupted, "Mr. Smith did not drive all the way out here to discuss politics."

"As usual, you're right, dear." Mr. Palmer dropped his head.

Mrs. Palmer looked at me with helpless eyes, "He rants whenever something else is bothering him."

As Mr. Palmer said, his wife was right, questions needed to be asked—but not before emphasizing a promise I hoped to keep: "Mr. and Mrs. Palmer, I *will* get Chris out of this mess." Then I asked if they knew Kathy Radney.

"No," Mrs. Palmer answered, "we only knew he was dating."

"And the Lakeview Manor Motel?"

"Never heard of it," Mr. Palmer said, "but I think there's something you need to know: Chris has problems."

"What kind of problems?"

Mr. Palmer glanced over at his wife who started to cry. He got up from his chair and sat next to her on the metal glider. Then after taking her hand and kissing her cheek, he continued, "Chris changed after his discharge . . . after Vietnam. Sleepless nights, and tremors during the day that he tried to hide." Chris's father slowly shook his head. "Bad nights, calling out when he did sleep. We heard him crying. I wanted to help, but he wouldn't let me, and he became angry when I suggested he talk to someone at the VA."

In 1979, no one wanted to hear about the Vietnam War, much less veterans' issues like PTSD. In fact, that clinical acronym wasn't adopted until a year or so later, having previously been referred to as combat stress reaction, shell shock, or battle fatigue. Hiding the misery became preferable to revealing a condition that some judged a weakness. And while many try to ignore the distasteful realities in this world, the attitudes nurtured by exposure to extreme violence—whether it be in a jungle six thousand miles away, or in one's own neighborhood—can't be turned off with the flick of a switch. Ironically, that argument would accompany the evidence the state's attorney would use to convict Chris.

It was after hearing about Chris's struggle with his emotional misery that I began to form a theory, a theory strengthened even further after meeting the friend who took Chris to the Manor the night of the murder.

◆ ◆ ◆

The warehouse where Chris Palmer worked was easy to find, and so was Tony Sellers. Mr. and Mrs. Palmer both disliked the man, and the justification for their feelings became immediately apparent. Their physical description was perfect: an overweight, filthy-looking excuse for a human being, smelling of cheap cologne—generously applied to conceal an apparent aversion to soap and water—wearing sloppy and shabby clothing, outrageous even for dirty and difficult work, and flaunting a constant and oppressive sneer as evidence of his demeanor. His appearance expressed an obvious desire to be left alone, and alone is how I found him eating lunch on the loading dock.

"Are you Tony Sellers?"

"Who wants to know?"

"My name is Jim Smith; I've been hired to help Chris Palmer."

"That guy's gonna need some help; in fact, he's gonna need a miracle." He laughed, but I didn't see anything funny about having a friend accused of murder.

"Then you won't mind answering a few questions."

"Hell no, I'll do anything I can to help a buddy."

"Why did you take Chris to the Lakeview Manor that night?"

He shifted his ample weight to one side—like someone about to fart—took a large bite out of his sandwich, then spoke without swallowing the mouthful, "Actually, it's kind of a crazy coincidence . . ."

*Coincidence!* I refused to accept this man as an instrument of fate.

"This friend of mine, who comes to town from time to time, went to the Manor 'cause he heard about finding some action out there. So he tells me he had this real good time . . . know what I mean . . . and it just so happens that, while he's telling me about it here at lunch . . . really, just like now . . . Chris's girl shows up, and all of a sudden he tells me she's the one. So I says, 'the one what,' and he says, 'she's the broad who showed me the real good time.' Know what I mean? Well, I hustled my friend out real quick so the girl don't see him, but it probably wouldn't have mattered anyway."

"What makes you say that?"

"Come on, man, a girl like that must have shown a good time to dozens of guys . . . and probably in the same night."

I ignored his assumption; naïve or not, there was no way I could picture Kathy with dozens of guys.

"Then what did you do?"

"I told Chris."

An involuntary grimace on my part immediately put Sellers on the defensive.

"What the hell, man, I had to. What would you have done?"

"I'm not sure; what made you think you had to tell him?"

"Hey, man, I don't care what anybody thinks, including his snobby parents (*snobby?*), it ain't right for some broad to make a chump out of a guy, especially a guy like Chris. He's the closest thing to a friend I have; these other guys are just ignorant bastards. He told me how much he loved that bitch, so there was no way I'd let her use him like that. And more than that . . ."

As he talked, I looked around the loading dock so I wouldn't have to make eye contact. In a word, the man was repulsive. Sellers never stopped feeding his face while he talked, spraying such a considerable amount of his lunch in my direction that standing to the side became the only way to keep the pieces of food from sticking to my sweat-soaked shirt.

I caught sight of a fly on the warehouse floor that seemed to be moving in a manner unlike a normal, healthy, annoying pest. Staggering across the floor, apparently unable to fly, the insect was obviously dying, one side paralyzed in such a way that only the other struggled to propel its body through a rigid and unalterable path, most likely a victim of some insecticide. I looked back at Sellers and tried to make sense of the baloney—no pun intended—that spewed from his mouth.

"Okay, so how did Chris take it?"

"Take what?"

Unbelievable. Could he be as stupid as Brewer?

"How did he take the news that his girlfriend might be a prostitute?"

"*Might be*? Hell, he took it like you seem to, he didn't believe me. I hated to break his heart, but I had to prove it to the big dope. That's why I took him to the Manor, to show him just what a wicked bitch his girl is."

The crippled fly spun more quickly, summoning some source of unknown energy, but now in a predetermined circle.

"During the drive up there, did Chris seem angry?"

"What do you mean?"

"Come on, it's not that hard a question. Was Chris angry, or was he worried that it might be true, and that Kathy was lying to him about her job?"

"Hell, I don't know. He didn't say nothin' in the car, and when we got there, I was too busy looking at all those good-lookin' broads to notice anything else. One thing I do know, the minute he saw his girl with that Hodges dude, Chris went nuts. I couldn't believe it was the same guy. He pushed the bitch out of the way and jumped Hodges. Chris is a big boy, if those two bouncers hadn't stopped him, Chris would have killed him right there and then."

The doomed fly moved more slowly.

"So you think Chris is capable of murder?"

"Aren't we all?"

I ignored his asinine attempt at philosophy.

"Where did Chris go after they kicked him out?"

"How the hell would I know?"

"You said he's your only friend; didn't you go after him?"

"Hell no. How would I know he'd need an alibi? Besides, there's no way I could have caught him. I did look outside, but he was gone. I don't even know how he got home, or if he went home at all."

I lifted my foot to step on the fly and relieve its suffering, but before committing the act of mercy, the insect surrendered to the inevitable, rolled onto its side, and died in the dirt and dust of the loading dock. In the meantime, Sellers chomped away on the roll that held a large portion of cheese and some kind of meat, no telling what kind, and not important either, it could have been horse meat and the fat slob would have devoured it. Animals eat with more manners. I looked down at the fly lying dead on the grungy warehouse floor that became its grave. The insect had more dignity.

I needed a drink. Why in the world would anyone befriend such an obnoxious lower form of life? The man sickened me. And the idea that Kathy would show any friend of Sellers a good time in the way he implied seemed ludicrous. Unlike the lunch he so easily gobbled down, the fat slob's story was hard to swallow. So, after that meeting, I considered the scant evidence concerning Hodges' murder and managed to put together a possible scenario.

My instincts screamed out that Sellers couldn't be trusted, especially since his version of the confrontation at the Manor differed from Kathy's, even though similar to Brewer's given that they both said Chris attacked Hodges. But in my mind, the unbelievable "coincidence" involving his friend and Kathy introduced the possibility that Sellers could be part of my developing theory that some person, or group of persons, set Chris up to take the fall for a murder they had already planned. Whether my reticent client was part of the original scheme, or just a lucky break that came along, remained to be seen, but some sort of preconceived framework seemed the only possible explanation for Chris Palmer's involvement.

I drove back to the refuge of my office, quickly poured the generous dose of Jack that I needed so badly, downed it, and poured another. My system needed a jolt and a sterile cleansing after the sickening encounter with Sellers.

My office is actually a small one-bedroom apartment located in southeast Baltimore County, but less than a mile from the city line, and not far from the marine terminals. It's a good location for my business, providing clients from the middle class, many of whom work in the port facilities supported by the harbor. The pay isn't great, but my needs are simple. Sergeant Polhaus wasn't wrong when he suggested that I get along better with the lower classes. The rich and entitled have very little in common with me. To my way of thinking, money is a necessity, not a desire, preferring the simple and self-reliant lifestyle inspired by Henry David Thoreau. Like him, I'd live in a cabin in the woods if I could find one.

Other than knowing about his struggle with PTSD, I had no realistic perception of my client's wants and needs. He may have never even heard of Thoreau. Just the same, I assumed that Chris also lived a simple life, a good part of which included searching for the woman of his dreams. And yet, if the fractured fairy tale given by Sellers had even an ounce of credibility, then Kathy certainly wasn't the right girl for Chris. More than that, and as much as it pained me, I needed to accept the possibility that my faith in the mystifying beauty bordered on naïveté.

A weakness for the opposite sex has been a problem since adolescence. Even though I am totally, and sometimes uncomfortably, aware that women are strong and more than capable of taking care of themselves, some obstinate compulsion to come to their rescue inspires my actions. So, when Kathy Radney first came to me, that impulse took over. In my judgment, my client didn't seem to me to be a prostitute—at least as described by Sellers—but to what extent did she actively participate in the escort business? And yet, if she was connected to the murder—even in the slightest—why hire a detective who might expose that connection?

Putting those questions aside, I concentrated on the more immediate problem: Chris Palmer suffering in jail for a crime he didn't commit. Inexperienced or not, something had to be done. Sellers believed that anyone could commit murder, and if I hadn't been in such a hurry to get away from him, I would have argued the point. Besides, there were more than enough candidates at the Manor with better reasons for wanting Hodges dead, much better than an angry outburst from Chris. And even though Sellers had no apparent connection to my new friends at the Manor, could it be possible that taking Chris out there was his role in a conspiracy?

I threw together a cup of instant coffee and a ham sandwich. Not that I was hungry, but the two quickly downed drinks were clouding my judgment and affecting my concentration as mental pictures of Kathy, Sellers, and the mob at the Manor danced around in my mind. Past experience handling combative personalities would be an advantage, but my lack of patience had already caused considerable pain, so a certain amount of caution became the order of the day.

After setting up a standing rotating fan to help the small one on my desk circulate the stagnant air, I sat down and found another legal pad—the first one with the names that Kathy had given me at our first meeting had mysteriously vanished. Its disappearance bothered me, but I ignored my carelessness and wrote down the names from memory:

Chris Palmer

Kathy Radney

Johnny Hodges (I drew a line through his name)

Brewer

Cliff and Pinkie

Tony Sellers

Listing names and related government agencies is my usual habit. The practice focuses my attention on an otherwise disorganized situation. I leave enough space between entries to record my thoughts and reactions as circumstances dictate, but in this case, there wasn't enough time to form any reasonable impressions. Other than the line drawn through the murdered man's name, I added "victim" next to Chris, "creep" next to Sellers, and a question mark beside Kathy's name. Where did these names take me? An aggressive and determined visit to some gutless bureaucrat wouldn't find Hodges' killer, but I couldn't believe that another impulsive confrontation with the beefy bouncers at the Manor was my only option.

Something was missing. I couldn't put my finger on it. Staring at those names pumped my adrenalin to a rush like the days in the jungles of Vietnam when I felt an NVA soldier hiding behind the treeline. I needed to slow down. Other than one job involving a missing teenage girl, none of my previous cases resulted in the kind of physical confrontation that took place at the Manor because the politicians and government bureaucrats I usually confronted promptly cooperated when faced with truth or exposure. Those successful negotiations came about because I had the facts to back me up. I needed evidence to free Chris, and so far, none was available. The visit to the Lakeview Manor Motel—the murder scene that held the secrets in the matter of Johnny Hodges' murder—surrendered nothing more than an undeserved physical pounding.

And then there was the newest character: Tony Sellers. The whisper in my ear that I'd heard so often grew louder, telling me that his connection was no coincidence. Was taking Chris to the Manor part of the plan that would bring about a confrontation between the two men, setting the framework in place? For that to be possible, I needed to connect Chris's disgusting friend to the crowd at the Manor which could only mean a visit to the secluded brothel and another confrontation with Cliff and Pinkie.

Leaning back in my chair, I said a silent prayer, then nodded off to sleep just long enough to fall into one of the many agonizing nightmares that took me back to my childhood home, the Blue Dahlia Bed and Breakfast. In the dream I'm watching as the once happy existence is being torn apart by rockets and mortars while scores of attacking Vietnamese soldiers are being cut down to pieces by some unseen army. I look down at the M-16 in my hands, but I'm not firing. Someone else is killing the enemy. Then, as always, I awaken, but not before standing alone among the ruins of my home with hundreds of dead enemy soldiers at my feet.

Somewhat unsettled after the dream, I noticed the lingering odor of the slop Sellers called lunch still stuck on my shirt. After taking a cold shower, I put on fresh clothes and went for a walk to clear my head.

Most of my friends think it's irresponsible, but my door is always unlocked. I learned the habit from my mom and dad who did the same with our B&B, leaving the front door open for anyone who needed shelter day or night.

Years earlier, I questioned my father, believing that too many people took advantage of my parents' generosity by showing up for handouts. Never one to let a teaching moment pass, my father had this to say:

"Don't you have enough?"

"Enough what, Dad?"

"Enough of everything you need."

"What do you mean?"

"Jimmy, you're twelve years old; there's much that you have yet to experience. Your mother and I have probably sheltered you too much. You don't know what it's like to struggle. The people who come here for what you call a handout are few in numbers compared to other parts of the country, especially down in the city. It all boils down to want and need. These people don't *want* help; they *need* help. You—and your mother and I—have been blessed with a comfortable life; these poor souls don't have the same advantages. We just try to do our part. Someday you'll learn that there are many greedy people in this world, immoral and selfish men and women who can never have enough . . . Don't be like them, son."

Of course, my father couldn't foresee the struggle I'd face six years later.

Just the same, leaving my door unlocked may be a little too trusting, but thanks to my appreciation of Thoreau's simple lifestyle and my father's teaching, there is little I own that would tempt even the most desperate thief. All I own of value—my bank book, tax records, and what little cash I keep along with my journal—are hidden under a floorboard in the corner of my bedroom closet under a pile of empty boxes and dirty clothes.

My casual walk turned out to be a bad idea for two reasons: first, the harsh intensity of the scorching afternoon sun, and second, an image of Chris Palmer suffering in jail that I couldn't get off my mind. It must have been unbearable in his cell. At that time, the county lockup that held Chris was actually the old jail built before the Civil War. As the need for more space demanded, the Department of Public Safety and Corrections found the money to build a new penitentiary but kept the older facility for any overflow without making what the bureaucrats viewed as unnecessary upgrades like air conditioning.

Something had to be done to get Chris out of that oven.

Unlike negotiating an efficient trash pickup, or retrieving back pay for a veteran, his case demanded a more urgent approach. Why did Kathy hire such an inexperienced detective? This case required a Sam Spade, instead she hired an unproven street cleaner with a fondness for Early-American literature and old movies.

I would have liked to walk farther, but the heat and humidity, along with the nagging obsession to free Chris, convinced me to head for home. As I turned toward my building, the overpowering reflections from the windows of the parked cars blinded me, their secondhand rays of light seemingly more intense than the radiance of the direct sun. Then, within that glow, I saw someone waving. In the passenger seat of my car with the door open sat Kathy.

"I was wondering when you'd see me."

"I'm sorry; the sun was blinding me."

"It is a beautiful day." Kathy glanced up at the sky without squinting, then looked back at me and continued, "I went to your office, but you weren't there."

"I know."

She smiled, but not because of the dry humor that she obviously missed.

"Anyway, I thought I'd wait in your car," she stroked the upholstery, "This is nice; I like the color."

I wondered how she knew the red Camaro was mine, but let it go because, once again, her looks became a distraction thanks to the black skirt that revealed a fantastic pair of legs. I did my best not to stare, but it was a challenge.

"Why wait out here? I don't lock my door."

"I'd feel funny."

"It would have been a hell of a lot more comfortable than out here in the heat, even if I don't have air-conditioning."

"Oh, I'm not hot."

Her surprising immunity to the oppressive heat amazed me as my client held out a dry hand for me to help her out of the Camaro's low seat. I stepped back to give her room, but she moved close enough that her face was inches from mine. She smiled; her eyes sparkled like diamonds. After a moment, I took another step back and watched her lean over to smooth her knee length skirt. Only a couple inches shorter than me, Kathy stood about five-ten and most of it looked like leg.

"Whatever you say. Why did you want to see me?"

"I thought of something that might help Chris, and I also heard that you had some trouble at the Manor yesterday."

The memory of the previous night's beating struck a nerve.

"I didn't have any trouble," I snapped, "Chris is the one with the real trouble, and without your help, Kathy, he *will* be convicted. I think you're holding back; in fact, I know you're holding back. There's no way you could have known about my visit to the Manor last night unless you were there. Now, all of a sudden, you just happen to think of something that might help Chris. What kind of game are you playing? In fact, why the hell did you hire me in the first place?"

Kathy flinched, then took a quick step back. She seemed comfortable enough during our first meeting, but now those seductive eyes stared at me with a heavy dose of apprehension. I prefer an amicable relationship with my clients, but given Kathy's reaction, I thought it might just be possible that an aggressive approach would prove more productive. I moved closer, and in a stern voice, "Well, what's it going to be?"

"What can I do?"

The words came from the scolded puppy I'd seen the day before.

"Tell me everything, and I mean everything. For a start,

tell me how you know about yesterday and why those animals came down as hard as they did. With the police and federal agents running around, a few more questions shouldn't have touched off that kind of response. Hell, for all they knew I could have been a cop. Did you warn them that I might be coming out?"

"No . . . No, I swear," she stuttered.

"Then tell me what you do know."

Kathy bowed her head and hesitated. I waited as patiently as possible while maintaining my aggressive attitude.

"Well . . . I don't have all day, Kathy."

"I went to see Mr. Barlowe; he owed me some money. But when I saw Brewer's face, he told me that some snoop came nosing around and assaulted him for no good reason. Then I saw Cliff and Pinkie. Mr. Smith, I didn't mean for you to get into any fights over this."

"What did you think might happen?"

"I don't know, but I didn't think it would ever come to that." She cocked her head in a sympathetic gesture and reached for my face. "You're hurt, too."

Not wanting to get suckered in, I pulled away.

"Don't worry about me. What else did Brewer say?"

"Nothing more than what I just told you, but be careful because they watched you drive away; that's how I knew your car." She looked at it, "It is a nice car. I always did like Camaros—"

"Yeah, Kathy, she's something special. Forget about the car, what else did Brewer say?"

"That's it, Mr. Smith. That's all we talked about. Honest."

"What about this thing you thought might help Chris?"

"Oh, I forgot when you scared me."

I started to apologize but thought better of it.

"So, what did you think of?"

"I think Johnny was blackmailing someone."

"Why?"

"For the money, I suppose."

Unbelievable. How could this many people be so damned stupid?

"Kathy, that's how most blackmailers work; I mean what makes you think Hodges was blackmailing someone?"

"About two weeks ago, Johnny took one of the regular clients aside and I saw the man give him an envelope. The man seemed real upset, but Johnny just laughed at him and walked away."

"Who was the man?"

"I don't know."

"How can you not know, Kathy?"

"The man wasn't my client."

"What did he look like?"

"I don't know, just a regular looking guy with brown hair. There was nothing special about him."

"Regular. Yeah, everything is too damn regular, Kathy. All right, here's what you need to do. Make some excuse to go back there and talk to Brewer. I think he knows more than the little he told me, and I surely can't go back and ask him. Either way, get the name of the man you saw with Hodges. Maybe Brewer knows who he is. Now, are you sure there's nothing else?"

Kathy once again adopted the deceptive prayerful bow of the head that tried my patience more than any client had done before. She wanted to tell me something else, but her game rules demanded that I force it out of her. Deciding to play along, and not strong enough to hurt, I grabbed Kathy by the arms, "Dammit, Kathy, I'm getting tired of this."

"It's the mafia. I think the mafia's involved."

"The mafia?"

"Yes, the mafia, you know, organized crime."

Of course I knew, but other than an alleged connection to the local waterfront, there were never any indications of a syndicate operating in the area.

"Are you sure?"

"Yes, I'm sure; I've seen them. Every month, three men in dark suits showed up and Mr. Barlowe would take one of them into his office."

"I guess for the payoff, huh?"

I said it facetiously; Kathy didn't get it.

"That's what I thought, too. The other two always stayed at the bar with Cliff and Pinkie, and when I asked Cliff who they were, he told me to shut up and mind my own business. I think he was afraid, and nothing scares Cliff."

For some reason, Kathy brought me a melodramatic fairy tale. Her suggestion of syndicate involvement was the heaviest dose of bull ever handed down by a client. Three men in dark suits? Kathy's been watching too many of the old movies I like so much. But why come to me with such an obvious deception? As much as I wanted Kathy to be innocent, her involvement gradually began to look more like a certainty. These new leads that had little or no credibility, and the obvious function of the well-hidden Lakeview Manor, convinced me even more that Hodges' murder was planned, and not by just one person.

I asked Kathy for her phone numbers that were on the original page of notes which had somehow gone missing. She gave me a quizzical look which bothered me for some reason. Then I told her again to get the name of the man Hodges may have been blackmailing while I contacted someone who might know if any kind of syndicate could be involved, no matter how unlikely it seemed.

It was time to check in with Sergeant Ben Quincannon.

❖ ❖ ❖

Ben is my friend. I'll never tell him, but he's my best friend and my guardian angel. We met in Vietnam back in '69 when I was being more than a little disorderly in the Da Nang NCO Club. On a search and destroy mission of my own, I was looking for the two sorry bastards who sent my platoon out on a night ambush intending to use us as bait just to make points with the brass. Intelligence reported a heavy concentration of regulars working out of the area, and if we got hit, the two glory hunters would go back in the morning with a larger force after calling in for air strikes. Meanwhile, the two bootlickers stayed behind, drinking in the club. We lost three good men that night. I didn't go back to base camp. I needed to get to the club before it closed.

Just like the two bouncers at the Manor, the worthless cowards sat perched on stools at the end of the bar like the carrion eating buzzards they were. I attacked, disabled one, then worked over the other, delivering the justice they deserved. That is until Ben, an Air Force Security Policeman, rapped me from behind with his night stick. I still don't know why he used his baton; then as now, Ben stands at least six-four and weighs in somewhere around a very muscular two-sixty. Then, after he dragged me outside the club, Ben beat me that much more when I laughed at his name.

"*Quincannon.*" I roared when I read the name on his fatigues. "What, was Victor McLaglen your uncle?" McLaglen played that character in a few John Wayne movies. "Come on, man," I said between punches, "You have to admit that's funny; you're the wrong color."

"Why can't a black man be Irish?" And then he hit me again.

"I don't know; it just doesn't seem to fit you. Besides, you hit like a girl, your name should be Gladys."

That wisecrack proved to be my final undoing. There were no more insults, and after I finally went down for the count, Ben picked me up, then escorted me back inside the club and to the bathroom where he helped clean off the blood and the mud. Then, while restraining my arm in his vice-grip, he forced me back into the bar with the idea that I would apologize to the two scumbags, which I had no intention of doing no matter what the consequences might be. Fortunately, they were gone, so he bought me a double that I quickly downed to ease the pain.

"Okay, what did those two do that got you so riled up?"

I told Ben about the doomed mission, "Well, it's a good thing they're gone; I would have joined in and we'd both be in the brig." He bought me another drink without buying one for himself; he was on duty and Ben never broke the rules.

"So, I have to ask. And don't hit me again, but come on . . . Quincannon? Not a typical name for a black dude. Anyway, I only laughed at it to piss you off." I rubbed the back of my neck and chuckled, "Like I needed to."

"All right, after the beating you took, I guess you deserve an explanation. My great-great grandfather was a slave, freed after the Civil War. He travelled west to find his fortune in gold, but as the story goes, was killed somehow. I don't know how or why, but anyone can guess. Anyway, he had a son who was adopted by the Quincannons. No, I don't know how he had a son, and I don't even know if it was a recorded adoption. In any case, my great-grandfather ended up with the name. He had a son, who had a son who came east to work in the steel mill. I was the result of that. Satisfied?"

"I guess so. But don't you ever get the urge to go back to

Ireland and find your family?"

I braced myself for another physical assault when Ben pulled back his fist, but he laughed instead, "You've had enough."

"Hell, I could've taken you if I wasn't tired from working over those two; anyway, you snuck up from behind."

Then he did hit me—but not too hard.

That night at the Da Nang Air Base, and in the years following, Ben taught me something about family honor. Under no circumstances would he allow anyone to tease him about his name—although I might get away with it from time to time— and he almost made me sorry that I changed my name to escape, if not erase, my family history.

After Ben got off duty, we sat and drank until the club closed, badmouthing lifers and talking about life after Nam. Isn't it funny how quickly a friendship can form, especially after finding common ground?

"So where are you from, killer?" He asked.

"Baltimore. How 'bout you?"

"Now isn't this a coincidence. I'm from Baltimore, too. That'll make it easy for me to keep an eye on you after we get out."

I took a sip of my drink, "Well, to be honest with you, Sarge, I'm not sure I'm going back."

"Why not, I'm sure your family wants you to come home."

Then, after another sip. "I haven't got any family."

Ben gently patted me on the back, "I'll be your family, Jimbo."

"Don't call me Jimbo; I don't like it, and I'll kick your ass if you do it again."

"Like you could. Anyway, why not Jimbo? The name seems to fit you."

"I know. For some reason, all my friends call me that; I don't mind it when they do, but anybody else . . ."

I looked hard at Ben, "You can call me Jimbo."

◆ ◆ ◆

And so, our friendship began and what a ride it's been. Ben never found another cause to rough me up after that night, managing to find other ways to beat me instead. At that time, one-on-one basketball and weightlifting were his favorites, his height and weight giving him the unfair advantage, but he would whine like a spoiled brat whenever I beat him at golf, making flimsy excuses every time he lost. My favorite came when he complained that his clubs were warped, so he bought an expensive set, upsetting his wife so much that she bribed me into letting him win before he bought a new wardrobe. It happens that Mrs. Quincannon makes the best meatloaf I ever tasted—and she delivers.

I knew where to find Ben anytime, day or night. Many times I needed his help, and many times he came to my rescue. That day he would be at the YMCA, where he works out every Monday, Wednesday, and Friday in an athletic routine he seldom misses. In fact, the only times I recall Ben skipping that habit had to do with either the job or his family.

On those three days, at three o'clock, Ben lifts weights for an hour, then runs for an hour more. Unless he's working overtime, my friend knows to be home for dinner by five-thirty or Mrs. Quincannon would make his life very difficult. I sometimes lift with him, but not seriously. Ben can press four hundred on the bench to satisfy his need for power while I work out with less weight to maintain quickness and tone. My job seldom gets as physical as my experience at the Manor, so I rely on speed and endurance with just enough muscle to get the job done. Still, in keeping with his competitive nature, Ben punishes me on the weights, then falls back on meager excuses when we run. You can believe that when confronting Ben, it's better to be faster, rather than stronger. I caught up with Ben at the Y a little after three.

"We're getting older, you and me," Ben said as I struggled with two hundred on the bench while he spotted me.

"What makes you think thirty is old?"

"Thirty may not be old, but it's time to start thinking about it. Muscle deterioration starts about now. Things have always come easy for you and me, Jimbo; that's about to change, and from the look of that busted lip, they already have for you. Come on, push that weight."

"Hey, I gave back more than this."

"Doesn't matter. Maybe you got away with it once, but what's going to happen the next time? Instincts might improve with experience, but our reflexes are slowing down, my friend. Come on, push that weight, two more. We need to work harder just to keep that edge. Push that weight, Jimbo. I see it every day; these younger guys are going to eat us up. *Push it, I said!*"

I wondered how old Cliff and Pinkie were. They didn't seem much younger than me, if at all, but even if I didn't deliver twice what they gave, our two bouts could be considered a draw. Ben noticed the wounds on my face, but as we worked out, I did my best to hide my pain so he wouldn't notice the rest of the damage. I got up from the bench and we made our way toward the dumbbell rack.

"Ben, Ben, Ben, you've been watching those daytime talk shows again, haven't you."

Ben swiped at my shoulder, driving me into the weights; I grabbed a thirty pounder.

"Okay, I'm sorry. It must be the soaps."

Huge hands clutched my shoulders, lifting me enough that I stood on my toes. I tried to conceal the pain.

"I'm serious, Smitty."

"I told you never to call me that."

The dumbbell I drove into Ben's gut convinced him to release his grip but caused so little pain that he only laughed.

"Jimbo, I'm going to dance on your grave."

"In that case, you'd better keep working out; I don't plan on dying for a while."

We finished our workout, jogged around the indoor track for a while, then took a free racquetball court.

It was time to get down to business.

"What do you know about the Lakeview Manor Motel and Chris Palmer's arrest?" I asked.

The question distracted Ben enough that he missed my serve, then gave me a puzzled expression while shaking his head.

"I know you like lost causes, but this one is too far gone. Take my advice, Jimbo, let it go."

"It's too late."

"I knew you were into something stupid when I grabbed you. Yeah, I noticed the pain on your face, but for once you've got to listen to me, this one is a slam dunk if there ever was one. A naïve sucker falls for a prostitute, loses his temper and kills her pimp. Open and shut—tight. He'll get sympathy at the sentencing, but he's definitely going down. I bet that pretty boy, State's Attorney Michael Blake, can't wait for this one to go to court—another conviction and more votes in his pocket."

"Well, first, I'm not convinced that the girl in question is a prostitute, and second, I have reason to believe that Hodges wasn't an ordinary pimp, in fact, he may not have been a pimp at all, but simply the manager of an escort service whose girls did some freelancing on the side."

"Sure, and I'm actually the Secretary of State, not a very good job these days."

"Okay, Ben, Hodges was shot in one of the cabins. How did Palmer know which one was his?"

"I don't know, and I can only guess that the homicide detectives have the answer. Maybe he asked somebody."

"According to the paper, there was no one there to ask . . . and at three in the morning?"

"I don't know, Jimbo, maybe he stalked Hodges at closing and followed him to his cabin, then waited until he was sure they were alone."

"Okay, why didn't they find a gun?"

"Maybe he dumped it in any one of the hundred dumpsters on that stretch of highway."

"Come on, Ben, either way that's at least three maybes; how many more did the detectives miss? There must be a lead or two that they didn't take the time to follow."

"Jimbo, the way I understand the case, Palmer was the only one who had motive to kill Hodges. Everybody loved the guy. There was nothing else to look for."

"Yeah? Like I said, they stopped looking. Real good detective work. Ben, I heard that Hodges was in the blackmail business and, come on, you can't tell me that a guy running a suspicious escort business hasn't pissed somebody off along the way, freelancing girls or not. There must be someone else who gained from Hodges' death. Have you heard about the FBI running an investigation at the Manor?"

"No kidding. That is something I didn't know. I'll check it out; I have a friend at the bureau."

"Is there any place you don't have a friend?"

"Not many, but unlike you, Jimbo, I'm a diplomat. If you were nicer to people, you could have some friends of your own."

"No thanks; you, Nora, the boys in the band, and my buddies down at the docks are all the friends I need, but there are a couple more in select high places that you don't know about."

"High places? *Bull*," he roared. "You're a reverse snob and you know it. You haven't changed since we met back in Nam. I've never seen anyone with such an inbred hatred for authority. When I make captain, you won't even talk to me. You need a shrink, son. And judging from the damage I see, you better start being a little nicer to people or you'll need a plastic surgeon, too."

"Speaking of my face, before the murder, were there any rumors at all concerning the Lakeview Manor?"

"To be honest, I didn't even know it existed. I take it that's where you got the treatment."

"Yeah."

"Then you know what it is. And that's why I can't believe you're not convinced those girls did a little more than freelance," Ben said.

"Yeah, you're probably right, but that's also the reason I know Palmer didn't kill Hodges. There must be at least a dozen people with a good deal to gain now that Hodges is out of the way."

"All I can tell you is that homicide couldn't come up with anything more. So, if there is someone else with motive, you'll have to find the evidence, and it had better be convincing."

I didn't tell Ben who hired me, but as we talked, the image of Kathy Radney as a woman for hire banged around in my head, bouncing off the walls like the racquetball in our court. Would I ever accept what seemed to be obvious? And then there was also her latest contribution.

"By the way, any chance of organized crime in the area?"

"Other than the probable connection to the waterfront, nothing, even though I do believe they have some business holdings, trucking and possibly some warehousing, but I doubt that it would extend to the Lakeview Manor."

"Yeah. That's what I thought, too."

We finished our game. Ben went home to shower. Thanks to me, he was a little late for dinner, but because she liked me, Mrs. Quincannon would forgive him.

I showered there, got dressed, and decided there was only one place left to go.

◆ ◆ ◆

It was after six o'clock. An entire day had passed since my trouble at the Lakeview Manor Motel and I still had no evidence to support my theory of a plot to murder Johnny Hodges. Though it wasn't a good idea, and without telling Ben, there would have to be another visit to the notorious establishment and a chance to meet Frank Barlowe, the man I neglected to add to the second list after losing the first. Kathy reminded me of him earlier that day.

The missing notes bothered me. Could they have been thrown out, or could I have taken the pad with me to the Manor the day before and lost it in the commotion? Doubtful, but not the immediate problem.

Forgetting about Barlowe could be excused, especially after taking into account the combative encounter with Brewer and the two bouncers. That confrontation demanded all my attention, putting aside any thoughts about the manager. In any case, I was still convinced that enough evidence to disturb the state's attorney's open and shut case existed at the Manor, so a meeting with Barlowe became a priority. After all, the manager might have had a reason or two of his own for wanting Hodges dead. On the other hand, there was also the possibility that Hodges may have been Barlowe's friend, a friend who would want to see the real killer exposed, especially if the murder interfered with the business at the Manor.

On the way, I stopped at a fast-food joint for a burger and some fries. After mentioning the pitiful food at the Manor, Kathy recommended a nearby diner that served good home cooking, but a sit-down meal would take more time than necessary. Barlowe had to be seen as soon as possible and I needed something on my stomach before facing Cliff and Pinkie again.

Unlike the night before, the parking lot was full, not one space available, a good omen that the manager would be there. I parked my Camaro on the side of the driveway and walked up the steps to the lounge.

The standing-room-only assembly within the smoke-filled room meandered like a swarm of bees working a busy hive as eager customers drifted from table to table where attractive girls sat on display like models in a store window. Loud music from the jukebox drowned out any negotiations that might be taking place between the Manor's clientele and their desires. None of the men appeared necessarily distinguished, but there were no stereotypical bikers or rednecks either. The size of the crowd must have had something to do with it being past seven-thirty on a Friday, or possibly that the regulars decided they had mourned Hodges' death the appropriate amount of time. Nevertheless, the preoccupied multitude worked in my favor since, once again, I neglected to carry my gun. Yes, another irresponsible lapse of memory, and going back for it was a thought, but with that many witnesses present, I decided against it, confident that Barlowe would answer a few harmless questions, after which I could take my leave before the bouncers found an excuse to repeat the previous night's performance.

From the door I could see Cliff and Pinkie sitting at the far end of the bar, and alongside them the scrawny bartender. Cliff's eyes were blackened—a result of the broken nose I gave him—while a sizeable bandage covered the impression of my dental work on Brewer's nose. It did look pathetic; I almost felt sorry for him . . . almost. Brewer must have been on his break because an older barmaid skillfully served drinks to the busy waitresses, all of whom were somewhat less than eye-catching. It seemed that the working girls, who—as Sellers said—were quite desirable, wanted no competition from the hired help.

My first thought was to work my way over to the manager's office before the bouncers noticed, but that idea quickly collapsed when Pinkie spotted me and nudged his partner. Both men stood, and like the night before, slowly started toward me. I walked the few steps to the corner of the bar, turned to face them, then stopped. The two big men kept coming. A few customers standing by the bar glanced at the bouncers, sensed the impending drama, and moved aside—they possibly had seen the two men in action before. Cliff and Pinkie came as close as six feet. I held up my hand like a cop holding traffic at an intersection. They stopped. Why, I didn't know, but took it as a promising sign that my meeting with Barlowe might take place without any bloodshed.

I smiled, "Hello, gentlemen."

Of course, there would be no response.

"Look, guys, I didn't come here looking for trouble, but since we've been through so much together, I thought you might be able to help me. I'm looking for Frank Barlowe. I understand he works here; in fact, I believe he's the manager."

Other than the unspoken stare of hatred that was as thick as the August humidity, Cliff and Pinkie gave no indication of being alive. Without a doubt, the two men heard me because I spoke loud enough that one waitress and a couple of the men turned to listen, their behavior almost comical as they looked at me, then at the bouncers, then at me, and again at the bouncers like they were watching a tennis match. Clearly, the group expected something to happen. Secrets are hard to keep, and Cliff's black eyes along with Brewer's bandaged nose must have created questions, so I wondered if word about our first skirmish had gotten out and the Manor's patrons hoped they might see a little action.

Though I believed Cliff and Pinkie to be the only two bouncers, I took a quick scan around the dimly lit room and saw no one moving in to back them up—not that they needed it. Still, these guys were professionals and they weren't going to underestimate my dirty fighting talent like the night before. I had to defuse any plan they might have, and it had to be quick.

"Come on, fellas, I'm truly sorry about last night and I know that we can never be friends, but you didn't give me a chance to explain. All I want is to clear Chris Palmer. I believe that you, and everyone involved—other than that fathead state's attorney—know that Chris didn't murder Hodges, and I don't think any of you would have killed him because it might destroy your meal ticket," I took another quick glance around the room, "even though, business doesn't seem to be suffering tonight. But none of that matters, I don't care who killed him; I only want to help Chris. Just give me something, anything that could help me get that kid out of jail."

Appealing to their nonexistent better natures triggered no response as the two bouncers, with the addition of Brewer who now stood safely behind his friends, looked like figures from a wax museum. Even the "fathead" remark concerning the state's attorney didn't change their impassive attitude. But at least they weren't trying to break my legs, hesitation that probably had more to do with the room full of witnesses than my tactful approach.

Before I had the chance to consider another option, a booming voice drowned out and virtually silenced the room.

The jukebox still played, but its music couldn't compete with the volume created by this massive monster of a man who easily pushed his way through the crowd.

"Brewer, I'm not going to tell you again; I want no more of your creepy friends in here."

Brewer's face lit up with excitement.

"No, boss, this is him; this is the bastard we told you about."

I turned to face the big man, a man much bigger than Ben, storming toward me. Whoever coined the phrase "mass of humanity" had this image in mind. I'm not usually affected by appearances, but I must admit that the size of the Manor's manager intimidated me.

"The boss, huh. Let me take a wild guess: Frank Barlowe, right?"

Once again, there was no response, so I muscled up and said to hell with diplomacy; if I was going to take another fall, I might as well go down swinging.

"All right, I'm tired of this bullshit. We can go at it like we did yesterday, or you can work with me and I'll get the cops, *and the feds*, off your ass at the same time."

"What the hell do you know about the feds?"

The air rippled with the manager's question that thundered like a police bullhorn, but with far less warmth. The big man stood tall and erect, easily six-five or six, his massive head jutting away from his body like a bull ready to charge. At one time, he could have been—and maybe he was—a bouncer at one of the famous strip clubs down in the city's red-light district. Just the word "out" would have sent trouble to the exit.

And yet, as I studied him more closely, it became apparent that any muscle he may have had, if he had any left at all, was covered by layers of fat. The imposing figure was a dozen donuts past obese. The time had long since passed when Barlowe, who looked about fifty, could work out with Ben; I noticed him breathing heavily after his walk from the office which was just across the room. The unfriendly giant had grown fat and lazy, left with the immenseness of his once proud body bursting at the seams of his expensive suit.

"I asked you a question, dammit. What do you know about the feds?"

"Slow down, Frank. We have plenty of time."

"I have plenty of time; you have what I say you have, so you'd better make it quick."

Okay, that declaration unsettled me, but I laughed as if it didn't, pausing for two reasons: to provoke him even more, and to collect myself so my voice wouldn't crack.

"I know that the feds are trying to bring charges against this operation."

"So what. Everybody knows the—"

"The cops didn't know about their investigation until I told them earlier today," I interrupted. "Oh, and by the way, since they know that now, some detectives might make their way out here for another visit."

Either my interruption, the surprise concerning the cops, or simply the fact that I had influence with the police seemed to confuse Barlowe as an overweight hamster slowly turned the wheel in the manager's mental cage. Other than the incompatible soulful ballad's melody coming from the jukebox, the room was still and quiet. I had everyone's attention.

We stared each other down, until Barlowe's eyes opened wide in an angry glare, "I don't give a damn what the cops know, what they don't know, or if they come back. Besides, how can a squirt like you influence a federal investigation? Is your mother an agent, or is she the cleaning lady, screwing all the men in the office so she can tell her little boy what's going on?"

The three stooges laughed along with some chuckles from the crowd, but the high school insult annoyed me. I'm too big to be called a squirt . . . and the shot at my mother crossed the line.

"That's right, asshole, my mother's a cleaning woman and yours is a fat ugly gorilla. You got names for my mother, I got names for yours . . . if you have one. Oh, and by the way, this squirt didn't have too much trouble the second time I faced your boys last night, and I'm ready for round three; so now, how about acting your age and show just a little intelligence. Yes, I do have influence with the cops, and the feds (a lie) . . . so, unless you help me, I will have them watch every move you make, along with every employee, and every customer who walks through that door."

The threat, though empty, caused an audible murmur in the room—even the jukebox had stopped. Someone must have purposely shut it down because, immediately after my warning, one of the customers ran out. In any case, my bluff still provoked no visible response from Barlowe. I wanted to anger him with the gorilla remark, hoping that my attack on his mother would annoy him enough that he'd say something revealing about the Manor's business and its connection to Hodges.

As the stare-down continued, I tried to guess what the big man might be thinking, then considered whether or not the manager could be involved in a conspiracy to murder Hodges. If he had played a part in any scheme, I had already given him more than enough cause to throw me out. So why would he want to hear anything I had to say?

But something must have piqued his interest. "I'll give you two minutes, then I'll have you thrown out for causing a disturbance, and there's plenty of witnesses here that will back me up, no matter how many cops you know."

"It won't take that long. What we have here, Mr. Barlowe, is the Lakeview Manor Motel where Johnny Hodges, the manager of a suspicious escort service, managed to get himself shot. An innocent man has been charged with the crime. Understand this, I don't care about your business or anything else that goes on out here at the Manor; all I care about is freeing Chris Palmer. I believe that a group of people concocted a scheme to murder Hodges and frame my client, but I can only guess why they killed him. Maybe he was skimming from his partners and got caught, or maybe they were skimming and he caught them; or maybe there's someone else hanging around, eager to take over. By the way who's next in line?" I looked over at Brewer and the two bouncers. "Also, I've heard that Hodges was in the blackmail business, which always brings out the best in people, and finally, maybe there's some truth to the possibility of a connection to some criminal organization who might have wanted Hodges to disappear. If that's not enough, the FBI is sticking their bloodhound noses into the rumor of illegal girls on the payroll. So, if someone hadn't framed Chris Palmer so neatly, there would have been more than enough reason for the cops to check out every bit of business that's conducted here at the Manor."

Barlowe said nothing. In fact, the proverbial pin dropping would have sounded like a clap of thunder. More than that, after hearing my theory out loud for the first time, I had to admit that the idea consisted of nothing more than conjecture without a bit of evidence. Sure, any part of the speculation was possible, but Chris's frame shut down any further investigation and took all the heat off the real killer. I struggled to regain some momentum with a sincere plea that, even if it didn't move Barlowe, there might be someone in the room with reason to help.

"Mr. Barlowe, give me one thing, one lead for the cops to chase, so I can get that innocent kid out of jail."

Barlowe stared at me without blinking. That bothered me.

Finally, the big man spoke, "Johnny didn't have a partner. He wasn't blackmailing anybody, and I have no idea what will happen to the escort service. As far as the feds go, they have the same thing you have, nothing but a bag of horse manure." He started to walk away, but turned back and said: "Oh yeah, and the only organization around here is me. Now get out."

I heard satisfied snickers from around the room. Why the hell did I come back with nothing? It was stupid. *I was stupid.* That stupidity fueled the anger raging inside me; the anger that I wanted to erupt from Barlowe burst forth from me instead.

"Hey, Barlowe, there is one more possibility."

He turned to face me.

"Maybe you're the anonymous partner who wanted Hodges dead."

Barlowe snapped his fingers, the signal for Cliff and Pinkie to get to work. I hadn't noticed that during my appeal to Barlowe, the two had taken up position near me, so before I had any chance to defend myself, a multitude of witnesses watched as the two bouncers, once again, worked me over before viciously bouncing me out of the lounge and onto the hot asphalt parking lot.

I hate getting thrown out of places; the embarrassment became something of a habit after Ben first escorted me out of the Da Nang NCO Club. But in my defense, I've never been drunk and disorderly, only disorderly like that night in Nam. I get thrown out because I'm either doing my job or being enough of an irritant to force a reaction.

Without a doubt, this latest visit to Lakeview Manor produced a definite reaction. My interference irritated and angered just about everyone involved, and even if I did pay the price for meddling, the painful experience clearly served a purpose.

Suddenly, a rush of anxiety overwhelmed me, intensifying the pain. I tried to stand but fell back down on my first try. The asphalt of the parking lot felt like the dirt and grass of the jungle floor. I heard an Asian voice, then noticed a couple passing on their way to one of the cabins. They laughed at me, the man's voice sounding like an echo, "The jerk got what he deserved."

The sun had yet to set, but the tall pines blocked its light. Then, out of the shadows, a voice whispered to me. It was my father telling me that everything would be okay. As always, he advised patience. His words calmed the tremors and my strength slowly returned.

I managed to stand and limp to my car, checking out my left leg on the way. At first, I thought it was broken, but feeling no exposed bones, convinced myself that it was merely a bad bruise. Warm blood dripped into my mouth from the broken nose that I straightened, triggering more than a little pain. It hurt to breathe; one of the two bouncers may have cracked a rib. Leaning against my Camaro, trying to convince myself that Ben was right and that the Lakeview Manor was out of my league, my father's voice came to me once again.

*Be smart. Drive away. Be patient. Get that rib checked out.*

I opened the car door and slumped in the seat, then turned to face my antagonist. It took some time before the hazy outline of the Lakeview Manor cleared in my vision. Two times I paid a visit to the scene of the crime, and two times I took a beating. Did that call for more drastic measures? Would going back expose some other evidence that would clear Chris Palmer? The characters inside the dark and smoky lounge had been sufficiently provoked, but to what end? Now aware that the stubborn detective wasn't going away, one of them—possibly a customer who knew a little more than he should, maybe the one who ran out—might be induced to help. My father's sound advice kept repeating in my mind: *Be patient.*

I stared down my nemesis, then winced with pain as I struggled to retrieve the loaded gun from its stash.

*Sorry, Dad.*

Once again, I climbed the steps to the porch and entered

the room that had resumed its business as if nothing had happened. The music from the rejuvenated jukebox muffled any bargaining over prices for whatever services would be offered as the customers and the waitresses picked up where they left off, much too busy to notice my return.

Strengthened by the adrenaline pumping through my veins, I zigzagged through the crowd with the .38 hanging at my side. The thought of Cliff or Pinkie stopping me was the farthest thing from my mind because my search and destroy mission had but one objective: Get that fat hog who insulted my mother, which would have infuriated me that much more if I knew who she was. But Barlowe didn't know her either, and I felt an obligation to defend the name—good or bad—of the woman who brought me into this world.

I made it to the office door, kicked it in, and aimed my gun at Barlowe's head as he sat behind his desk. "You're a fat son-of-a-bitch and I'm gonna blow your fucking brains out."

Kicking in the door silenced the crowd. The pair of predictable footsteps could be heard rushing toward the office while others ran for the exit. I stepped in the office to the open side of the broken door so Cliff and Pinkie couldn't get behind me.

"If they come in, you're dead."

"Hold it, Cliff." Though loud enough for the bouncers to hear, Barlowe's command lacked the intimidation from our previous encounter. Their feet skidded to a halt on the hardwood floor.

Without taking my eyes off the fat man, I said, "That's right, Cliff, go wait by the bar; I'll deal with you and your buddy after I finish with your boss."

The door hung on the hinges just enough to close it. Barlowe looked unconcerned, flashing a crooked and defiant smile that seemed to say, "What now, squirt?"

I didn't like being called a squirt either out loud or under the fat man's breath, imagined or not.

"How do you like me now, fatso? I'll bet you didn't think this squirt had it in him, did ya."

Barlowe didn't answer, which was pretty much to be expected. It would take more than a snub-nosed revolver to ruffle the big man's feathers. But while my ill-advised decision to confront the Manor's manager might not have been the best move I could have made, the severe pain kept pushing me. I was committed; walking away wasn't an option.

"All right, Barlowe, start talking."

"I told you all I know."

"Which is absolutely nothing."

"And that's all I know."

"Bullshit!"

I walked over, stood beside him, and pressed my .38 against his temple, though doubtful that he would break as easily as Brewer.

"Is this where you plugged Hodges? A quick and efficient shot to the head?"

"I didn't kill him."

Barlowe didn't seem to be breathing.

"You know, I could blow your brains out and there's not a jury in the world who would convict me. Your boys assaulted me two days in a row. Right now, I'm out of my mind with pain. Oh, it might take a good lawyer, but one look at those two monsters and the jury will understand why I went crazy enough to do you in. Anyway, twenty to life would be worth it just to send your fat ass to hell."

"What do you want from me? Do you want me to make something up?"

It was my turn to be silent, so I tightened my grip, and pushed the muzzle against his temple.

"Dammit, let's get this over with. Johnny ran the service on his own. I did take a percentage, but that doesn't make me a partner; it was more like rent. I have no idea what will happen now because the girls are freelancing, but they don't have Johnny's connections and I'm not about to let the Manor become a cheap whorehouse. There are a couple new faces, but I look for one of the older girls to organize things."

Kathy immediately sprang to mind, but I couldn't let Barlowe know she hired me.

"I planned to wait another week before getting involved. Oh, and I don't know where he found them, but Johnny did bring in two girls from Thailand who are legal. Hiring them must have brought out the feds, and I questioned Johnny about it. His answer was somewhat evasive, but because I trusted Johnny, I let it go. In any case, the agents checked out the Asian girls and left."

I heard a noise from the door. The broken jamb slowed down whoever was trying to get in. Thinking it might be Cliff and Pinkie, I stepped behind Barlowe, but kept the gun pressed firmly against the back of his head. Then came a voice:

"Jimbo?"

It was Ben's baritone.

"Come in, Sergeant Quincannon."

He pushed the door the rest of the way and it fell over. After inspecting the damage, Ben shook his head at me, then flashed his badge as he stared down the manager. "Do you want my *friend* to pay for these damages . . . and do you want to file any charges?"

The emphasis on friend and its implication couldn't have gone unnoticed; after all, I did tell Barlowe that I knew people on the force.

"No, we don't need any more publicity, but you should consider a leash for this animal."

Ben and I both chuckled; it was one of the first things Ben said to me back in Nam.

"Yeah, I've heard that suggestion before. Come on, Jimbo."

"Just a minute, Ben, I have one more question for Mr. Barlowe. Where were you when Hodges was killed?"

Barlowe looked at Ben who responded, "Go on, tell him."

"I was sleeping with one of the girls."

"What's her name?"

"Brittany."

"I wouldn't mind talking to her; where is she?"

"Visiting her mother in Annapolis."

"Now isn't that nice," I said. "Cute name, convenient alibi; I wonder if she'll be the girl who takes over the escort business."

"That's enough, Jimbo. Let's go."

I left the lounge led by Ben's vice grip on my arm like a father taking his son to the woodshed. Cliff and Pinkie stood by the door scowling at me. They probably would have laughed if not for the fact that they were about to catch more than a decent share of hell for letting me get to their boss in the first place. Scanning the room as we left, I confirmed that those two were the only bouncers, which was all the Manor needed . . . until a certain nosy detective came around. I giggled.

*They might need reinforcements when I come back.*

Ben read my mind, and dragged me to my car, where he threw me against the fender. He didn't care if it hurt or not—which it did.

"Man, I've about had it with your temper. Look at you; you won't survive another session with those two beasts standing by the door, and the day will come when I won't be around to save your sorry butt."

"It's your fault, Ben. I listened to what you said about getting older, so I came here and tried some of your diplomacy, and it didn't work. That fat slob tried to bullshit me, Ben, and you know how much I hate bullshitters."

Ben shook his head. "I'm serious, Jimbo. You have to stop."

"Not until I get that kid out of jail. Which reminds me, isn't it a little past your shift?"

"Somebody called in that there was trouble at the Lakeview Manor. I told dispatch that I was in the area; it was more than obvious who the trouble was. Lucky for you, Sergeant Morgan's wife decided to have her baby tonight, that's why I'm on duty . . . to cover for him."

"That call must have come from the guy who ran out when I threatened to bring the cops back."

"How could you do that?"

"By being a total nuisance."

"Which is what you constantly are."

"I have to be a nuisance if I'm going to do your work. You know that kid's innocent as well as I do, so how can you call yourself a policeman?"

"Because I have connections at the Bureau. I checked out their investigation."

"Don't tell me, dead end, right."

Ben nodded. "Hodges hired two Asian girls for the business, but they were clean, and by the way, so was he. Hodges kept meticulous books."

"Yeah, I'm sure he entered every trick his girls turned."

"Let's put it this way, he recorded all the appropriate entries that made the business appear to be nothing more than a legitimate escort service. Anyway, Jimbo, it was an anonymous tip that brought out the feds."

"There you go. Now, doesn't that make you curious?"

"I'm a cop, I don't get curious, I get facts, and so far, there are none."

"Yeah, I know that now."

Ben drove away, leaving me in the parking lot feeling the pain from round three. I leaned against my car, once again staring at the source of my dilemma. He knew I wanted to go back and trash the place, but he ordered me to go home and trusted me enough to know that I would follow his command.

Still, I was determined to free Chris Palmer, and nothing would stand in my way. Not the beatings from Cliff and Pinkie, not the denials from Barlowe, and not the questionable leads from Kathy. Not one of those obstacles would keep me from finding the real killer. The answer had to be in the secluded hideaway standing in front of me. Someone in there knew the truth. I would be back. Maybe that's what Ben meant when he said he liked the way I bounced. It's hard to keep a good man down.

But I wouldn't go back that night. Even though I knew it would be a struggle, Ben talked me into a round of golf in the morning, which meant another meatloaf delivery.

# SATURDAY

## August 18, 1979

Mrs. Quincannon didn't have to bribe me to lose that morning because every swing of the club brought about a significant amount of pain, so apparent that Ben showed some uncharacteristic compassion when he suggested we quit after the first nine. Nevertheless, while walking the course—and suffering through Ben's laughter every time he sunk a putt to win the hole—I considered my latest conversation with Kathy. Reasoning still vetoed any organized crime association, but blackmail seemed a more than likely motive for murder, especially since prostitution was involved. But what about Barlowe? With Cliff and Pinkie as enforcers, the porky manager could be running a little extortion racket of his own. Another question for my client.

If Kathy could get me the name of Hodges' blackmail victim, I thought Ben might help by digging up whatever dirt the murdered man had on his target, but my friend refused to get involved, complaining that he was entirely too busy to be chasing any of my wild geese. That left only one other person who might be able to help.

At the time, Nora Rutledge was an assistant state's

attorney, and a dear friend. While most people believed us to have little more than a business association, the unseen love affair known only to our closest friends suffered from the burden of emotional baggage. Struggling with scars from dysfunctional and tragic family histories, neither one of us could find the courage to make a commitment. Those complications gave rise to sincere discussions and heated arguments that took place only behind closed doors. Nevertheless, we deeply cared for one another, and frequently tried to figure out just what the hell we were doing and where we were going. After all, a certain PhD hadn't yet told us that men were from Mars, and women from Venus, a concept I never could understand.

Nora didn't answer the bell to her apartment, but knowing that she'd be in, I persisted. Staying out late, and sleeping in even later, became acquired habits while attending an upscale New England law school. Nora's father, a partner in a prestigious firm in our area, arranged a prominent position waiting for the graduate, but Nora had made up her mind to enter public service and subsequently declined the offer after she passed the bar. I'm sure that decision brought about more than a few uncomfortable family dinners.

Three rings and as many minutes passed before the door finally opened. Nora was not in one of her better moods.

"I absolutely despise it when you come over without calling."

"Since when do I need an invitation?"

"Since our last 'are we an exclusive couple, or not' argument, and I thought we got that straight. What if I had someone over?"

"Aw, come on, who would sleep with a girl who looks like you in the morning?"

"You've spent the night often enough," she snapped.

"That's only because I can't do any better."

I walked past her and into the kitchen, went to the fridge, and poured a glass of orange juice. She must have remained by the open door trying to control one of her temper tantrums because I finished the first glass and was pouring another when the door slammed and the pounding of footsteps accompanied her into the kitchen. It amazed me that Nora could maintain perfect control in the courtroom while I could set her off with as little as a cross-eyed glance.

"I'm tired of your attitude, Jimmy. You use me. You take me for granted and I'm sick of it. You're not the only man in my life, you know."

"Getting back with the husband?"

"You know better than that."

I smiled and drew her close to me. She responded as always, squeezing my shoulders, cuddling her head into my neck, and relaxing her body against mine. Fortunately, her embrace didn't hurt too bad—it turned out that the rib wasn't broken as I suspected—but I still couldn't let Nora know what I'd been doing. Like Ben, she disapproved of my methods.

Nora was right; I treated her badly. Without question some psychobabble quack would blame my behavior on the way my family abandoned me—even though it wasn't their choice —but there could be no excuse for mistreating one of the few people who stood beside me no matter what.

After a moment, she tried to push me away, but I pulled her back and we kissed. Nora was truly beautiful. Her natural blonde hair fell loosely, just touching slender shoulders while framing a flawless complexion that required no make-up and— like my attractive client—turned heads when she walked in the room. And yet their beauty differed. The elegant and unique Kathy Radney could compete for and win the Miss America crown, while the more natural and popular Nora would run unopposed as candidate for homecoming queen.

"Why the hell did Bill divorce you?"

"Because I'm a bitch to live with."

"I know better than that."

"If you feel that way, why not ask me to marry you again?"

"What? Propose to an irritable bitch like you, besides, you turned me down, remember?"

Nora stepped back and clipped my chin with a quick left. I flinched just enough that she noticed.

"Aw, come off it. I didn't hit you that hard." She cocked her head and gave me that expression of displeasure I'd seen too many times. "Oh no, you're on another case that needs my help. I thought your nose looked funny, and there's a cut on your lip. I should have known this was no social call."

"Hey, I was here just last week."

"It's been two weeks. One night and gone."

"You kicked me out."

"I had to get to the office; some of us have to work for a living, you know."

Nora turned away and headed for the living room where she flopped down on the sofa like a little girl about to be lectured. I followed, sat beside her, and took her hands. Those beautiful blue eyes peered into mine as their enchanting glow replaced the confrontational disposition from the moment before. I liked her like this, not that I felt in control, but more that we were communicating with the possibility of finally reaching an agreement.

"Nora, you know how I feel about you, and I know how you feel about me, and also that we're both afraid to change things because neither one of us wants to ruin our friendship. But Nora, isn't that a good thing? Being friends, I mean. Yes, we both have problems that are no secret, and Nora, I'm not Bill."

"I know you're not Bill . . . if you were anything like him, you wouldn't be here."

"Okay. That's settled. So why not step it up a notch? There doesn't have to be a proposal or a ring; I'm not about to get down on one knee again, not yet anyway, but Nora, we love each other, and we enjoy each other's company—"

"If you mean screwing, that's right."

"This isn't a court of law; you don't have to be blunt for the sake of the jury. So, what I'm saying is . . ."

I stopped and shook my head; the scene suddenly became all too familiar.

"Nora, this isn't working. It's the same damn thing, the same dead-end discussion. It's not your fault, it's mine." I got up to leave, but Nora pulled me back.

"I'm sorry; I shouldn't have interrupted. We'll talk later; I promise. It's just that this has been a bad week in the office. But you know I'm here for you, so how can I help?"

"You can't help . . . forget about it."

I tried to stand, but Nora still wouldn't release her grip, "Please don't leave, not like this."

And so, the same inevitable outcome began.

It's not easy for me to talk about sex—must be my strict Catholic upbringing. The least explicit description would be to simply say that our lovemaking was physical and demanding, driven by an outpouring of emotion, ironic for two people with such a fear of commitment. Regardless, the seldom planned passion quickly started, then slowly finished. Afterwards, we usually slept, if only for a little while.

That day, I couldn't sleep, not even for a minute. Too much confusion in my mind and in my life. Time after time, Nora and I would argue, settle nothing, and then work out our frustration in bed as if making love resolved all our problems. In a way, it did. We forgot why we fought and returned to our comfortable, although ambiguous, relationship.

Nora appeared to be sleeping so I tried to leave without waking her, but as soon as I stirred, she grabbed me in a playful manner: "No, no, no. You're not getting away that easy."

I leaned back in bed and kissed her.

"Sorry, but I have to go; this time I have work to do."

"Okay, but you came to me for help. There must be something you want me to do."

"Probably not. I'm not even sure I can help this kid myself."

"*Kid.* I don't believe it. Could we be working the same case? Chris Palmer?" When I nodded, she laughed, "I guess we were meant to be together."

"So that's why you've had a bad week; you know he's innocent."

"No. I don't know he's innocent, Jimmy, look at the evidence."

"To hell with the evidence; look at that kid, there's no way he shot Hodges."

"And there's another thing, stop calling him 'kid.' Even though I knew you were referring to Palmer because of his baby-face, you need to remember that he's a man, and he's a big man."

"And that means he's guilty of murder?"

"Possibly . . . and he's also a combat veteran which—"

"Don't do that! You do not have to do *that!*"

"If I don't, I'm not doing my job."

"To hell with your job if it means using a man's service record as capability to commit murder. It amazes me that people who never fought in Vietnam, or any other war, think they know how it feels. How can anyone understand what it's like to come home with memories that can never be forgotten unless they lived through it themselves? Not only that, but to come home and be spit on. Who can know how that feels? I met Chris Palmer, and I spoke to his parents; Chris has nightmares, and he is not about to live the war over again by killing some worthless pimp."

"Jimmy, you can afford to be emotional, I have to look at the facts. He threatened Hodges, Hodges died. No alibi, and plenty of motive. The state's attorney sees nothing more than that evidence and salivates over a guilty verdict that translates into a win and more votes come Election Day."

"Michael Blake. Of course, the distinguished state's attorney who cares more about public opinion than justice. How are you going to explain the federal investigation and the likelihood of blackmail?"

I purposely left out the claim concerning organized crime.

Nora shook her head, "We've heard rumors, but defense counsel can't introduce them on cross-examination unless we bring them up on direct, and that's not going to happen. Jimmy, the escort business is squeaky clean on paper; I looked into the operation and its employees myself. Besides, hearsay can't be used as evidence. And if that's not enough, his public defender isn't going to bring up those rumors even when he can, in fact, the defense is practically nonexistent . . . I believe you know Ron Myers."

I knew Ron Myers. The man was an ignorant moron, a talent he perfected since we first met in elementary school. His arrogance and lack of morals imprisoned the lowlife snake in the public defender's office after certain unethical, but not quite illegal, maneuvers banished him from a downtown partnership, branding him with a reputation that kept him out of any other respectable firm. Even the public defender's position wouldn't have been available if not for his uncle who served on the county council. Myers also used his political connection to hand-pick only those cases that gave him the opportunity to cheat unfortunate victims with no alternative but to trust him.

So why would Myers represent Chris Palmer? There was no naïve girl to seduce, or gullible relative to deceive. Kathy Radney would be too perceptive to fall for Myers' customary scam, and since his name never came up during our meeting, I doubted that he ever met with Mr. and Mrs. Palmer. Myers must have drawn the case from the workload and, unable to squirm his way out of it, reluctantly accepted the assignment with the intention of going through the motions until he could move on to a more lucrative case.

"When is the arraignment?"

"Already done. With the elections coming up next year, my boss wants any win we can get. After I told him that there would be a guilty plea, Blake didn't even look at the case. He told me just to go along with anything Myers wants. We go to trial a couple weeks from now."

"Knowing Myers, I can see why, but isn't this a little quick for your office?"

"It is unusual, but the indisputable evidence and Palmer's state of mind left me no choice, especially after Myers pushed for the first available court date, saying that it was in his client's best interest."

"I can understand that, too. Palmer's case keeps him away from his usual . . . Well, you know how Myers works."

"Yes I do, which is why it bothered me that Palmer didn't request another lawyer after seeing Myers' negotiations, but my hands are tied because of his attitude."

"Yeah, I've seen that attitude for myself."

"Well, there you have it. If nothing happens to change Myers' defense, Chris Palmer will go to jail."

"Well, I guess it's up to me to see that something happens.

I'll call you this week."

I got up to leave and noticed that we had been discussing the whole matter while totally naked. I stood there in my birthday suit with Nora laughing at me.

"Rushing out a little quickly, aren't we?"

"Should I dress first?"

"That might be a good idea."

I dressed while Nora put on her robe and together we walked to the door. I held her close and kissed her.

"Still friends?" I asked.

"Forever."

"You know, it might be a good idea to refrain from sex for a while. We could get back to taking our walks down at the harbor."

Nora pulled away just far enough to lightly punch me in the stomach.

"No way," she said, "No sex, no friendship."

"You're using me."

"I don't hear you complaining."

"I look at it as a public service. You know, taking care of the underpaid civil servant."

I knew she'd hit me again, but I said it anyway. I must be a glutton for punishment because the punch aggravated my sore ribcage. . . But some things are worth it. We kissed once more and I left.

The public defender's office happened to be just a few blocks away.

◆ ◆ ◆

Nora recalled seeing on the docket that Myers had a court hearing on Monday and that he scheduled a meeting with one of his clients that morning at eleven. If I hurried, I might catch him.

Ron Myers, public defender, occupied a small cubicle that I considered a snake pit where the treacherous predator would lie in wait for some unsuspecting prey to happen by so it can sink its fangs into the unfortunate creature. But, unlike the snake that would quickly kill and devour, death would come slowly to this prey as Myers sucked the life from his victim before discarding what little he left.

I heard laughter coming from Myers' cubicle.

"Mr. Myers, are you sure you can get me off that easy?"

"Don't worry, Miss Lupid, I can get you off."

The girl giggled like a twelve-year-old, Miss Lupid missing the obvious double entendre as Myers nibbled at his quarry. But after I entered his cubicle and got a good look at the young lady, it became clear that the public defender's client knew exactly what the snake had in mind. Stereotyping people is not an obsession, nor even a habit, but after you've seen so many individuals from as many walks of life, profiling becomes something of an involuntary impulse. Miss Lupid, with her exposed and bulging bosom, cheap jewelry, generous make-up, combined with an out-of-date miniskirt that was two sizes too small, advertised her profession as if she wore a billboard. Most likely arrested for solicitation, she would surely pay the devious reptile; I wondered if she knew how much, or if it even mattered.

I interrupted their conference, "Making new friends, are we?"

"Jimbo, Jimbo, Jimbo . . . tsk, tsk, tsk," he hissed.

He knew that only my closest friends call me Jimbo even

though I never liked it, but drawing on my early morning golf temperament, I controlled myself.

"How are you doing, Mr. Public Defender? You're looking well." Ben would have been proud of my latest attempt at diplomacy.

"I am doing just fine, thank you for asking." He smiled at Miss Lupid, "Please excuse us, dear. I'll see you tonight."

The snake's latest prey gave me a playful wink. I remember thinking that I may have misjudged the young lady's lack of intellect a little too quickly because her engaging smile clearly said: "Yes, I've been here before and I know exactly what I'm doing." And as she shimmied away, I wondered what questionable life experience influenced the young woman's career choice, doubting that her "What I Want To Be When I Grow Up" essay included prostitution as her life's ambition.

"So, what brings you here on a Saturday?"

Myers' interruption stopped me before I could chase after Miss Lupid in an attempt to rescue her from a life of decadence. I turned to face the snake.

"Chris Palmer, but I'm guessing you already knew that."

"Of course. I took that loser's case knowing you'd show up, especially after noticing that your girlfriend was the prosecutor. After all, a Vietnam vet who gets suckered in by some whore . . . had your name all over it." He shook his head as if in sympathy, "Jimbo, I will never understand why you work the southern section of the county when up here you'd get all those husband tailing jobs, and the please-save-my-child-from-drugs cries for help. How are you ever going to make anything of yourself?"

"I'm all I want to be."

"That may be true, but I wonder if Miss Rutledge feels the same way."

Bringing up my relationship with Nora after that

morning's quarrel provided the straw that broke this camel's back; all too quickly the golf mentality abandoned me. I wanted to tee off on the son-of-a-bitch with my nine-iron.

"All right, enough of the bull. Are you going to help that kid, or just go screw your whore while Chris Palmer goes to jail for a murder he didn't commit?"

As usual, Myers was as calm as I was agitated, which angered me that much more. He leaned back and wiped his brow, as if he worked that hard.

"Jimbo," he said slowly with an irritating and purposeful emphasis, "What can I do? Palmer won't even talk to me. I tried to plead temporary insanity, but the state's attorney office wouldn't go for it, and the judge took their side. It's such a simple case that Blake didn't even show up; your girlfriend handled the arraignment herself."

"So that means you already cut a deal."

"We compromised. Your girlfriend's office agreed to lower the charge to second-degree murder even though Palmer did go back which indicates premeditation. But given his state of mind . . . Well, I'm sure you've seen that for yourself, Jimbo. Anyway, Palmer will be sentenced to thirty years with the possibility of parole for good behavior . . . in fifteen years or so."

"And you're good with that? How the hell do you sleep at night?"

"Oh, I sleep all right, especially after my meeting with Miss Lupid."

I wanted to chop the head off the snake now striking at me. The devious reptile had been a curse since high school when Myers, who was much bigger than me at the time, had no trouble kicking my ass—especially with his friends around—until my junior year.

He was one of the cool seniors at the time and I thought that fighting back would destroy my social standing even though my size and strength had increased by that time. After one of the beatings, I talked to my dad at breakfast when he gave me his usual good advice:

"Why should you care who likes you or not? People are going to like you if you like and respect yourself, and those who don't . . . Well, son, they're just not worth it. When you deal with people honestly, they respond in kind. It's simply a matter of social justice, and that justice has nothing to do with who's popular, who's bigger, or anything else for that matter. Justice is simply a matter of right and wrong."

I went to school that day, confronted Myers, then beat him until he cried and ran for the nurse. After that, the snake changed his tactics, verbally attacking me, but only with an escape route already planned out. So, when I reached for the gutless wonder, he immediately pushed the security button on his desk.

"I'll get you, Myers. You can't hide from me forever."

He pressed the button again. "Yeah, Jimbo, I am so scared."

After our last altercation, Myers' uncle—the politician who got Myers the job after nearly being disbarred—threatened to ban me from the building if I touched his pathetic nephew again. Because I often needed help from the other attorneys who worked there, I backed out and quickly made my way to the elevators, but as the doors opened, there stood security.

"Been to see that son-of-a—"

"Now, now, Harold," I cut in before my friend lost his Baptist religion, "Where's that Christian forgiveness you and Ben always preach about?"

Harold was a good friend and another veteran who strictly practiced his faith. For him to spit out obscenities, there must be exceptional motivation.

"You're right, and I am sorry. But that guy makes it so da . . . I mean *darn* hard to practice what you preach. So, don't do as I do, do as I say."

"You and Ben know how hard I try."

Harold laughed and shook my hand, "I'll tell the rat that you got out before I could catch you."

Rat, snake, either way, Myers was an animal.

"Lying, too, Harold. I'll remember you in church."

That playful rebuke led to the inevitable shot to the stomach. All my friends love to hit me.

The day that began with a pleasant though somewhat painful golf game turned into a nightmare and neither the playful punch from Harold nor the elevator ride did anything to calm me down. Anger is one thing, rage is another, or so my dad said. All the battles I fought before the Lakeview case were handled without losing control of my temper—even in Vietnam —all because of my father's advice after I killed a copperhead snake.

"Why did you kill it?" Dad asked.

"It attacked a baby bunny and I just lost it; I took the whittling knife you gave me and cut off its head before it could swallow the poor thing."

"So you lost your temper; is that right?"

"Yes, sir. I couldn't stand seeing that slithering bas . . ." My father's disapproving frown stopped me in my tracks. "I mean the snake trying to swallow that baby bunny."

"Okay, so you killed a snake that was actually doing what it needs to do to survive. If you had stopped long enough to think, you would have realized that a copperhead is venomous and could turn on you to protect itself. You ignored the danger because you lost control. Yes, the snake's action appears brutal to you, and it's natural to feel anger when you witness cruelty, but losing your temper gives your enemy the advantage. How did you feel after you killed it?"

"I don't remember; I was shaking so bad."

"You were shaking because your emotions tightened your muscles. Rage not only affects you mentally, but physically as well. Think before you act and restrain your rage, even when angry. What happened to the rabbit?"

"I brought the little guy home, but it died; I just buried it."

"I'm sorry to have to tell you this, Son, but the sad truth is that you're going to meet more than a couple snakes in your life," Dad slowly shook his head, "and you won't be able save all the baby bunnies of the world."

After our talk, clashes with my anger became a common occurrence, but I won more than I lost . . . until Cliff and Pinkie's second beating. That previous night, while lying on the Lakeview Manor's asphalt parking lot, and as the whisper of Dad's teaching resonated loud and clear, my unbridled rage nonetheless accompanied me to Barlowe's office. I was trying to save a bunny.

The meeting with Myers enraged me in the same manner. Speeding out of the county garage, an intense fire drove me to the mall where Kathy Radney worked. With my insides still shaking, I made my way past the stores, trying to compose myself by repeating a silent prayer that Harold would have prescribed—it didn't work. I saw Kathy and tried to act as though nothing was wrong.

A middle-aged customer listened as Kathy recommended two dresses from which to choose. Clearly, this business suited my client better than wet nursing some old geezer, or . . .

I continued to fight my suspicions concerning the

beautiful girl's involvement in Hodges' murder, and also the role she played in the escort service. Could it really be possible that she and Miss Lupid had anything in common?

My client saw me then turned back to her customer, "Will you excuse me for a moment; I need to speak to this gentleman."

"We need to talk."

"Sure, let me get Betty."

Kathy went to the back of the store and returned with another saleslady. The customer expressed her concern that such a helpful fashion consultant was leaving, but the woman's attitude changed after Kathy handed her one of the two dresses, then said, "This blue dress brings out the color of your eyes, and it will be perfect for your son's engagement party. You'll be the envy of everyone there. Betty will ring you up."

After assuring the customer of her purchase, Kathy grabbed her pocketbook, took my arm, and led me out of the shop. "You're as tight as a drum. What's wrong?"

"It's nothing. I let some people get to me from time to time, but that's not your problem, and it sure isn't Chris's. Look, Kathy, we need to clarify a couple things before I can go any further."

"What things? I've told you everything I've seen and heard since Johnny's murder."

"I know. You've told me about the business at the Manor with all its rumors, but you haven't told me anything about you and Chris. How and when did you meet?"

Kathy walked over to a bench and sat down; I followed but remained standing. She bowed her head in that familiar pose, playing the part of the mannequin, motionless and barely breathing. Finally, she looked up and spoke.

"I first noticed Chris last April in the library when I was looking into some classes at the community college. They keep all the catalogues there. I know my job at the Manor won't last forever, Jim . . . I've never called you Jim before, may I call you Jim?" I nodded. "Thanks, that's much better. Anyway, when I did see Chris, that cute face of his just made me smile and I tried some innocent flirting, but he didn't give me a second look. This might sound petty, but I was hurt. Men come on to me all the time, so I decided to approach him. I'll admit that it was a game at first, but not for long. It's not only his boyish features and shyness that attracted me, it was his kind and generous nature after I got to know him. You wouldn't believe how much he gives to all the panhandlers down at the harbor." She laughed. "He's definitely not the kind of guy I'm used to dating. He didn't even kiss me until our third date, and that was only because I kissed him first. But he was so tender . . ."

Once again, the annoying bow of the head appeared, accompanied by the extended pause. Just before I could ask her to go on, Kathy looked up with tears streaming down those lovely cheeks.

"I'm so sorry; I miss him so much." Then she bowed her head again.

"Kathy, I don't have all day."

If my impatience affected her, it didn't show. She smiled through the tears, searched for and found a tissue in her pocketbook, then wiped her eyes.

"I don't know why I didn't tell him about my job at the Manor, but when I did explain that I worked as a hostess and that I sometimes accompanied clients to business functions, he didn't seem to mind. I don't know how he found out about the rumors, unless it was that guy he works with, the one who brought him to the Manor that night."

"But are you sure Chris had no suspicions before?"

"I'm sure. The first time he brought up the rumors was at the Manor the night Johnny was murdered, and you know what happened after that, but I'm positive Chris didn't go back to kill Johnny."

"How can you be so sure? You only dated a few months."

"You met him once, what do you think?"

She had me there, but her answer raised the question that bothered me since I first visited Chris: "If you miss him so much, why haven't you gone to see him?"

"I'm afraid, Jim. I'm afraid he won't see me. My only hope is that you can free Chris, then we can be together again."

"I still don't understand why you made no attempt to go after Chris that night, or even give him an alibi. Sure, it would have been a lie, but at least the police wouldn't have stopped their investigation so quickly. The leads you gave me would have kept them busy for a while."

"I couldn't go after Chris, and I couldn't give him an alibi because I was with a client until early that morning."

My expression asked the question before I had the chance to put it into words.

"I know what that looks like, but so many of my clients come to me for . . . I don't know, I guess they come to me for some kind of therapy. I have a way of making men feel comfortable, and I spent most of that night with a man who is more than a client. He's a good friend, a friend dealing with terrible personal problems. I just couldn't leave him."

"Chris needed you more."

"How could I know that? I never thought something like this would happen."

"Okay. Let's forget about that for the moment. What about the blackmail you mentioned? Did you ask Brewer about the guy you saw with your boss?"

"No, I haven't gone back."

"And you still can't remember his name?"

"No, I never knew his name . . . but there is someone who might know: Brittany. That man used to be one of her clients."

"And Brittany is one of Johnny's girls?"

"She used to be until she got with Mr. Barlowe."

Then I remembered the name: Barlowe's alibi.

"Barlowe said she's out of town."

"She should be back."

I ignored the fact that Kathy still knew quite a bit about the happenings at the Manor, especially since she supposedly hadn't gone back.

"Could you set up a meeting with her without Barlowe knowing?"

"No, we don't get along, but there is a chance that you might catch her at the gym; she works out every day except Sunday with Cliff and Pinkie."

"Just what I need."

◆ ◆ ◆

I drove to Brad's Body Shop. Though the name sounds like an auto repair garage, it was definitely a gym, but not the kind you might think. This gym's membership pumped iron, not to bulk up, but to brute up. Bouncers and badasses practically lived there. Not long before, the police suspected the business of running an illegal prize fighting circuit, but despite all the bruised and battered faces, the investigation resulted in the same dead end as their investigation at the Manor, every bit of the operation squeaky clean.

The building stood alone in the middle of a large shopping center. I knew the layout because I went along with Nora when she needed to question one of the club's members over an alleged assault and battery charge. She didn't want me to go with her, but the police wouldn't escort the assistant state's attorney and I could only imagine what she'd do if one of the boys tried to get a little too frisky or friendly. Also, I knew the owner, Brad Jacoby. We met when I worked at the port with his brother Jack, a nickname shortened from Jacoby; I never knew his real first name. I liked Jack but didn't care much for his brother. Still, knowing the owner got Nora safely in and out, even though she fared no better than the police.

Kathy said that Cliff and Pinkie knew my car, so I parked behind the building, then walked to a place in the parking lot where the gym was in view without anyone inside seeing me. The front, nothing more than a sheet of glass, kept me from getting close enough to look for Brittany, but did present a clear view of the two bouncers spotting each other on the weights. Their workout routine would have impressed Ben, and I considered myself lucky that I managed to put them down that first night at the Manor—even if it did take dirty fighting and my .38.

There were no girls to be seen, and since the troubling sight of the two beefy bouncers along with about twenty other monsters prevented me from going inside to ask around, I uncharacteristically decided to be cautious. This time I would follow Dad's advice to be patient; there had to be a better way to meet Barlowe's girlfriend.

But I believe it was a golfer who said that it's better to be lucky than good. A cute and what I suppose could be described as just-a-little-bit-better-than-buffed girl walked out by herself. Kathy described Brittany as a well-built pretty blonde who always wore pink and this girl easily fit that description. After all, how many blondes who wore pink worked out in this particular gym that catered to the brutish and brutal? It had to be Brittany—but how could I get close to her without being seen?

I wondered if I shouldn't take a chance that Cliff and Pinkie would be too involved with their routine to pay attention to anything other than their reps. But before I had the chance to take that risk, luck continued to be on my side when Brittany walked away from the glass façade to the side of the gym where she lit a cigarette and relaxed, casually leaning against the concrete wall. Assuming that my name came up after the episodes at the Manor, she might have heard about me, so I quickly devised a plan, then ran around the lot, away from the front of the building, and came up behind her.

"Excuse me, is your name Brittany?" Kathy didn't give me her last name and I didn't ask, hoping it wouldn't matter. Slowly, she turned toward me while taking a deep drag, then blew the smoke in my face.

"Yeah, why?"

"My name is Ron Myers. I'm the public defender defending Chris Palmer on the Hodges murder case."

"Oh yeah, I know you."

My heart sank. Could Myers have met her before?

"I don't remember you; where did we meet?"

"Oh, we never met, but you defended a friend of mine, Sheri Peters. You must remember her. She had to screw you five times before you got her a court date, and then she still had to pay a fine."

Hardly a shock there, Myers took whatever he could from his clients—Miss Lupid would receive the same hands-on service —but fortunately, the charade seemed to be working, so I continued to act the part.

"Hey, lady, do you know how little this job pays? Why would you begrudge me a couple fringe benefits? Besides, I did the best I could for Sheri. She could have gotten worse."

"Either way, I got your number, pal. That Palmer guy has nothing to offer, so you thought you could hit on me. Well, you're not screwing me, so get lost."

Brittany threw down the cigarette, stomped on it, and started to walk away. I couldn't let her get around that corner. Putting my speed to good use, I jumped in front of her and held up my hands.

"Okay, wait a minute. Please. You're right. I heard about you from Palmer's girlfriend and I thought we could work something out, but if not, then that's okay, too. Brittany, I have to be honest with you, this case has upset me more than any other I've had. Anyone with any sense at all can see that Palmer didn't kill Hodges. All the police and that asshole state's attorney think about is throwing the book at this kid. Hell, the only thing Chris did wrong was to fall for that whore."

As soon as I said it, I thought "whore" may have been the wrong choice of words, but I imagined Myers saying it, and even though it had no effect back at the Manor, I still believed the asshole reference to the state's attorney would be a nice touch. I looked into Brittany's eyes as compassionately as possible without blowing my imitation of the rotten bastard. She barely moved before finally letting out a slow breath.

"Yeah . . . Kathy. That too good for the rest of the world bitch. I showed her that she wasn't so great when I hooked up with Frank. I'll bet that's why she dropped my name. She's been jealous of me ever since we got together, and she'll do anything just to piss me off."

"Do you mean Frank Barlowe?"

"Yeah, I love that big guy and he loves me; so now I don't have to work for nobody. Let's see where that bitch ends up." Brittany gave me a hard look and laughed, "I bet you hit on her and she turned you down."

"Come on, Brittany, give me a little credit; even I have

standards. Heaven knows what that nice guy saw in her; in fact, I still wonder if she's not the one who set Palmer up."

There, I finally said it. The thought that had been in the back of my mind for quite some time but refused to say out loud. In my journal, I wrote down everything that happened since my first meeting with Kathy, along with any conclusion I could draw from the encounters with everyone involved—good and bad. One by one, I considered every question that came to mind, questions that, in any other case, wouldn't affect me. Something about Kathy, other than her looks, made me want to protect, rather than implicate her—maybe it was that calming influence. Nora and Ben both had to look at the facts. I didn't. For me, only one indisputable reality existed: Someone fabricated the frame to implicate Chris, and it was time to admit that Kathy could very well be a part of that framework—but was she a willing or unwilling participant?

In the meantime, Brittany stood there, obviously deep in thought, her mind's engine turning unaccustomed RPMs. Suddenly, her eyes opened wide with the arrival of what appeared to be a pleasurable thought.

"Hey, I never thought of that, but it might be possible. Hell, I bet she's into it up to her scrawny, snobby neck."

"That's why I came to you, Brittany. If you can give me something that'll throw the slightest doubt on the state's attorney's case against Chris . . . anything you can think of that could help me get him out of jail would be great. I don't care who killed Hodges; I only want to free Chris."

I added the last statement in case Barlowe was involved and Brittany knew it.

"He does seem like just a good guy who got screwed around by that bitch."

Once again, I nodded as compassionately as possible without compromising my masquerade. Brittany looked down at her shoes, scratched her head, then pulled back her bangs. It seemed like hours passed while her thought processing engine remained in neutral, before finally popping the clutch to reveal an idea.

"Frank doesn't tell me a lot, but I pay attention to everything that goes on. I watched Johnny working the room every night while that bitch followed him around. Is there something in particular that could help?"

"Well, I know you were sleeping with Barlowe the night Hodges was shot, but what about—"

"Wait a minute, I wasn't with . . . Oh yeah. Yeah, that's right. I was sleeping with Frank. Go ahead."

What the hell was going on? Could Brittany be another empty-headed character, or was she playing a game like everybody else? I needed to strap a lie detector on my back just to talk to these people. How could I separate stupidity from intentional deception?

"I was going to ask if you knew anything about blackmail. I heard that Hodges was putting the squeeze on somebody."

"No, most of our customers come from out of town. You know the type: respectable traveling businessmen trying to get away from their old ladies. They probably use fake names, especially since Johnny only took cash. One of my regulars even told me that . . ."

The motor that drove Brittany's brain was working overtime. I thought it had slipped back into neutral at this latest pause, but after no more than a few seconds, her face lit up with a devilish grin.

"There was one guy. Damn, I wish I knew who he was. He was one of Kathy's regulars, but I never saw his face. Whenever he did show up, which wasn't that often, it would be just before closing. He must have been expected because Johnny and Kathy would take him into Frank's office before anyone could get a good look at him. He never went to a table or the bar. And I never saw him leave either. Kathy must have taken the guy out through the back door of the office because she would be gone the rest of the night. Rumor was that he was a local politician."

"Thanks, Brittany. You've been a great help."

My Ron Myers imitation hadn't finished thanking Brittany when someone lifted me up from behind and threw me against the wall. As I fell to the ground, I saw Pinkie standing over me getting ready to attack. These guys get fiercely aggressive when they work out. I shook my head, struggled to my feet, and kicked him squarely in the groin. Nothing happened—the giant was wearing a cup. He grabbed me again and lifted me off the ground, but Brittany stopped him before he could do any more damage.

"Pinkie! Put him down."

"Heth's a fuckin' thnoop, Brith."

Pinkie spoke with an incompatible crackling soprano and a distinctive lisp. The high-pitched tone of his voice, accompanied by the speech impediment had to be the reason for the nickname that probably saddled him through high school, and which would have been comical if he wasn't holding me a foot off the ground in what I hoped wouldn't be a death grip.

"It's okay, Pinkie. He's trying to help."

"The bosth don't like him, Brith."

"Pinkie, I said put him down."

The well-trained goliath released me and I took off the second my feet hit the ground. Pinkie and Brittany could decide who and what I was after my escape. I ran to my car and sped out onto the road hitting eighty in record time, lucky that no cops were around or Ben would be fixing another ticket, even though he swore he'd never do it again.

Once safely away, I began to think about the problems Brittany presented. All these bewildering women. Those familiar with the great movies from years past would understand why I cast the mystifyingly gorgeous Mary Astor as Kathy, the alluring and amusingly madcap Judy Holliday as Brittany, and, of course, the beautiful, yet remote Lauren Bacall as Nora.

But Humphrey Bogart wouldn't fit my part in this story line, only because I lacked his confidence. I did have his tough, gate-crashing mentality, but not the positive and decisive line of sight. Yes, I would take a giant leap into a massive quicksand hole, or worse, step on a land mine as I did twice at the Manor, but I failed in any attempt to distinguish the lies from calculated chess moves. Who were the queens and who were the pawns?

From then on, I decided to consider everyone a liar until he or she proved different.

All but one.

◆ ◆ ◆

Chris Palmer was the only person who could tell me the truth as to what happened the night Hodges was killed. But convincing him to trust me might prove to be just about as difficult as watching Tony Sellers eat without gagging. Ben and Nora both said that I could talk a judge out of his gavel. Chris would put their claim to the test.

Ed Polhaus looked up from the desk and smiled, "Not you again."

"Hell, yes. I've got to get that kid to open up."

"You keep dreaming, Jimbo; I hear it's good for the heart."

"Then I must have a pretty healthy heart because my only dream is to get Palmer out of here. Sarge, I'm telling you: He's innocent."

"Just the little I've seen of him," Ed said as he nodded, "I believe you're right. But first, you've got to get him to talk. How are you going to do that?"

I grinned, "My friend, I am going to pull some of that good old brutal in-your-face service mentality on him. You know military discipline never leaves us."

"Good luck, buddy, but I still think you're going to need more than a traditional butt-kicking to get that kid to budge."

"It's worth a try, especially since it's my only chance to get to the bottom of this mess."

Once again, I made my way to the visitor's room and waited. The history of the old jail came to mind. Surely, Chris wasn't the only innocent man these walls held through the years, and if the old bricks could talk, I'd wager that you'd hear many sad stories about other unjustly accused inmates.

Chris entered the room, and without looking up, walked over and practically collapsed on the bench across from me. The fresh bruises and cuts on his face told me everything I needed to know. The beating could have occurred in any number of ways, and I could only imagine what Chris dealt with on the other side of the cellblock door. But no amount of sympathy would solve his crisis. I took a deep breath to destroy my compassion and did what I came to do.

"I came here because I thought you might like to know how my investigation is going."

I waited for any kind of reaction, but Chris's demeanor remained stoic, extreme, and rock hard, just like the walls that held him prisoner.

I stood and leaned toward him, "You know what? Your best friend Sellers is a piece of shit. Your defense attorney is the ugliest slime I've ever had the misfortune to meet, and Kathy Radney. . . Well, hell, I don't know what she is. But I do know one thing for sure . . . you're no better than the worst of them.

The only guy who had any guts at all was Johnny Hodges. That's right, he did what he wanted to do and the hell with anybody who didn't like it. But you had to go back out there that night and kill him. *Didn't you.* Yeah, you did it; nobody else could be that *fucking stupid!*

"So, all I have to say to you, pal, is that it's been a real pleasure meeting you. You made me enough money to pay this month's rent."

I turned to leave.

"Wait."

He spoke softly, but loud enough to stop me. I turned to face my client who looked up at me and finally had something to say.

"I didn't kill Hodges."

I smiled, "Hell, I know that."

I sat again on the bench across from Chris with the intention of patiently waiting for him to continue. I didn't have to wait long.

"No one's been here but my parents."

"I know."

"I should have treated them better; they deserve ..."

His head dropped.

"Chris, listen to me. They understand; I've spoken to them, and their only concern is getting you out of here."

"Mom told me that you came to see them," he said, looking back up, "I appreciate that you took the time, especially after the way I treated you."

"Not a problem. Since you weren't talking, I thought they could help."

"Yeah, I am sorry about that ... Mr. Smith, I have to get out of here."

"Well, Chris, let's be honest, you're the only one who can help me. I've spoken to just about everyone involved and believe me, there are too many conflicting stories. You're the only one who can unravel this mess so I have something to go on."

"I'll do anything I can."

"Okay, start with the night of the murder. Tell me everything that happened and everything you saw and heard, even the smallest thing might not mean anything to you, but you never know how it could possibly help."

Chris slowly tilted his head like someone trying to recreate a scene from memory, then after less than a minute, he began:

"This whole mess started that day Tony told me about his friend's . . ." He paused, let out a quick breath, shook his head, then continued, "his encounter with Kathy. I didn't believe him, and I wanted to wait until I saw Kathy, but Tony kept pushing me to go. I don't know why, but I gave in and he drove me out to the Manor. I was hardly inside the door when Kathy came over to meet me. We started to talk. Kathy told me again that she was just a hostess for the most part and sometimes an escort who accompanied businessmen to corporate functions. Now, maybe I'm naïve, Mr. Smith, but I was okay with her explanation, even after seeing the inside of the Manor. Anyway, I told her that I would go, and that we'd talk later. But I never had a chance to finish. Hodges came over and grabbed my arm. Push came to shove and we got into it, but two big men broke it up before any damage was done. Now here's the part I don't understand: Hodges confronted me like he thought I was there to start trouble even though we had never met. And as far as I could tell, no one else in that room knew me either. I didn't even know who he was at the time. In any case, Hodges couldn't have known I was coming because Tony didn't talk me into going until just before we left work after stowing a late load that came in. I barely had enough time to go home and change before he picked me up."

Chris stopped there and took another breath.

"Mr. Smith, I'm not going to lie. I'm not much for fighting, but I wanted to lay Hodges out. I heard that there are witnesses who said I threatened him, but that's not true. There wasn't enough time; those two guys, I guess they were bouncers, threw me out before I could even say anything."

"First, call me Jim, and I met the bouncers, too."

Squinting his eyes, Chris took notice of the effects of my visits to the Manor, "Your face doesn't look a whole lot better than mine."

I laughed and my client smiled; that felt good.

"Go on. Where did you go after they threw you out?"

"I walked all the way back to my apartment, got in my car, and drove to the Inner Harbor. Kathy and I used to go there, and she said that's where she'd meet me if she could get away."

"Did you see anyone who might remember seeing you?"

"Nope, just walked around until I got to our bench. I stayed there all night hoping she'd show up."

Slowly, Chris shook his head; the "our bench" memory got to him. I waited, but time mattered more than patience.

"Come on, buddy, didn't you buy anything. Not even a drink?"

"No, I didn't . . . Wait a minute. *Buddy!* That's it. I don't know if he'll remember me, but there's an old guy who's always there with his dog. He sits on a bench not far from where Kathy and I used to sit; in fact, the two benches are right next to each other. We talked a little, not much, but a little. Most people think he's crazy."

"That's okay, crazy is my second language."

◆ ◆ ◆

I ran to my car and bolted for Baltimore's Inner Harbor making the trip in record time, fortunate that it was Saturday with no rush hour traffic to battle on I-83. After parking in a garage six blocks away to avoid paying the exorbitant rates closer to the harbor, I zigzagged through the streets, nearly getting pancaked by an impatient young girl running a red light. But safety didn't concern me; Chris had an alibi that would clear him of Hodges' murder.

One worry came to mind: What if the old-timer didn't remember my client? After all, the senior citizen didn't appear to have a concrete grasp on reality. He sat on the same bench every day, never moving, ignoring all those who snubbed or mocked him, talking to his dog as if she were human. Like Chris and his girl, Nora and I would often stroll on the developing waterfront walkway checking out the changes the city planners had in mind by tearing down the old piers, markets, and warehouses. The new construction didn't appear to affect the old guy, but I wondered what he'd do if they moved his bench. Relocate probably, because the old man impressed me as someone who dealt with whatever comes without complaining.

It was just after five when I reached the promenade and mingled in with the large weekend crowd wandering around the concession area. I hadn't eaten since breakfast, so I stopped at a hot dog cart and bought two of the overpriced delicacies.

I walked toward the far side of the harbor marveling at the yachts in the marina, calculating the amount of wealth the owners must have in order to afford the boats and their slips, deciding that it would add up to more money than I could ever have, or want.

On the other side of that opulence, and away from the

construction, the old timer and his dog would be camped out. It was during those years that the inseparable couple resided on the same bench never moving from the stake they claimed as their home. I often wondered how he lived, where he slept, and where he carried out his personal business. The dog, his untethered faithful companion, never strayed far from his side, and together they existed in contradiction to the wealth and prosperity surrounding them.

The picture-perfect setting of pristine rolling hills and slowly rotting docks that serviced the first trading ships and many fishing vessels since the seventeenth century was slowly falling victim to urban development. The destruction of that serene antiquity sickened me, not only because of the indifference toward the past, but because profit motivated the destruction, which I suppose should be understandable. A thirty-one-story-high World Trade Center already dominated the water's edge. Soon, two pavilions, a science center and an aquarium, along with pricy hotels and upscale condominiums would replace the once peaceful natural landscape of the harbor. And yet, with all this immeasurable source of tax income, the mayor and city council will still cry poverty. The city's bureaucracy probably tried to tax the old guy, his dog and their bench, but that would be about as successful as getting a straight answer from a politician.

The squatter's faithful companion, something of a lab mix, feasted on the charity of the regular visitors and tourists who gave the dog something to eat, so much in fact, that you'd think she'd weigh a ton. Instead, the old guy's sidekick looked trim and healthy, unlike her scruffy owner who wore dingy military fatigues that were as much a part of his body as his skin. His face, mostly hidden by a shabby beard and an Orioles ball cap, appeared pale and gaunt, weathered from years of exposure. The dog may have been well-fed, but I never saw her master take or ask for a handout. In fact, most of his social interaction took place with his furry comrade.

"Sit." She stood.

"Lay down." She sat.

"Stop scratching." She scratched.

"Good dog."

That was their existence. A constant training session that the dog ignored, doing as she damn well pleased.

I gave the dog the last bite of my hot dog, then turned to her master, "That's the best trained dog I've ever seen."

"Damn right she is, buddy," he said in a low and scratchy voice just a couple decibels above a whisper. "Takes constant work, hard work, trained her myself. But it's worth it, buddy. Yeah, buddy, I'll bet she's the best trained dog in the universe. Yes sir, buddy, that's what I'd say."

"Well, you have to be pretty sharp yourself to train a dog that well."

"Yeah, buddy. Yes sir, I'll go along with that even though most people think I'm pretty damned useless . . . but I'm not useless, buddy. I *am* sharp, buddy, just like you know I am."

"Yes, I know you are. By the way, do you remember me? I come down here from time to time with my girl."

He looked hard at me, then smiled, "Yeah, sure. I seen you around, buddy. You feed Sally, and you don't laugh at me like some of these youngsters. You're more like my buddies back in the Nam."

Isn't it strange that we can look at something or someone so often without noticing who and what they actually are? In all my visits to the harbor, not once did I really see him. Not once did I closely examine his clothing or take notice of his features. He was just there, occupying a space in time, just like the bench he occupied. The veteran existed as a fragment of hardship scraping by in those prosperous surroundings. That day, I looked into his eyes and finally recognized this man for what he truly was.

Embarrassed for failing to notice before, the Vietnam veteran was slender, but not unhealthy; his weathered face was pale, but not sickly, and in spite of the heat, he seemed surprisingly comfortable, even with his military field jacket buttoned to the collar. Not all casualties of war come home with visible scars or missing limbs, some simply have that distinct vacant gaze. What I presumed to be age, turned out to be that look of experience.

"You are sharp, my friend. I also served in Nam, and so did a friend of mine, a friend who needs your help."

He sat up and became more animated, "Hey, buddy, we got to help each other; we're all we got, man. I'll do anything to help a brother."

I showed him a picture of Chris that I cut from the paper Sergeant Polhaus gave me back in the jail; it was all I could dig up on such short notice.

"This is my friend. He was here the Friday before last. Do you remember him?"

The veteran looked at the picture and slowly nodded his head, "Yeah, buddy, sure I remember. He's my friend, too. Always feeds Sally. Comes with a real pretty girl, but she wasn't with him that night. I asked where she was, but he didn't answer, fact, he didn't say nothin' . . . just sat there. I was gonna take Sally for a walk, but I was too scared to leave him. He looked real bad, buddy. I figured it was probably the girl."

"When did he leave?"

"Never, buddy. Well, not never. I mean he stayed 'til morning . . . stood reveille with me. So come on, buddy, how can I help?"

I assured my new buddy that he'd already helped and not to go anywhere because I'd be back. He chuckled and said that he would need to cancel all his travel plans, but he could work it out. I shook his hand, ran to my car, then raced to Nora's apartment and rang the bell four times until she finally answered. But before she opened the door completely, I pushed my way in, took her in my arms and danced around the room until we fell over the couch and onto her coffee table, breaking one of the legs beneath us.

I laughed while Nora swore. The busted table, apparently something of sentimental value, angered Nora that much more, but I didn't care. Chris had an alibi, and my favorite assistant state's attorney could get him out of jail in the morning . . .

Or so I thought.

"It won't work."

"What the hell do you mean it won't work? Didn't you hear me? Chris has an alibi."

"Yes, I heard you and I also heard who the alibi is. Michael Blake would tear his testimony apart."

"You mean that *you* would tear his testimony apart."

"That's right, Jimmy. I have to do my job."

"Please tell me you're kidding."

"No, Jimmy, you're kidding yourself if you think I can ignore what that old guy is. He's a fruitcake."

"He's not a fruitcake, and he's not old, either."

"He's a fruitcake, and that's all that matters to a judge and jury."

"Okay, let's say he's a little eccentric."

"*A little!* Jimmy, you are so hardheaded. You can't be this blind."

Nora was losing her temper more by the minute, and then I lost mine.

"Thanks, Nora, thanks a lot. He's a veteran; he served in Nam."

"I know that means a lot to you, and maybe he'll draw some sympathy because of that, but compassion won't help Palmer because your friend's credibility will go flying out the window as soon as he calls me his buddy twenty or thirty times. The judge will think the defense paid him to testify."

"That's just great. And you say you fight for justice."

Then I noticed that Nora was wearing the robe she throws on when she leaves her bed, and also that the bedroom door was closed. I wondered why it took so long for her to come to the door at that hour.

"A little early for you to be in bed, isn't it?"

"I was . . . I was tired." She was stuttering, unusual for Nora. "It's been a long day."

"Busy Saturday, huh?"

She didn't answer; the robe answered for her.

I left Nora's apartment with nothing but hate, frustration and more than a little confusion in my heart trying my best to rationalize her reason for wearing that robe. Could she be as tired as she said? But it was Saturday; Nora didn't work weekends, and she never went to bed early unless it was with me. Just as I refused to accept any thoughts of Kathy Radney's involvement in Hodges' murder, I bitterly fought the possibility that there was a man hiding behind the closed door to Nora's bedroom. After all, we were together just that morning. But what other explanation could there be? She said I wasn't the only man in her life. Had we drifted that far apart?

In that moment I hated Nora for wearing the revealing robe as much as I hated her for being part of the injustice that blinded everyone but me surrounding the case against Chris Palmer. If I couldn't find justice for my client in the courtroom, where could I go? Just as the mystery man in Nora's bedroom remained hidden from view, so did the murderer who shot Johnny Hodges. And while I could make a couple of what I thought were mighty intelligent guesses—none of which I could prove—that one indisputable fact kept gnawing: Chris Palmer had to be released and it was up to me, and me alone, to take care of business.

I drove around for a while, even heading toward the old bed and breakfast that was once my home, the route taken whenever my past beckoned, wishing that the roads led to a time portal capable of returning me to the days of my youth and the treasured advice my father always provided. I often heard his voice telling me to be patient and think things through before acting, and it was his teachings and guidance that encouraged me during my time in Vietnam and after I came home. But I didn't hear from Dad that night; he and Mom were missing through no fault of their own and I was stuck in the inescapable corrupt and unjust world.

It was dark by the time I got home. Turning on the lights of my office is a waste of electricity. Many late-night arrivals, blind from the overindulgence of alcohol, taught me the location of each piece of furniture in the room, especially my favorite, the worn swivel chair behind my desk that I found in an antique store. It was during those dark evenings when I easily made my way to that chair and the waiting bottle of Jack Daniels to sit and curse the world's insanity, often daring to question God's plan. There were even times when I almost came to terms with the death of my parents along with my friends in Nam.

Almost.

That night, the chair that usually inspired my reasoning failed. The harder I tried to concentrate, the more unintelligible each thought became. I stared at the bottle of Jack on my desk, its silhouette outlined by the streetlight peeking through my window. Even my liquid friend couldn't help.

I placed my hand on the legal pad, sliding my fingers across the page as if reading braille, reviewing the names of the players I couldn't see, their roles as indistinct as the writing on the paper. I considered my theory and the leads Kathy provided hoping that at least one would expose the conspiracy someone used to frame Chris. Any one of the persons involved in those leads had more than enough reason to eliminate Hodges. All but the mafia.

The only sound in the darkened room came from the two fans until a knock at the door interrupted my thoughts—a soft, muffled knock that I hardly heard. Too late for my neighbor's son, and too emotionally drained to see anyone, I ignored the interruption hoping they would go away.

The knob clicked and the door slowly opened. One short, not quite stocky man, maybe five-six, stood in the doorway, his figure outlined in the light from the hall. Then two men, big men, appeared behind him.

While my few valuables are safely hidden under the floorboard in my closet, I keep one other item taped under the center desk drawer: another snub-nosed .38—this one loaded at all times. Ben talked me into keeping the gun close at hand in case one of the public officials I managed to offend might be driven to drastic measures. But I hid it there thinking it would be something that Spade or Marlowe would do.

The two big men weren't Cliff and Pinkie, though I'm not sure why I believed this since their faces were indistinct. It may have been because the smaller man wasn't Sellers, Barlowe, Brewer, or anyone else I had recently met. So where in God's name could another character come from this late in the game? Then I thought that it may just be possible that they had nothing to do with the Manor at all, but potential clients who simply wanted my help with some other matter. That thought quickly disappeared into the darkness.

The shorter man entered and approached my desk while the others kept their place. It bothered me when he sat down in the chair across from me as if he knew the layout of the room. I felt him staring at me. My hand tightly gripped the .38 I had silently taken from its hiding place.

"Don't turn on the light," he said.

"I have no intention to. I can see well enough to take care of you and your two friends standing in the doorway."

"Your bravado is well-known, Mr. Smith . . ."

*Bravado—who talks like that anymore.*

". . . but I would advise against any imprudent action. The sole purpose of my visit is to offer our assistance in the present crisis facing you and your client."

He spoke slowly and distinctly, like a teacher making a point to a third-grade class. My journal didn't clearly state my feelings of that moment, and I don't remember if it was his manner, or the two men standing in the doorway that intimidated me, but I do recall my palm sweating as my grip instinctively tightened even more around the gun.

"And just how can you, and whoever else you're talking about, help me?"

"I possess valuable information pertinent to your investigation."

He didn't pause there but stopped. What the hell was this? The two of us sat in silence while his escort held their place in the doorway. The only sound in the room continued to be only the two fans blowing, but not cooling, the humid air. Without knowing the nature of the intruder's purpose, I decided to wait until the devil delivered ice before reacting to what seemed to be a prompt. It took some time before the visitor realized that I wasn't about to perform like a trained seal.

"Mr. Smith," he began, "Mr. Barlowe and the Lakeview Manor Motel are a small part of the organization I represent as well as the silent partners who wish to remain nameless. I must stress that neither the business at the motel, nor Mr. Barlowe himself, are in any way involved in the murder of Mr. Hodges. The Lakeview Manor is strictly a monetary holding of my clients, and nothing more. They have no other interest in the business, especially that of the escort service of which the partners had no knowledge, believing that the establishment operated exclusively as a motel and restaurant."

Once again, my visitor hit the brakes. He had accomplished his mission. But his information wasn't assistance—it was a threat. The pause gave me enough time to consider his presence, which I assumed to be an obvious ploy validating the mafia association suggested by Kathy. I stared at the messenger, then glanced at his escorts who still hadn't budged. Why would any criminal organization send a courier? Why not have his oversized companions deliver a physical message similar to the kind delivered by Cliff and Pinkie? Or why not just shoot me in the hallway before I opened the door, or as I sat behind my desk, leaving an untraceable gun on the floor like they do in the movies?

*Leave the gun; take the cannoli.*

I concluded that the little man came from one of the local dinner theaters and that his two friends were most likely rent-a-brutes from Brad's Body Shop. They even fit the description that Kathy gave of the three men who came to the Manor for their "piece of the action." No, this performance had to be another part of the plan, and it would take more than this elaborate second-rate dramatic acting to convince me otherwise.

Tightly gripping the .38 in my hand, I said, "You're not here to help me and Chris Palmer; you're warning me to back off. Well, buddy, that's not going to happen. Give this message to the organization you represent: Chris Palmer did not kill Johnny

Hodges and I am going to do anything I can to prove it. If my investigation takes me back to the Manor, that's where I'm going. Right now, I believe that your friend Barlowe had something to do with the murder, and if he didn't, he certainly knows more than he's saying, maybe even who did it. And another thing, if you are who you say you are, your organization might have had more than a couple reasons of their own to eliminate Hodges. Either way, I promise you, I will find the truth."

I intended to pause just as the messenger had done, but he immediately stood and started for the door, turning to face me before leaving.

"We understand that you are a man of sterling character, Mr. Smith, and that you do much to support the people in your community who need help. I would hate to see that reputation jeopardized."

He left with his escort, closing the door behind them.

*Bullshit!* Sorry, but there is no tender way to describe what I felt. Nevertheless, I did laugh at myself when I turned on the light, then walked over and locked the door before returning to my desk to record the notes of the day. I retaped the .38 and placed the legal pad in the center drawer; later I'd rewrite the day's puzzling episodes in my journal after taking it from its hiding place. I went to bed and drank enough Jack to put me to sleep for a while, then with each awakening, I repeated the self-prescribed medication until morning.

# SUNDAY

## *August 19, 1979*

I attend Mass every Sunday . . . Well, almost every Sunday. The pastor of St. Rita's at the time, Monsignor Patrick Sauer, didn't regard me as a good Catholic, but not for my occasional absence. The stern priest disagreed with my opinion that the Roman Catholic Mass was more impactful celebrated in Latin, along with my criticism about the amount of gold everywhere you look. Monsignor Sauer insisted that you do as Rome directs, or else. He never told me exactly what he meant by "or else," but his implication was clear. There were other doctrinal disputes, but my more grievous faults, he maintained, existed in periodic lapses of morals along with my weakness for a certain Tennessee sour mash whiskey.

I attend Catholic services simply because the nuns who educated me would appreciate the effort. They taught me to pray, not solely for my welfare, but for the needs and comfort of everyone—even my enemies. So, during early Mass on that Sunday morning in August, I did just that, even though I sometimes feel like a hypocrite praying for people like those I met during the previous few days.

There was a time when I denied the existence of God, or

any other kind of deity. I lost my faith after it abandoned me. I grew up loving a mother who tenderly cared for me, and a father who taught me all I needed to know about running the small bed and breakfast that was our home. Then, in the summer of '67, just after my high school graduation, the two wonderful people I believed to be my biological parents died in a tragic traffic accident. I had no idea that they adopted me as an infant.

But dying young wasn't part of the plan, and the only parents I ever knew died without leaving a will. Then, three days after the accident, at my parents' wake, my mother's sister vehemently declared that no bastard—that would be me—would inherit the business her sister and husband had worked so hard to build. Embarrassed by the stares her outburst touched off, I ran out without saying a word, angry with any kind of God who would create such a pathetic existence.

Grief stricken, no longer a part of a family, I lost my faith. So, with the help of my Army recruiter, I changed the spelling of my name from Smyth to Smith and enlisted, directing my outrage at the North Vietnamese who I hated no more than the rest of the world. The Army trained me to be a soldier, and like so many others, I did a soldier's job.

Then came the night of the doomed patrol. When it was over, I stared at all the lifeless bodies, but especially the face of my childhood friend Gary who died in my arms, and who —unlike me—had a family and a future. How could God allow him to die instead of me? For the first time since childhood, uncontrolled emotion exploded as tears ran down my face. I cried for Gary along with the other dead, friend and foe . . . and for the first time, I cried for my mother and father. What was the use in living? My life had no purpose.

After that night, I tried my best to correct what I considered God's mistake by taking reckless chances, but rather than receiving death as a reward for my actions, the Army handed down commendations and promotions for my efforts.

After each battle, I'd walk among the dead wondering why I wasn't another casualty lying on the ground next to them. I asked God why He wouldn't let me die. That question turned into a prayer. So, during one of the many sleepless nights in the jungle, I decided that God must have a plan, and rather than search for an explanation of His actions, I would wait for the answer without helping.

After mass that morning, I went back to my office, sat at my desk, and stared at the legal pad waiting for it to talk to me. Of course, it didn't. I felt worthless. Monsignor Sauer's sermon stressed that moral weakness destroys spiritual conscience. I stared at the bottle of Jack.

The phone rang. I hated to work on Sundays, so I didn't pick it up. But the damn thing wouldn't stop ringing.

"Jimbo, it's Ben."

"Dammit, Ben, you know not to call me—"

"Barlowe's dead." Ben's interruption floored me. "I thought you might want to come out for a look."

I drove to the Manor lost in a dream. During my Sunday morning meditation, I decided to concentrate on Barlowe, whose guilt—no matter what the previous night's visitor claimed—seemed to make more and more sense, even though adopting that strategy meant another challenging visit to the Manor and a possible rematch with Cliff and Pinkie. The way I saw it, the play put on by the actor masquerading as a syndicate messenger only strengthened my assumption of the manager's involvement. But his death blasted that idea to kingdom come.

I forced myself to slow down and consider what Barlowe's death meant. To my way of thinking, his murder cleared Chris who had spent the night innocently tucked away in jail. Our buddy's testimony for Chris's alibi now acquired some credibility whether the state's attorney's office wanted to admit it or not. I recalled Kathy and Brittany's assertion that Hodges had been blackmailing someone. Each said the other knew who he was. No matter which one lied, I could try to convince Ben that Hodges' target might also have a good reason for wanting Barlowe dead.

And then there was Kathy's absurd implication of organized crime. That bizarre assertion reinforced my conspiracy theory. Why would someone send the actors guild to me if they weren't following a script—and a pretty bad one at that? But even though I doubted the credibility of any syndicate involvement, I could still suggest that improbable possibility to free Chris.

My shoulders shivered when I turned into the Manor's driveway. The previous three days reeled through my mind like a movie I had already seen. In no more than a passing moment, every detail, every confrontation, every encounter with Kathy, Chris and the others flashed by. I parked and made my way around the multitude of police cars toward Ben standing by the lounge door scribbling in his notebook.

"Did you need an army for this job?"

"You know how Sunday mornings are," Ben answered, "just trying to keep busy."

"So how did my friend die?"

"Single shot to the temple, just like Hodges. His girlfriend, too."

"Girlfriend?"

"Her name was Brittany, but from that look on your face, I'm guessing you knew that. I remembered Barlowe naming her as his alibi."

I didn't answer. Barlowe's death didn't bother me as much as it should have, but Brittany's murder troubled me—killed simply because she was there. Wrong place, wrong time.

Ben led me through the office where I threatened the

manager two nights earlier, then into the small bedroom. The two bodies were lying facing one another as if sleeping, only a trickle of blood visible on their temples—there would be more underneath. Reminiscent of the humid mornings in Vietnam, clammy air crept through an open window creating an otherworldly atmosphere. And then there was the odor, that indescribable scent of death that filled the room. I'd seen many dead bodies in Vietnam, most were the enemy I felt little sympathy for at the time, especially since they were doing their best to kill me. And though I felt the same lack of compassion for the Manor's manager, looking at Brittany brought back the vision of my innocent brothers who lost their lives for no good reason. They died, like Brittany, murdered as collateral damage, destroyed by greed.

Ben didn't notice when I shook my head to dismiss the haunting memories. I needed to get my head out of Nam and back in the present—the dead were dead, gone forever, nothing could change that.

I turned my attention to Barlowe, and then back to Brittany. I imagined that the way the two lovers faced each other, they probably shared a goodnight kiss, fell asleep, then died at peace—if that's possible.

Ben disrupted my speculation: "Obvious, isn't it."

"What? Dead? Yeah, man, they are definitely dead."

"I guess you've never seen one before. It's an execution."

"An execution?"

"The mob killed them."

"Come on, Ben, how the hell do you know that?"

"We already sent the guns to ballistics, but it's likely that the same caliber killed Hodges. The killers left both guns beside the bed, taped up so there would be no fingerprints. I'm sure the serial numbers, if there are any, will be dead ends. And just like when they killed Hodges, the motel had no overnight guests.

They cleared the place out, Jimbo. Nobody's going to say a word."

I could only stare at Ben in disbelief. I mumbled something about the cannoli being gone.

"What did you say?"

"Nothing, Ben."

But, if the mob actually had an interest in the Manor, the manager should have been aware, or at least suspected, that they eliminated Hodges, and that his life could also be in jeopardy. And yet, because they're not clumsy enough to leave any loose ends hanging around, it did make sense that the mob would finish anything they started. So, could it be possible that my visitors from the previous night were authentic gangsters and not the actors I suspected them to be?

*No!*

Okay, while true that I had no experience dealing with any kind of criminal organization, if their brutal reputation was at all deserved, I would have been eliminated the minute they opened my door. What crime syndicate would pay a friendly visit to some apparently inept investigator, warn him to back off, then assassinate the man they claimed to be innocent of any involvement? I couldn't convince myself that the visitors from the night before were anything but imposters, actors playing a part in the three-act drama I suspected. But if Hodges' death occurred in Act I, and Barlowe's death in Act II, what would happen in Act III?

My silence annoyed Ben who gave me the look I'd seen before, "What's bugging you now?"

I stared at the bodies without answering.

"Are you kidding me? I know you. You are never satisfied. Listen to me, Jimbo, you brought up the idea. We know that the Manor is owned by some conglomerate, and even though it's next to impossible to prove, I'll bet I can link it to the organization. They're doing their dirty laundry, man."

"Too neat," I mumbled.

"*Too neat.* Did you honestly say that? What is wrong with you? These murders clear Chris Palmer. Isn't that what you wanted? Isn't that what you've been working for these last few days?"

I told Ben about my visitors.

"There you go. That proves it," he answered.

"But they told me to stay away from Barlowe because he was not involved."

"Yeah. So what."

"So why order me to back off, then eliminate him?"

"I can tell you why. What did you say after they gave you your marching orders, Mr. Smith? I'll bet you told them to pack a lunch. Right? Man, you are a certified nutcase. You're a one-man wrecking crew, Jimbo. Now, you can do what you want, but in the meantime, I'm going to file my report that agrees with the homicide detectives, a report that relies on the facts that are staring you in the face, but ones you choose to ignore. You should be grateful."

Ben left me alone to question my ingratitude. He and the homicide detectives would file their reports accusing the killer who could never be brought to justice, and Ben was right: I should have been grateful. But the vision of the dead bodies, especially Brittany's, ate away at my reasoning. Whether they intended to kill Barlowe or not, the men who knocked on my door should have eliminated the bumbling investigator who was screwing up their business interest, especially since a suitable patsy was already indicted for Hodges' murder.

My heart pounded just like it did when I stood over the bodies in the jungle wondering why all those men died and I didn't. Once again, I tried to convince myself that my survival had a purpose, both here and in Nam. Despite Ben's conclusion, I believed that the men who came to see me acted out their roles in the drama meant to validate the mafia connection. I, too, unwittingly played my part which incriminated, and then indicted, the indistinct and untouchable organization in such a way that the police, and the state's attorney's office, would write the murders off as housecleaning. Nevertheless, even though I doubted the easy solution, Ben's report could provide the justification needed for Chris's release . . . that's if Nora forgave me for the broken table.

My emotions required a small adjustment before I could face Nora, so I drove home where only a liquid tonic could rescue me from the hazy world that held me suspended in time between the past and the present. The medication went down easy. I leaned back in my chair, took two deep breaths and repeated the familiar mantra from the days in Nam:

*It don't mean nothin'.*

Life goes on no matter who lives and who dies.

*It don't mean nothin'.*

I called out to my father for advice, followed by the repetitious prayer that began in the jungles of Vietnam. Of course, there would be no response from God or my father, but the liquid therapy did begin to take effect. About an hour later, my survivor's guilt had been pacified, at least for the moment. I needed to get back to work.

But it was Sunday. Chris's release would normally have to wait until Monday, so I needed the assistant state's attorney to perform the same kind of miracle I'd seen her work before.

I drove to Nora's, she came to the door, but refused to open it enough to let me in.

"Did I wake you?"

"Jimmy, it's not a good time."

Her brief response, spoken through the half open door in a hushed monotone, was accompanied by a guarded glance over her shoulder.

"Nora, I'm sorry about last—"

"Stop it, dammit, I've heard it all before." Even with so much anger, her voice rose no louder than a hoarse whisper. "I love being with you when you're not an asshole, but you're an asshole entirely too often."

Her attack hurt, but I wouldn't let Nora know. And then the obvious struck me. The explanation for the glance and the whisper. She was not alone. Suddenly, I didn't feel very apologetic.

"Barlowe and his girlfriend were murdered last night."

"You're kidding."

I explained Ben's theory without adding my skepticism.

"Their reports should be filed by now; he said it should be enough to release Chris. Can you help?"

Nora's pause gave me reason to brace for another disappointment. Then finally, "Sunday's not a good day, the county offices are closed, but under special circumstances like Ben's report, I might be able to work something out."

"I can take care of any bail."

"There won't be bail; I should be able to convince my boss to formally drop all the charges tomorrow." She paused, obviously thinking of some way to work it out, "I'll call Judge McCartney," she smiled, "He likes my legs. Since the police reports clear Palmer, I should be able to convince him to let Chris out on his own recognizance."

"McCartney likes any woman's legs, but yours are exceptional."

For some reason, that compliment erased Nora's smile.

"Jimmy, Michael Blake might not be happy that I let Chris go before . . ." Again, a pause that I hoped wouldn't be a second guess; I wanted Chris out that day, not the next. Nora slowly shook her head. "Dammit, Jimmy, the things I do for you. Go home and wait for my call . . . but no promises."

I saw no reason for concern because Nora knew what she could and could not do. More than that, she knew how to take care of herself, and getting Chris out of jail mattered more than anything else—even the identity of her anonymous house guest. I drove home confident that my client would be released.

The phone was already ringing when I opened my door. Nora had worked another miracle; I could pick up Chris any time after two. I immediately called the Palmers who were naturally overjoyed, and then I called Kathy at home.

The phone rang at least ten times before she answered, sounding barely awake. By then it was after one, much too late to be sleeping in, even for a Sunday. First, I told her about Barlowe and Brittany, which had no effect, then about Chris. To my amazement, that news evoked the same lack of emotion followed by a moment of silence.

"That couldn't be better news," she finally said in a mechanical tone.

"I'll be picking him up in about a half hour; I could come get you."

Another moment of silence.

"No . . . No, I don't think that's a good idea."

"I understand. I'll call you later."

During the drive to the jail, I couldn't get Kathy's last words out of my mind. Hell no, I didn't understand. She hired me to free Chris and I did it. Kathy should have been bursting with joy. Seeing Chris would be the perfect time to clear the air; instead, she greeted the news like a favorable weather report. It didn't make sense.

Chris was already out of his cell and waiting for me when

I arrived at the jail. We shook hands and walked to my car.

"You must be responsible for my release, thank you."

"I wish I could take the credit, but I had little to do with it. Frank Barlowe and Brittany were murdered last night, and the police believe their killer also knocked off Hodges. Since you were enjoying the hospitality of the county at the time, it couldn't have been you."

"Faultless logic, but who were Frank Barlowe and Brittany?"

It occurred to me just how little Chris knew about the people responsible for his trouble.

"Don't worry about that; I'll give you all the bloody details later. Right now, let's get you home, but I want you to remember that you're not completely in the clear. Those murders merely muddle the state's attorney's evidence against you. He still has to drop all the charges."

"So what can I do?"

"You can do nothing. You go to your parents' house and stay there. I want you to have an around the clock alibi. And I want the house locked up at night. I'm not trying to alarm you, and I don't think you or your parents are in danger, but I don't like taking any chances with these kinds of people."

"What kinds of people do you think they are, Jim?"

"I'm not sure, but after three murders, a little caution won't hurt."

The conversation ended for the moment as I struggled with the persistent question that had plagued me for days.

Kathy Radney.

I couldn't get her off my mind. I didn't want to mention my suspicions to Chris, but still wondered what he thought of her.

"Are you okay?" I asked.

"Yeah, I'm good. I was just thinking about what a fool I've been. Jim, do you think she used me?"

Even without mentioning her name, Chris had been considering the same troubling question.

"That's funny, I was asking myself the same thing."

Since neither of us had the answer, little more could be said.

As I turned toward Chris's home, I could see his mom and dad waiting by the curb. I gave him one last piece of advice.

"Listen to me, Chris, go inside and rest; don't go back to your apartment. Do not think, do not question anything that's happened since you met Kathy. Read a book or watch TV, but not the news, and don't dwell on anything to do with the Lakeview Manor Motel or any of the people involved. I don't know why, but I think something's going to happen in the next few days and I don't want you to be a part of it."

"Don't worry, Jim. I plan on sitting down for a while with Mom and Dad. After that, I'm going to put on some old blues music while sipping on Jack Daniels."

"Chris, we have more in common than I thought."

I drove away with the sight of the family reunion in my rear-view mirror. Although heartwarming, their happiness did nothing to erase the serious question that haunted me. What if all my suspicions were wrong? What if Ben was right about the mob's involvement? What if it wasn't the local actors guild, but an actual delegation from some underground syndicate "suggesting" that I keep my nose out of their business? And what if I accepted Ben's belief that it was my reaction to the messenger that forced the mob to eliminate Barlowe and his girlfriend?

That last bit of speculation bothered me most, because if it were true, my life would definitely be in danger. And yet that whispering voice in my head kept nagging. Something just didn't seem right. Ben's mob involvement theory looked like a jigsaw puzzle that, once all the pieces have been securely locked in place, the picture remains distorted like a Picasso painting.

Why wasn't I dead like all the rest?

For a year and a half, the Vietnamese had numerous chances to kill me but failed. In the lowest moments of my life, I even tried to help. Now, the syndicate, with all their experience, missed the perfect opportunity to . . .

Or did they?

During the drive home, I realized that Ben's interpretation of the murders did my job by fulfilling my promise to Chris's parents. The police report freed my client, and as Ben said, I should have been grateful. Why not accept the obvious?

*Go home and get drunk, Jimbo. If a mob assassin shows up . . . What the hell, nobody's gonna miss you anyway.*

And yet that whispering voice lingered, turning my suspicions into the conviction that this was no syndicate scheme, but the intricate plan I first theorized since my meeting with Sellers. Someone connected to the Manor put all the events, along with my actions in motion, a mastermind with a plan, but more than a plan, a dramatic play designed to assign roles to each character. I doubted that the director could be Kathy, or any of the boys at the Manor, but a behind-the-scenes writer giving each actor their lines—including mine. Sellers didn't seem bright enough to concoct such an intricate conspiracy, and neither did Brewer. What about one of the many influential clients of the escort service? The man who ran out when I confronted Barlowe crept back into my mind.

Then I wondered if part of the play yet to come would add my name to the list of the dead, written off as another mob hit. Also, very possible. But after considering each murder, a plausible answer came to me:

*I'm still alive because the playwright needs me.*

The heat of the day, oppressive and breathtaking, beat the life from me as I walked to my building. Mentally exhausted, I slowly climbed the stairs, mulling over my dilemma. Every idea took me back to the Manor and, more than likely, another encounter with Cliff and Pinkie who I believed had nothing to do with the murders. On the other hand, Brewer, though not the playwright, should know something, because if I read him correctly, the foul-mouthed bartender was the kind of guy who listened at keyholes.

The strategy session came to an abrupt halt when I reached my office and noticed a young woman standing by my door. *Come on, lady, it's Sunday.* After all that happened in the last few days, taking on another case would be out of the question. The Manor was my priority. I started to explain, but the girl spoke first.

"Are you Jim Smith?"

"Yes, but I'm not sure I can help—"

"Please, I just need to talk to you. It won't take long."

"Okay. Come on in."

Curiosity and my incurable weakness for a damsel in distress prevented a rude refusal. I would listen to her problem, let her down easy, then recommend another investigator.

I still hadn't acquired the responsible habit of locking my door, so without being obvious, my paranoia and I inspected the kitchen, bath and bedroom. Once satisfied that no assassins were lurking behind any doors or under the bed, I returned from my search, and found the young lady seated across from my desk —and she was drinking my Jack.

"Help yourself."

She said nothing in return, but finished what I hoped was her first before pouring another two fingers—Jack isn't cheap.

Somewhat attractive, the young woman wore no makeup. Her hair was combed, not styled, and her clothing appropriately conservative in a classy understatement of fashion except for the large, expensive-looking diamond ring on her left hand.

"I didn't think you'd mind." She swallowed the last of the whiskey. "Besides, I thought you owed me a drink if nothing else."

"I'm confused. What are you talking about? Have we met?"

"No, we never met, but I came here to find out what kind of jerk you are." She took a deep breath, then slowly let it out. "But it doesn't matter now, because while waiting outside your door, I realized that it's probably not your fault, anyway."

"What's not my fault?"

"Johnny's murder."

"Johnny Hodges?" She nodded. "What's he to you?"

"I'm . . . I was his fiancée."

The unexpected twist stunned me. I took the seat at my desk across from her.

"I'm confused. First, I didn't know Hodges had a fiancée, and second, he was already dead when I accepted the case. So how could you blame me?"

"I had to blame somebody, and some of the things that happened lately made me think you were involved."

"What kind of things?"

"I don't know exactly," she said, "Johnny never discussed

business in front of me, but I knew something was wrong when I overheard him arguing on the phone with a man who had something to do with a couple of the new girls that Johnny didn't want to hire. Whoever he was talking to must have had some kind of leverage concerning the hires because Johnny apparently lost the argument. But before hanging up, Johnny said that it wasn't over, and his tone was a definite warning of some kind."

She leaned over and placed the empty glass on my desk, then shook her head like someone trying to erase a memory.

"Anyway, that happened about four months ago, and I knew that their disagreement bothered Johnny because he started drinking every night. I told him to sell the business, that we'd go away, but he said he couldn't . . . not then anyway, but maybe soon if he could work something out. Then . . . Then he got killed."

She began to cry; I reached across the desk and handed her a tissue. "Who was on the phone?"

"I have no idea."

"Then how do you know it was a man?"

"His voice was loud and husky; I heard it from six feet away."

That description could easily fit Sellers.

"You said Johnny started drinking every night, do you mean before he went to the Manor?"

"No, when he got home."

"But I was given the impression that he always slept at the Manor."

"That's another thing. Johnny had the same routine every night. He would set up the girls, then leave around nine to come home except for once a month when he'd stay late because of a business meeting. But the night he . . ." She paused a moment.

"That night, he told me that he wouldn't be home because he had an early-morning meeting with someone involved with the escort service, but he wouldn't say who."

"The police never came to question you?"

She shook her head. "Kathy Radney is the only person who knew about me and Johnny; he didn't want me involved in his business. I doubt that my name ever came up in their investigation."

"Then when did you hear about his murder? Please tell me you didn't read about it in the morning paper, or hear about it on the news."

"No, I slept late that morning because I had a drink and took a sleeping pill the night before, so I didn't know anything about his murder until Kathy came over and told me what happened. She was very comforting. I knew she helped Johnny in the business, but we had never met. She seems to be a very nice person; she even checked in on me later that week when she brought over some money that belonged to Johnny. I asked if she was sure that the guy the police arrested was the murderer; she said that she wasn't convinced, but that you were working on the case. Then she told me that it would be better if I left town before anyone found out about my relationship with Johnny. After that, I put two plus two together and came up with five thinking that you were involved. Sorry. In any case, it was nice of her to give me the money; she could have kept it for herself. It was a little over four thousand dollars."

"Yeah, I'd say that was pretty nice of her. So, other than that money, are you okay financially?"

She nodded. "Johnny kept a savings account in both our names, and he had some life insurance that I'll have to straighten out. It won't last forever, but I'll be able to find work when I get home."

"Where's home?"

"I grew up on a farm not far from Topeka, Kansas. Three years ago, I came east to study for my MBA, and then I met Johnny when he needed someone to keep his books. We felt a connection right away; after that, life seemed so perfect. We even talked about having kids and moving to Kansas. Johnny liked the idea of working on my parents' farm. That's why I couldn't understand why he wouldn't leave when the trouble started."

"I'm sorry, I didn't ask, what's your name?"

"Dorothy, but everybody calls me Dotty."

Dorothy from Kansas. Appropriate. Surely, the poor girl must have felt that she'd been through a tornado, and as for me, I seemed more like the scarecrow looking for a brain with no one to guide me down the yellow brick road in the land of Oz.

"Well, Dotty, I am sorry for your loss, and I wish you all the luck in the world."

"I'll make it. I had no great love for my hometown, but I have missed my family. It will be good to see them again."

"Dotty, I want to be sure, are you positive that it was a man on the phone with Johnny?"

"I'm positive. Johnny never cursed like that, especially around me, besides, from the way he talked to the man, it sounded like they knew each other for some time because Johnny said something about 'over there.' From that I guessed that they were in the service together; Johnny never did tell me one way or the other. I can imagine what you must think of him, Mr. Smith, but Johnny was a decent man. He told me that I might hear bad things about the Manor, but not to pay any attention. You're wrong if you think he ran whatever kind of business the newspapers implied. He managed an escort service for out-of-town businessmen; if it became something else, Johnny either didn't know, or he couldn't stop it."

I offered Dotty another drink, but she refused and left,

so I grabbed a clean glass and poured one for myself while considering this new picture she painted of her attentive and loving fiancé. Her story echoed Kathy's original insistence that the escort service was intended to be nothing more than a legitimate business. But what would make Hodges lose control? The off-color atmosphere of the Manor certainly wasn't one that screamed high-class, so the interior decorations couldn't have been his idea. And where did my client get all that money? Did she have access to the business as I inferred from our first meeting? And why was Kathy giving Dotty enough money to get her out of town before anyone found out that Johnny had a girlfriend? As far as that goes, why would her existence even matter? I wondered why the police investigation didn't turn up that tidbit of information, secret or not.

Convinced more than ever that my theory was on target, it still lacked something, or rather someone: the playwright who first put the finger on Chris, then effectively cleared my client with the subsequent murders that conveniently blamed the syndicate.

Dotty contradicted Brewer's assertion that he took Hodges a bottle every night, establishing his role as yet another actor with a part in the script. He undoubtedly told the same lie to the cops, which would explain why they never questioned Dotty. But I still doubted that the foul-mouthed bartender was capable of manufacturing the elaborate scheme, and I felt the same way about Sellers. Who else could there be?

Kathy Radney? Why did she come to me? Could it be that she needed my cooperation to underscore the mob's implication?

*Okay, Dad, talk to me. Are her looks and intoxicating power pushing me in the wrong direction? Could she possibly be involved in the murders? Talk to me, Dad.*

But Dad and Mom were gone. Twelve years had passed since they were alive to counsel me.

Too tired to consider any more possible conspiracies, and without my father to untangle the knots in my theory, I drank the remainder of the Jack that Dorothy from Kansas left and went to my bedroom to rest.

◆ ◆ ◆

I awoke around eight that night, my clothing and bedding soaked with sweat. A hazy color of gray cast a dismal shadow over the room. Too tired to change the sheets and my shirt, I closed my eyes and drifted back into sleep . . . a sleep spoiled by another recurring nightmare.

Standing on the side of a country road, I screamed.

*"Mom!"*

*"Dad!*

*Get out of the car!"*

Then suddenly, I was in the jungle.

*"Gary . . . Gary, get down!"*

Gasping for air, I fell out of bed and landed on the floor where I smelled gunpowder and burning elephant grass. Screams and cries for help hollered all around me.

*Where's my M-16!?! Where's Gary?*

*Kill 'em! Kill all the bastards!*

I woke up and looked around. No one was there, but I called out their names anyway: "Mom . . . Dad . . . Gary?"

Trembling and dripping with sweat, I finally managed to recapture a shaky grasp of reality, realizing that I wasn't on a country road or in the jungle, and that Mom, Dad, and Gary, along with so many others were all dead.

I showered, then retrieved a new bottle of Jack from the closet thinking that with all the comings and goings of late, it might be a good idea to hide my supply. Then an uneasy caution set in. Slowly and quietly, I walked to my desk, set down the bottle, and reached under the center drawer. I removed the thirty-eight and looked around my office. The room, silent as death, felt like a crypt. I stood motionless and rigid, clutching the gun, my finger nervously massaging the trigger, listening for any sounds of danger.

Nothing but the sound of the fans moving the humid air.

I don't know why, but I wanted to check the hallway. I remember walking toward the door, thinking that it might be a good idea to invest in a deadbolt.

Suddenly, a noise came from outside my open window. I spun toward it only to catch a cardinal settling onto a limb of the dogwood tree just outside. Now this may sound crazy, but that bird's appearance calmed me. I stepped toward the window. The bright red bird turned and looked at me before flying away. I went back to my desk and retaped the gun under the drawer.

I drank my first Jack, then poured a second. For this one night, I intended to follow the same advice I gave Chris by forgetting all about the Lakeview Manor.

That particular Sunday, like every Sunday night during those years, my favorite band had a weekly gig at the club in the Holiday Inn that was within walking distance from my apartment. Not that they enjoyed playing in front of the drunken out-of-town businessmen who hadn't yet heard of the Lakeview Manor, but steady money for a musician is a good thing. So even though there would be no record company executives or talent scouts in the otherwise occupied crowd, the gig supplemented their day jobs and helped pay the bills.

I often went to the club on Sunday nights, so often that I became something of a celebrity with the staff. I did enjoy the attention; it was nice to feel wanted without having to work for it. So, after the beatings and the frustrations, I decided to reward myself with this peaceful diversion.

My favorite bouncer, appropriately named Big Sid, greeted me at the door. Unlike other bouncers I've encountered—like my two friends at the Manor—this big man had the ability to prevent a disturbance rather than contributing to any commotion with a combative attitude. Sid kept the peace in one of two ways: The first was through the immediate intimidation of his impressive stature, and the second, by imposing his infectious sense of humor—the cooler who made everyone laugh until the cause of the altercation is forgotten. Of course, there was a third method: He simply beat the crap out of any aggressor who refused to succumb to the other two approaches.

"Hey, Jimbo, why you lookin' so down, man?"

"Don't know, Sid, must be this damn heat."

"Yeah, man, it sure is hot out there, so you just come on in where it's cool and we'll get you some happy."

I shook his hand and climbed the few steps to the second tier where the acoustics were better, and where my usual table was far enough away from the one-night-stand negotiations.

"Hey, Jimbo, how are you doing?"

It was Tommy Abbot, the club's owner and a friend I've known since high school. Without pausing for an answer, he raised two fingers to Bonnie, the somewhat less-than-sociable waitress.

"Big Sid said the heat's getting to you," he continued, "But knowing you, I'm guessing it's something more. Anything I can do?"

That quickly, Bonnie set two generous pours of Jack on the table.

"As usual, you're just in time, young lady, even if you are grumpy." Tommy liked to make fun of the remote demeanor of his most popular waitress.

"Thank you, Bonnie." I accepted the cute waitress as whatever she chose to be, and since all the other girls joked with me, her detached manner meant very little, even though, like every still-breathing male, I was extremely attracted to her. Bonnie didn't need personality to earn her tips.

I sipped my drink while ignoring Tommy's previous question.

"Look, I won't push you. Not that it does any good, but you know where to come if you need anything."

"I appreciate it, Tommy . . . You never can tell; I may be a little short of cash someday."

"Yeah, right. You live such an extravagant lifestyle that I can see your cash flow running low. You make your hero, Thoreau, look extravagant." Tommy stood and swallowed the last of his drink, "Anyway, like I said, I'm here if you need me."

With that he was gone and I was left alone to put my mind at ease while listening to the music. The action at the bar and on the dance floor looked like a minor league Lakeview Manor as the patrons meandered around in search of a friend for the night. I gulped the rest of the first Jack to erase the mental picture of the Manor, but before setting the glass on the table, Bonnie took the empty from my hand and replaced it with another.

"Thanks again." Our eyes met for just a moment before the captivating waitress walked down to the floor below with my gaze following, her perfectly petite body teasing me.

With my attention intently watching Bonnie walk away, I failed to notice the customary assault coming from the boys in the band who had finished their set. They climbed onto my tier like a bunch of monkeys, taking turns slapping and punching me, the tradition all my friends seem to enjoy. I should have been prepared; it's the same routine every week. Sam squeezed in next to me while the others gathered around as if I were about to reveal the secret of the universe. The leader of the band spoke first.

"Big Sid said you ain't doin' so good."

"Sid has never been very good at keeping secrets."

Sam put his arm around my shoulders and shook me like a father comforting his son after striking out with the bases loaded, "Come on, Jimbo, tell your old buddy all your troubles. I know what you need: You need a broad. A little nookie can fix anything."

Sam lost touch with reality immediately after puberty.

"Or is that your problem? Is that lawyer girlfriend driving you insane again? Man, I keep telling you that she's a strange one, she is. Dr. Sammy knows what you need. You need a meaningless, knock-down, drag-out, dirty, and vulgar physical relationship. I'm telling ya, buddy: You need to get screwed."

I could only laugh, but his simple answer to any problem— Sam's cure-all prescription—stimulated the effect of that great-tasting sour mash whiskey, and it was that combination that delivered the remedy I went to the club to find: The Lakeview Manor, along with all the players in the drama, had completely disappeared from my thoughts.

Sam and the rest of the band provided all the conversation, most of which dealt with funny stories from the old days, exaggerated beyond all recognition. Stevie, the drummer in the band, gave his customary fractured version of the time he spiked the punch at a school dance, then blamed it on the class bully, who found out and promptly kicked his ass. Stevie never knew, but I paid a visit to that bully, my friend Ron

Myers, and explained that it wasn't nice to pick on little guys.

When the band took the stage for their last set, Bonnie brought me another drink which was, as usual, on the house. Tommy never let me pay for anything. Not long before, I fixed an issue for my friend without charge and, despite my objections, he refused to consider his debt paid in full, even though his problem took barely a day to rectify.

I put a twenty in Bonnie's tip glass that she tried to refuse, but I pushed it back, "That's for the rest of the night."

"It's too much." She complained courteously, but without a smile.

"You might not say that an hour from now; I plan on working you pretty hard tonight."

Bonnie flashed a quick smile, not a generous one, maybe a notch above the famous painting, but the curious gesture seemed to speak to me. Then she added another new and unexpected twist to her personality when she placed her hand on the back of my neck and applied a gentle massage. Between the drinks at my office and the generous pours in the club, my mind stumbled, trying to translate the alluring girl's actions into language, but without success. I knew what Sam would say, and yet I couldn't believe that the enigmatic waitress would actually come on to me.

The band finished their final set and the last-call lights brightened the room blinding the few of us who remained. Bonnie came over, took my empty glass, and wiped the table without taking her eyes off mine. Intoxicated enough to be physically affected, but not mentally impaired, I said nothing, staring back at those big brown eyes seemed to be all I could do.

"You've had a lot to drink, Jim."

That was the first time she ever called me by name.

"I'm okay."

"I'm sure you are, but just the same, I think I should drive you home."

"That might be a good idea."

I could have told her that I walked there, but—I'm ashamed to admit—decided against it. The Lakeview Manor and every other trouble in my life had been replaced with the sudden desire to be with Bonnie.

On our way out of the club, Tommy repeated his blank check offer, Big Sid hugged me, and Sam . . . Sam practically yanked my arm out of its socket when he saw Bonnie holding my hand, then he whispered, "See, I told you. All you need is a good piece of—." I pulled my hand away and punched him in the stomach before he could finish.

Bonnie led me to her car, opened the passenger door and helped me in as if she thought I was too drunk to help myself. Then she leaned in, gave me a little peck on the cheek, pulled back to rub noses, and kissed me again, this time full on the lips. She closed my door, then walked around and got in behind the wheel.

"Where to, boss."

Somewhere in the twilight zone, confused by my chauffeur's actions, I stuttered, mumbling something stupid like "w-what?"

Bonnie tilted her head and smiled: "I don't know where you live."

"Oh . . . The Heritage Apartments."

"I know where they are. You could have walked here."

I broke out in a wide grin.

"You stinker. I should make you walk home."

My grin widened even more.

"How can I refuse that smile?"

We didn't talk during the short drive until I showed Bonnie where to park. I took two deep breaths in an attempt to regain a better measure of sobriety, then met her by the front of her car where I kissed her. I didn't want Bonnie to have the idea of putting me to bed while she watched a late-night movie.

Though he tried hard to convince me, I never accepted Sam's theory that sex cures everything from a head cold to acne, and I refused to sleep around simply for sexual gratification. Nonetheless, I take full responsibility for the times love at first sight got confused with lust at first eye contact or a gentle touch on the arm. So that night, walking hand in hand with Bonnie, that mystical intangible called love teased me. I knew Bonnie from numerous trips to the club, but we had never gone to a movie or had dinner together. I didn't know where she lived or where she came from. How could I be in love? Was I trying to convince myself of that elusive emotion so I wouldn't have to confess to Monsignor Sauer?

I kissed her again.

*Sorry, Monsignor, I'll see you in confession.*

# MONDAY

## *August 20, 1979*

Bonnie slept through the night while I tried to lie as still as possible during each waking guilt trip. Our embrace lasted until morning when Bonnie awoke.

"Good morning, Jim," she said with the reappearance of that rare, attractive smile.

"Good morning."

"How are you feeling?"

"If you mean do I have a hangover, no I don't. How are you?"

"I'm fine, but let's talk later."

With that she kissed me and we made love once more. Being with Bonnie was both satisfying and comforting, but when we finished, my thoughts produced an eight by ten color picture of Nora. Still, it was she who wanted to see other people, and the unseen man in her bedroom proof that she meant it. Why should I feel guilty?

Bonnie interrupted the moral skirmish.

"I'm glad we did it again," she said with a smile, "I was

afraid you wouldn't remember last night."

"Bonnie, I have a confession to make."

"Don't tell me because I already know," her smile disappeared as she sat up with a serious expression, "I heard Sam talking about your girlfriend and the way she treats you. If she does treat you like that . . . Well, I just wanted to take your mind off her, if only for a little while."

"No, I wasn't thinking of her," I lied, "but it is about last night."

"Wait, Jim, you don't owe me any explanations. We're both old enough—"

"Please, Bonnie, let me finish." I interrupted her because she started to sound like Nora. "I just want you to know that I wasn't as drunk as you might have thought."

"Actually, Mr. Smith," the smile came back, "I'm very happy to hear that, but what does that have to do with anything?"

I thought for a moment. "Well, nothing I suppose. But I wanted you to know because I despise pretense, especially among friends, and I didn't want you to think that acting drunk was some kind of plan."

Bonnie kissed me, more gently this time.

"Yes, I did think you were too drunk to drive home (a kiss). Oh, and that was a nice trick by the way (another kiss). But it wouldn't have mattered. Do you know how many guys come on to me? (The question was, of course, rhetorical.) There are times when I need someone to hold, and you're different from those other shallow creeps. It's easy to see how much you care about people. And that's why I chose you."

Another kiss followed, but longer this time.

"You make it sound like you picked me out of a herd."

She cocked her head with a quizzical expression, "I

suppose I did. I am attracted to you, Jim, you are definitely good-looking, and I wanted to meet your body up close and personal . . . very nice, by the way, even with those scars and bruises."

"I feel so used." That remark brought about the predictable punch in the gut.

"Jim, I hope this won't be just a one-night stand, but either way, I know I can depend on you not to brag to your friends about it."

"Can't I even tell Sam?"

Bonnie sure could hit hard for a girl her size.

"How 'bout Tommy or Big Sid?"

I must be a glutton for punishment. We made love once more before Bonnie and the pleasant distraction left me alone. My temporary vacation was over.

After Bonnie left, I scrambled a couple eggs and brewed some coffee. Then I recorded the previous day's events in my journal before placing it back in its hiding place and returning to my desk. While sipping on my coffee, I studied the names on the legal pad like one might brood over a puzzle with missing pieces. I added Frank Barlowe's and Brittany's names to the list, then crossed them out with a single stroke like the shot that killed each. Two more deaths.

Why wasn't I satisfied? Chris Palmer was free. Why couldn't I accept the apparent facts as Ben had? Why couldn't I accept the evidence that implicated the unseen and untouchable organization? Especially since I met them . . . or did I?

I still believed that, if an actual mob delegation visited me, this stumbling detective would have been assassinated the previous Saturday night instead of, or along with, Barlowe and Brittany. My execution would have tied up every loose end, allowing business to return to normal once suitable replacements were installed.

In my mind, nothing existed but that puzzle, and yet the solution would never be found as long as I fixated on those names. So often I relied on my father for clarity and advice. He was my go-to guy. But there was one other . . . it was time for a haircut.

◆ ◆ ◆

Mr. Joe was my father's closest friend and the one man I could rely on to bring me back to reality when times got tough. With a slight, self-manufactured Italian accent and bushy gray mustache, he appeared as more of a Disney cartoon character than the treasured friend and barber who gave me my first haircut. Born and raised in the Little Italy section of Baltimore, the accent was just an added personality feature I believe he adopted to enhance his calling as an old-fashioned Italian barber capable of belting out occasional renderings of Italian operas which were surprisingly impressive. I saw Mr. Joe every month of my life until I joined the Army, feeling so close to him, that after learning of my adoption, I entertained the possibility that he might be my biological father. Mr. Joe quickly set me and the record straight.

"As far as I know, and for all I care, Daniel Smyth was your father and that's all she wrote. I can't believe you changed your name. What the hell were you thinking? I'm sure it had something to do with that she-devil who claims to be your mother's sister, especially with that crap she pulled after the accident, but I still don't get your reasoning. People like her prove that blood don't mean nothin'. It's what's in here that counts," he pounded his chest. "Your heart's the only thing that matters."

Mr. Joe would occasionally scold me like that, stern and

purposeful, but never degrading, more like a life lesson delivered by a concerned uncle. Every month, I'd stop in for a haircut whether I needed one or not, straying from his services only during my enlistment in the Army. Through the years, my mentor could be relied on for support and dependable advice anytime it was needed, and after Dad and Mom died, he became my trusted source of clarity and reason.

"Oh no, not you again. Hey boys, it's Mr. Hot Shot Detective."

Anthony and Doc, the two ageless fixtures who were as much a part of the shop as the chairs and mirrors, sat by the window and either laughed at, or agreed with, everything Mr. Joe said. The two men never wandered from their assigned seats, Anthony lopsided from the missing leg he lost on D-Day, and Doc, another WWII veteran, chewing on an ever-present giant unlit cigar. I never heard either speak—Mr. Joe provided all the dialogue.

Something of a friendly curmudgeon, if there is such a thing, the greatest barber in the world once had customers standing in line at the door, but I never had to wait. He would proclaim to those waiting that I was a dignitary from a foreign land on his way to Washington to speak with the president, and I would play along by speaking with an outrageous accent that resembled no dialect other than gibberish.

But times change, as they always do, and it was during the seventies that trendy hair salons took the business away from the traditional barbershops.

"Come on, big shot, sit down before the crowd gets here."

"Sure, Mr. Joe, lucky for me I missed the rush again."

"So what's on your mind, my boy?"

"Nothing in particular, just thought I'd drop by for a trim."

"Now, Jimmy, I may not be the smartest man in the universe, but I'll bet something's bothering you, and I'll also bet it has something to do with girls."

"You're wasting a talent Mr. Joe; you should be a mind-reader."

"Being a barber is more than cutting hair, kid. So, what's the problem with the ladies?"

"I'm not sure that it's exactly a problem; it's more that I don't understand them—"

Mr. Joe interrupted me with a laugh, "In the name of all the saints in heaven, why would you want to understand women?"

"I don't know. I mean, how else are we ever going to get along? Just when I think I have a handle on what she . . . I mean, they, want. . ."

I stopped and shook my head trying to clear the confusion. The "she" referred to Nora, and the "they" to Bonnie, Kathy, and Dorothy from Kansas, along with every other girl I ever met. But my long-time friend and advisor didn't need me to finish the thought.

"Son, Marge and I were married for more than thirty years, and not once did I try to understand that woman. Besides, what difference would it make? You know how she was, always yelling at me for one thing or another. She didn't know why she was yelling, and I didn't care. If she had something to complain about, she was happy, and I'd like to think she was happy 'til the day she died."

Sadly, I remembered that Miss Marge wasn't happy until she died. Joey, their only son, died in Vietnam two weeks before his flight home. A few years older than me, Joey quit college and volunteered for the draft because volunteering meant only a two-year commitment, after which he could finish his degree with the help of the G.I. Bill. Mr. Joe would never admit it, but his wife never raised her voice after their son's death, in fact, she hardly said a word. She died not long after they buried Joey in

Arlington National Cemetery.

Mr. Joe's demeanor changed whenever his wife and son drifted into the conversation. It didn't happen often, but often enough that I would struggle to change the subject.

"But I still don't understand how you always know what's on my mind."

"You're too easy, kid. I knew you had problems the minute you walked through the door. Come on, Jimmy, you were here just last week. I know that barbers and bartenders are unpaid psychiatrists, but anybody can read you. The only thing that ever troubled you was women. Now, there's that lawyer woman. Oh yeah . . ." He smiled, leaned over, and whispered in my ear so Doc and Anthony couldn't hear, "Remember when you thought you were in love with your cousin?"

Of course, I remembered my beautiful cousin who, as it turned out, wasn't really my cousin, but that's another story.

"So, here's my free advice: Find yourself a nice girl, settle down, and get a decent job. Your friend Stevie got you a job down at the port before; go back there, it's a good living. I hear people talk about your business. I don't know how much money you make doing other people's dirty work, but no amount's worth it."

"Come on, Mr. Joe, that's not exactly true. I help people with problems they can't handle. It's not dirty work."

"You say that, and I'm sure you believe it, but I see something changing in you, Jimmy. You were always a good kid. You and Joey were the only kids Marge and I never worried about. I know you got screwed out of your house and the family business, but you can't let people like that make you bitter; you can't turn your life into a crusade to change the world. Your mom and dad were honest and decent; that greedy woman and others like her are garbage, and there's nothing you can do to change it—"

"I can try," I interrupted.

"Trying makes you nuts! Look, from what I hear, the house and the business are both crumbling down. That woman is getting what she deserves. What goes around comes around. That's a fact of life just like breathing gives life, and you can believe that life has a way of catching up to people like her. It may not look like it at the time, but sooner or later, the Lord's justice takes over, maybe not in this world, but in the next."

Anthony and Doc nodded at everything Mr. Joe said, and with good reason—he was right. The woman he referred to was my mother's sister who, with impeccable timing, rudely informed me of the adoption at my parents' wake.

But in that brief moment of silence, I asked myself: What if I didn't try; what if no one tried?

"Now, about these girls, any mixed up in your work?"

"Yes, sir. I think my client's playing me, but I can't be sure. She has me running around in different directions chasing leads that may or may not be credible. I can't be sure because . . . well, because—"

"Because women are your weakness, Samson—maybe I shouldn't cut your hair," Mr. Joe and his friends laughed. "Look, Jimmy, even though I don't know the circumstances, I have to believe that this girl hired you because she heard about your connections with the police. She tells you what she wants them to hear, and off you go. Now, is it because she wants to help you or use you? Sincerity is a difficult thing to hide. Is this girl that good an actress? What do you feel when you talk to her?"

"Even from the beginning, I felt that she was holding back."

"That first impression was probably right."

As Mr. Joe trimmed the hair he had cut the week before, I thought it over. It appeared to be more and more evident that, once again, a pretty face had manipulated me. Kathy Radney used me to influence the investigations of all three murders.

I shouldn't have been surprised when Brittany's testimony contradicted much of what Kathy told me—the innocent blond had no motivation to lie. My client cleverly maneuvered me into chasing down the false leads that implicated organized crime in the neatly packaged framework that I delivered to Ben.

And yet, I still couldn't convince myself that Kathy was a murderer, and my reasoning also doubted that she could be the creator of such an elaborate scheme. Two different guns killed Barlowe and Brittany, which meant two killers. So, if I was right and Kathy wasn't one of them, two other people had to be involved. A couple obvious names stood out: Brewer and Sellers.

The foul-mouthed bartender seemed the easy choice. After all, Barlowe's murder could conceivably catapult Brewer into the manager's job, a position he must have coveted. But what about Sellers? No tangible evidence connected him to the Manor's operation. There had to be something more than my natural dislike for the man. So I considered the night Hodges was killed. Sellers insisted that Chris confront Kathy at the Manor, not wait for the next day. Too much of a coincidence for the fat man not to be involved in some way.

I went home for a bite to eat, then drove to the police station to check in on Ben to see if their investigation turned up anything useful and to be sure that he didn't find anything that might send Chris back to jail.

"I told you," Ben triumphantly declared from his desk as soon as I entered the squad room.

"Told me what? And what is that?"

"Our new computer system. I used it to link the Lakeview Manor Motel to the syndicate."

"You're kidding."

"Nope, got it right here. I was skeptical when the department shelled out so much money for this contraption, but it turns out I was wrong; you wouldn't believe what I can get out of this thing. A world of information is at my fingertips. Heaven knows what'll happen if the government lets these things go public. Anyway, I thought you could use some good news after all the beatings you took. Just look at this."

Ben turned the monitor so I could see where he typed *Lakeview Manor Motel and Lounge: ownership search.*

"Just follow the bouncing ball. The Manor is owned by this company, that's owned by this company, which is owned by this company, and so on until you get to this: Freeport Warehousing, Inc., which also owns the warehouse where Chris Palmer works. Now, you read the papers, you know how many times the feds have tried to sink that outfit for racketeering, but they can't prove a thing. I wish those people would stay up north where they belong. We've got enough trouble . . . Wait a minute, I know that look. That's the look you get whenever you're about to say something stupid."

"No, Ben," I said, "Looks like you nailed it."

"*Bullshit.*"

"Hey, watch your mouth."

Ben jumped out of his chair and turned toward me, shaking his head. I thought he was going to hit me.

"You have shit for brains, Jimbo. You *still* don't believe it."

"Ben, stop sending yourself to Hell long enough to think about it. The Manor is a small operation that wouldn't demand much attention. If there was a problem, the mob would have handled it differently. People would have simply disappeared."

"Dammit, Jimbo, I know what you're going to do. Go on back out there." He pointed a finger at me. "But don't expect me to come running to the rescue, mob or not. If you show up again, someone's liable to blow your head off."

"Now why would they do that when you have the case tied up in that neat little package?"

"Oh, I don't know. Maybe because you're that pleasant, accommodating person they've come to know and love."

I laughed and turned to leave, but Ben stopped me.

"Oh, I almost forgot. Nora's been looking for you. She wants to see you in her office right away."

I turned again, but Ben reached out and grabbed my arm: "Hey, crap for brains. Be careful, okay."

Ben had good reason to worry.

❖ ❖ ❖

I drove to the county office complex, parked in the garage, signed the register at the desk, then made my way through the crowded corridors where all the bloodsucking lobbyists attached themselves to their targeted bureaucrats like leeches on an open wound. I used the stairs rather than take the elevator where many of the predators cornered their prey.

Running up the seven flights to Nora's floor didn't replace my usual morning run but it lifted my spirits as exercise can do. I knocked on her door, then after no response, slowly opened it. In her capacity as an assistant state's attorney, Nora could be inconsiderate for any number of reasons, like ignoring visitors and phone calls until she caught up on her daily responsibilities. As I suspected, she sat at her desk, ferociously typing, each stroke a knockout punch to the chin of some doomed criminal.

"Hey, girl, are you busy?"

Nora looked up and smiled, "Come in, Jimmy, I've been trying to find you. I called you at home, and when you didn't answer, I thought you were out running."

"No . . . Not this morning. I left home early to get a haircut.

Ben just told me that you wanted to see me."

"Another haircut? What do you have, a weekly appointment? How is Mr. Joe?"

"Same as always. What did you want?" It had to be business; Nora never discussed our personal life in her office.

"Come in and sit down. My boss wants to see you about the Palmer case, but I wanted to talk to you first."

"Oh, I know, you have to instruct me as to what I can and cannot say to the big jerk."

"Not in this case, at least I shouldn't have to. I just wanted to tell you how proud I am of you."

"What the hell for?"

"Jimmy, everybody's talking about the way you handled the Palmer case. If it hadn't been for you, Chris Palmer would have been convicted. I thought Michael might be angry because he didn't get the credit for clearing Palmer, but he was actually quite pleased."

"Nora, I didn't have anything to do with it; in fact, I hardly did a thing."

"How can you say that? It's because of your stubborn nature that the syndicate had to act."

"Yeah, that's what I got from Ben."

She gave me the same look Ben gave me in his office, "Jimmy, I don't know what's going on in that suspicious brain of yours, but—"

Before I could take a seat to endure the same lecture I had just heard from Ben, the phone interrupted Nora mid-sentence.

"Okay," Nora said to the receiver, "Tell him we're on our way."

She hung up, then returned her attention to me. "Dammit, Jimmy, I'll say this one time, and one time only: Say thank you, then shut up!"

Nora stood and walked around her desk where I met her and—I don't know why—tried to kiss her. She pushed me away.

"Not here. You know that. What's gotten into you?"

We walked down the corridor to Michael Blake's office and were immediately waved inside where the state's attorney, in his usual ceremonious manner, strolled out from behind his desk to greet me with an open hand and a smile bright enough to light up the city.

I knew Michael Blake. In fact, everyone in the state of Maryland knew Michael Blake. Like Nora, he grew up in privileged surroundings but never learned to respect the struggles of those without social advantages, even after spending time in the service. Seriously lacking in what I consider moral judgment, Blake excelled in backroom negotiations with outcomes that promoted the state's attorney's agenda, or they simply wouldn't happen. He had that power because he knew how to play politics.

"Mr. Smith, it is indeed a pleasure to meet you." He squeezed my hand without releasing his grasp.

But we had met before. Blake knew me from the time our paths crossed when, as a county administrator, he came out on the losing end of a public works issue that I settled for our community after some allocated money managed to get itself "lost." A lesser official took the blame for what was said to be an error in accounting, and the matter was quickly swept under the carpet.

"Thank you," I said obeying Nora's order. "But I am puzzled that you wanted to see me."

"I wanted to thank you in person, my friend. You, and citizens like you, are an underappreciated, albeit more than valuable asset to our community."

He continued to shake my hand, grinning as he glanced

over my shoulder. Then, when I turned my head in the same direction, a camera flash nearly blinded me. After a second, my eyes cleared and I noticed three reporters in the corner of the room intently scribbling on their pads while the cameraman shot away, his lightbulb flashes reflecting off the walls that displayed Blake's diplomas and pictures of the state's attorney shaking the hands of prominent figures in business and politics. There was even one with President Jimmy Carter.

"Mr. Smith, it is with heartfelt gratitude that I applaud your actions. Your professional diligence supports the law enforcement community in their efforts to uphold and enforce the law. In the meantime, I will do my utmost, as I have promised, to increase the funding for our police department whose numbers are stretched to the limit."

And with that unpaid political announcement, the grandstander released my hand.

"Now, if you'll excuse me, there are matters that demand my attention, matters that, as of yet, Mr. Smith, have not crossed your desk, so I'll have to tend to them myself."

The blowhard laughed, so everyone else laughed— everyone but me, and to her credit, Nora, who grabbed my arm and pulled me out of the room before I could say anything.

"My time is just as valuable as his," I said as soon as we reached the hallway.

"Keep your voice down; he'll hear you."

"I couldn't care less, Nora. Look at the windbag, busy selling himself, he wouldn't notice if I stripped to my underwear. That was a setup at my expense."

She pulled me even farther into the corridor, "Jimmy, you know how the game is played. You did his job, so he had to make the best of it."

"Bullshit, Nora, he threw Ben under the bus with that stretched to the limit crap. That's not a game to me. Well, I promise you, that's the last time that jackass uses me."

"You can be so damned unreasonable. I've got to get back to work. Goodbye."

Nora stormed away until some three-piece-suit stopped her in the hall. Her expression immediately changed as her body relaxed and a smile came to her face. The man was no casual acquaintance. I became suspicious; the hair on my neck bristled. I never liked a man who could wear a three-piece suit in that kind of heat. Looks meant more to him than practicality. Was he the man in her apartment the morning before after spending the night?

It became difficult to control my temper. First, the crafty state's attorney used me, and then I had to see Nora with a Blake wannabe.

◆ ◆ ◆

With no idea what to do or where to go, I left the county garage. Dad's voice was missing in action, Mr. Joe wasn't an option, and my gut churned with self-doubt. Should I let it go? The police and the state's attorney believed what they considered the obvious solution to all three murders, why shouldn't I? But was their conclusion obvious or merely apparent? The difference nagged. The boys from out of town *apparently* assassinated Hodges, Barlowe and Brittany, and they *apparently* came to see me. Not *obviously*.

Once on the road my Camaro had a mind of its own. I shifted gears but had no control over the steering until turning into the drive that led to the Lakeview Manor Motel. Still early, the lot was empty. I parked and sat in the car wondering what imperceptible force compelled me to return. Should I go in? Like Ben said, another professional treatment from my two favorite bouncers would most likely be waiting inside and I doubted that my body could endure another pounding.

I got out of the car and walked through the unrelenting heat toward the building that was becoming all too familiar. Once inside, I saw Brewer stocking the bar with his back toward the door. After completing a thorough scan of the room—making certain that Cliff and Pinkie weren't around—I silently made my way to the end stool by the door.

The empty room held a somber atmosphere as if it grieved for the victims. Even the air conditioner couldn't dispel the gloomy mist that hung in the air. Brewer didn't hear me come in. God, he was skinny; no wonder I could lift him so easily over the bar. And what a nose. He was perfect for the part of Ichabod Crane running from the headless horseman. The thought brought about a chuckle that he must have heard.

"Haven't you had enough?" he said.

"No, I don't think I have."

Silence shrouded the room as we stared at each other with obvious hatred; neither of us knowing what to do or say. With the murders so efficiently pinned on some untouchable crime syndicate, Brewer probably didn't expect the meddlesome detective to return. And as for me, I really had no good reason to come back. But there I was.

Finally, Brewer broke the stalemate.

"Well, what do you want? You should be happy. The Palmer kid is out of jail. You did what you were supposed to do."

That remark interested me.

"What does that mean?"

"What does what mean?"

"You said I did what I was supposed to do. What do you mean?"

His complexion suddenly turned cherry red and his eyes

opened wide. Clearly agitated, the skinny little man feverishly chewed on his gum as he moved from side to side in a matching rhythm like the first night we met. He regretted those words and, unlike a polished politician like Michael Blake, he struggled for an explanation.

"Well," he said after an awkward pause, "Your job was to get Palmer out of jail and you did it. You did what you were supposed to do. Now get the hell out before I call the boys."

He turned away from me and returned to his duties. I pushed my luck, taking a chance that if the bouncers were close by, Brewer would have already called them. I attacked what appeared to be an open wound.

"You know, Brewer, I'm surprised you're open."

"Why?" He responded without facing me.

"Oh, I don't know. Maybe you haven't heard, but the manager and his girlfriend were murdered the night before last."

"I've learned not to ask questions." The answer was quick. Not wanting to repeat his mistake, he probably had that response planned for whatever I might say. But I couldn't let him off that easy.

"So, who's the new boss?"

The direct question hit a tender nerve. He quickly spun around to face me with a defiant look, "None of your fucking business."

"I will find out. Sooner or later."

"What if you do? What's it gonna prove? Man, you are an ignorant asshole. Look, wise guy, I don't want any more trouble. Besides, the police are happy, why aren't you satisfied? And I'm telling you right now that if you don't back off, you'll have more trouble than—"

"There's that threat again."

"That's right, *trouble*. It's more than just a threat; this trouble is for real, man, and I hope that pisses you off. Do you know how tough these guys can be? You've already seen what they're capable of. Believe me, the same thing can happen to you. And I wouldn't lose any sleep over it if it did."

"If you're talking about the organization that owns this place, I'm not worried. But I am wondering about your part in all this."

"Me. I know you're nuts, but how do you figure that?"

"I think you may be more involved than you care to let on. I might even guess that you're in line for a promotion. Maybe you jump in as manager of the Manor while Kathy Radney takes over Johnny's operation."

"Kathy! Yeah, man, you are a fucking nut. I hate that uppity bitch. I can't wait for her to get . . ."

He abruptly stopped. Obviously upset with himself, the actor almost revealed part of the last act. Breathing heavily now, nervously chomping on that wad of gum, Brewer wanted to step back from the line he crossed. What was he about to say?

"What about Kathy?"

"Nothin', man. Nothin' at all. In fact, I'm done with you. Now get the fuck outta here."

We stared at each other, the loose-lipped, foul-mouthed bartender and the bumbling detective. The fact that he knew something about my client convinced me of his involvement. I needed to find out what it was. Bogart playing Sam Spade would have beat the truth out of him, but this was no movie. I tricked him twice—he wouldn't screw up again. Maybe I could wait him out.

I threw a twenty on the bar. "Jack on the rocks."

"We're closed."

"I don't care. Give me a drink."

The bartender did his job.

I sat there, nursing my pride and my drinks along with crazy thoughts. Was Kathy in danger from the mob I believed not to exist? That was Ben's theory and Brewer's remark made me reconsider the idea. I kept grilling the player who knew the secret, but other than a few vulgar insults, the bartender stubbornly refused to talk.

Brewer was liberal with his pours, so when my speech began to slur after the second drink, I gave up talking—but not drinking. After finishing the third Jack, I tilted the glass and sucked out the last cube, then wiped my finger around the inside to remove the remaining liquid. But no matter how hard I tried, a shiny residue remained. For some reason that shimmering glimmer teased me.

I wasn't conscious of the time when a few customers and a couple of the girls shuffled in, but I couldn't have been there much longer than two hours. After toying with the idea of having another drink while waiting for the two monsters and round four, I wisely concluded that I was in no condition to fight and thought it better to leave.

Sitting in my car, I tried to make some sense out of everything that happened up to that point. Should I just take Kathy's money and run? Like Brewer said, everybody was happy. Ben was happy, Nora was happy, even that bastard Blake was happy. What the hell, Chris and his family were happy. So what if some crook got away with murder? What's that to me? All those killed were crooks, anyway.

No. Not all. Maybe Brittany was an opportunist, but not a criminal. And what about Dotty? She described Hodges as a decent businessman instead of the felon I first believed him to be. Even Ben's investigation aided by his new computer system couldn't implicate him as a criminal. Maybe he just turned his back on the girls' extracurricular activities like Kathy told me in our first meeting.

I shook my head in an effort to clear my mind from the

overwhelming turmoil created by the three Jacks. Either those heavy doses that Brewer poured, or the stress from the case, pushed me beyond the usual alcohol-induced ecstasy and into an uncomfortable chaos. I needed to put something on my stomach. Going back inside for the tasty cuisine that the Manor had to offer was not an option, so there had to be another choice. Then I recalled the local diner just up the road that Kathy mentioned.

Unlike the Lakeview Manor Motel, the brightly lit sign marking the location of Meg's Diner couldn't be missed. I parked in the overcrowded lot, got out and staggered a bit as I made my way toward the entrance, then climbed the few steps to the door.

Also unlike the Lakeview Manor, I was supposed to wait for the waitress to be seated, but as soon as I noticed the couple seated in the front of the crowded diner, I scurried to a booth in the back, fortunate that one was available—and I also sobered up in less time than it took to take my first sip.

Kathy Radney sat at a table in front handing out envelopes to attractive girls, envelopes I assumed to be either instructions, paychecks, or both. No surprise there, for days I harbored the suspicion that sooner or later Kathy would move in. But the sight that reassembled a large part of Picasso's puzzle into a clear portrait was the person sitting with her—stuffing his fat face.

Tony Sellers was the film on the glass that teased me.

I was in shock. Not because Kathy had apparently taken over the escort business—that probability existed almost from the beginning—but I never considered the odds that she would have any connection to the obese vermin sitting across from her.

My timing was fortunate because just as I sat down, Kathy stood and handed some money with the check to their waitress who broke out in a bright smile when she counted the bills. Business must be good. In the meantime, Sellers shoved the last helping of pie in his mouth and pushed himself away from the table. The two conspirators turned to leave. I slumped down so they wouldn't see me as they headed towards the door.

The ducking maneuver kept my client and Sellers from seeing me, but not the waitress who had made her way to my booth. Totally different than the hostile encounter at the Lakeview Manor, this neatly uniformed middle-aged woman greeted me with a generous smile, then asked, "Are you checking out that couple who's just leaving?"

"Is it that obvious?"

"That look on your face says it all."

"Well, I'd be grateful if you wouldn't say anything."

"Not a word. You're no policeman."

I shook my head. "No, ma'am."

"It wasn't a question because I knew you weren't," and she laughed.

"Why the laugh?"

"Your picture was in the evening paper. You look better in person."

"I don't do well with publicity. Do they come here often?"

"Just the last few nights. There hasn't exactly been a parade of the young ladies, only a couple here and there, but it's obvious what they're doing. I was getting ready to put an end to it. I don't need business that bad, even if the fat man does eat like a horse."

"Something tells me your name is Meg."

"Wow, deductive reasoning, no wonder you made the

news."

"Well, Meg, I don't think you'll have to worry about them much longer. In fact, I have a feeling that tonight may be the last time you'll see them."

"That won't break my heart. So how 'bout it, sweetie, what can I get ya?"

"Steak and eggs would be great."

"They will be, but keep an eye on your cholesterol; I understand there's a link to heart disease."

What was cholesterol, I wondered. But that didn't matter. What mattered was that I could now connect Sellers to the business at the Manor. Be that as it may, handing out envelopes at the diner didn't make either Kathy or the fat dirtbag guilty of murder, but rather the two of them—regardless of how unlikely the pairing—taking advantage of Hodges' untimely death to gain control of the business. Nonetheless, one obvious reality stood out: Their association was no mere coincidence.

With the operation apparently over for the night, I watched through the window as they spoke to a couple of the girls in the parking lot for about ten minutes. Their conversation looked amicable enough, like businessmen discussing a strategy. After that, my client and the fat man got into a new Lincoln that Sellers drove away. Quite an expensive car for a warehouse worker. Yes, business was indeed good. Meg interrupted my thoughts.

"It's been the same every night. They never stay late, just long enough to conduct their business with the girls and feed the fat man who takes very little time chewing his food. But how 'bout you; will you have time to eat?"

I looked at the food on the tray, "Yes ma'am, besides, I think I know where they're going."

I stayed for dessert, every scrap the best I ever tasted. I'll never tell her, but Meg's cooking was just as good as Mrs.

Quincannon's. I left at eight thirty and drove to the Lakeview Manor Motel to confirm my suspicions.

The Lincoln was there.

# TUESDAY

## *August 21, 1979*

Sleep would have been a blessing that Monday night, but Picasso's distorted masterpiece of Kathy Radney and Tony Sellers sitting in a booth at Meg's Diner kept me from nodding off even for a moment. Though part of the painting fell into place with Kathy and Sellers' alliance, certain facial features still needed to be rearranged. I got out of bed around 3 a.m. and brewed a pot of coffee when one of Thoreau's quotes came to mind: It's not what you look at . . . but what you see. What would Thoreau see if he looked at Kathy and Sellers working together at the diner when there had been no previous indication that they even knew each other? Kathy only remembered Sellers as the man who brought Chris out to the Manor that night . . . or so she said.

I knew what Ben would see, he would see Sellers and my deceitful client taking advantage of the murders committed by the syndicate. But after considering the events of the previous few days, that conclusion just didn't work for me. What criminal organization would commit such a sloppy crime? Any problem with the Manor's operation would have been handled silently. More than that, there would have been no need to frame Chris

Palmer whose appearance, I believed, was no coincidence. Sellers took him there on the fateful night, purposely placing my client in the crosshairs of the murder investigation. But I would need a solid argument to convince Ben that Sellers was guilty of something more than teaming up with Kathy to take over the escort business.

Oh yeah, and what about Kathy?

While fighting the conclusion that my client and the fat man scripted the drama, a vital question remained: Why weren't they afraid of the syndicate? After all, Ben's research traced the ownership to an alleged gangland holding. But that connection was at least four times removed. The Manor was a stepchild in the organization's family. I doubted the ownership even knew about the coup.

And yet, the extent of Kathy's involvement troubled me. Facts are facts. Two separate guns without silencers killed Barlowe and Brittany—two killers firing in unison so neither would awaken with the sound of each shot. While my client's access to the business pointed to her guilt, I still couldn't convince myself that she pulled that second trigger, playwright or not.

Brewer.

It had to be Brewer, the foul-mouthed bartender who talked too much and who knew a secret concerning Kathy that he wouldn't reveal, a secret that bothered me since he nearly gave away that part of the play, placing him in the middle of the conspiracy.

Okay, so they used the rookie detective, but if that included thinking that I would lie down and give up . . . well, they missed that part of my résumé. It was time for another search and destroy mission, which meant creating a plan of my own that would bring Ben back to my way of thinking. My first move that morning was to call Kathy at work.

"We need to talk, but not there, here in my office."

"What about? Chris is out and everybody's happy."

No surprise that she echoed the "everybody's happy" refrain.

"I'll tell you when we meet. What time can you be here?"

"I'll have to leave work early, but I could be there by three."

Kathy sounded curious but not alarmed. I could only guess that she forgot about her casual mention of the diner. After Barlowe's and Brittany's death, they needed a nearby place to set up the girls until the smoke cleared, and given his enormous appetite, Sellers probably chose Meg's as the perfect place to gorge himself until they could safely move the operation back to the Manor.

Now that Kathy and Brewer fit nicely in the picture, I needed to connect the fat man to my client before talking to Ben. How and when did he appear? Before catching Sellers and Kathy at the diner, they had no apparent previous association, but their newly revealed business relationship earned him a major role in the play.

In order to satisfy Ben, I needed to place Kathy with Sellers before the murder. Only one person could make that connection.

❖ ❖ ❖

I found Chris Palmer on the porch looking as if he lost his best friend, then it occurred to me that he had. The sight of him sitting on that metal glider with his head hanging down so low made me want to slap both Sellers and Kathy, but especially Kathy, woman or not.

"It's not all that bad, you know."

"Oh. Hi, Mr. Smith."

"Remember, it's Jim."

"Yes, I know. I'm sorry; my mind's in another place. It probably would have been better if I went to work today."

"Do you need money, 'cause I—"

"No, please," he interrupted, "You've done enough. My parents have already taken care of this month's rent and there's nothing else I need. So, what did you want to see me about?"

"Just a few questions. First, how did you meet Tony Sellers?"

"Tony? On the job. He's a strange guy. After the company hired him, he would talk to some of the other guys, but it wasn't long before he would only hang out with me. Why do you want to know about Tony? Is it because he took me out to the Manor that night?"

"Yeah, I'm just checking up on the time frame. When did he start working with you?"

"I'm not sure. Sometime in April or May I suppose."

"And Sellers became your friend?"

"Yeah, but to be honest with you, Jim, Tony kind of forced himself on me. I never liked the guy, and we surely don't have anything in common. But I felt sorry for him, especially after he told me about his time in Vietnam."

"What about Vietnam?"

"He said that memories of fighting in the Mekong Delta with the $9^{th}$ Infantry Division give him nightmares and that's the reason for his eating disorder."

"Chris, your parents told me that you saw combat, too."

He nodded.

"Did you tell Sellers?"

"I don't know ... probably."

"Now, for the tough part. When did you meet Kathy?"

"We met about the same time Tony came to work at the warehouse."

"Did you meet in the library?"

"Yes, but how did you know that? Oh, I forgot that you know her, too. Jim, why did she hire you? She hasn't talked to me since ..." Chris's voice trailed off and his head dropped.

"I'm not sure, Chris." He didn't need to know the truth. "Just one more question. Did you tell Kathy that you served in Nam?"

"I don't know; I suppose it came up, but what difference does that make?"

"Oh, probably nothing."

I got up to leave, then remembered something else.

"I'm sorry ... I do have another question. Did Kathy ever visit you at the warehouse?"

Chris shook his head in a negative reply.

"Then how did he explain his friend seeing the two of you together?"

"Tony said that his friend saw us walking around the harbor ... I guess I should have believed his story."

"Chris, I can't explain now, but I don't think there ever was a friend."

I left Chris a little after eleven which gave me time to kill before seeing Ben. Part of my plan involved using my old friend and his new computer system. But there was also the forgone conclusion that he'd get angry the minute I asked for his help. He would echo the "everybody's happy" refrain before suggesting that I find more suitable employment. So, since I hadn't eaten any breakfast, I thought it might be nice to take a breather before facing the wrath of Quincannon.

Stevie and the guys from the docks would be having lunch at the VFW down by the marine terminal. After my discharge, my friend set me up with part-time work in his stevedore gang whenever I needed spending money while using the G.I. Bill to study journalism in college.

Those were the days before workplace urine testing, so many longshoremen enjoyed a beer or two with lunch before heading back to work. That may sound irresponsible, but with only one exception, the guys never overindulged unless they were done for the day. So, while relaxing at the bar, we talked about sports and exaggerated love affairs, but steered away from turbulent subjects like politics and union disputes too argumentative to debate until one extreme radical with a drinking problem made them impossible to ignore.

On that day, I walked in on a heated discussion about the next presidential election which meant that Eddie —the outspoken radical I mentioned—had been there a while. Everyone knew Eddie was an alcoholic. His license had been revoked years before, so one of his three brothers drove him to and from work while keeping a close eye on him. His job as a freight clerk posed no danger to himself or others, and even though he drank too much, he did his job surprisingly well, better than most in fact.

"Hey, guys."

"Look, boys," Stevie said, "it's the wandering soldier."

Wayne asked how I was doing, Eddie—distracted from his ranting—waved at me while sipping on his beer, and George chimed in that it was my turn to buy.

"When is it ever your turn?" I asked the notorious scrooge. He just answered with a childish grin. I took my usual spot at the end of the bar next to Stevie then motioned for Darlene to set up a round before trying to steer the conversation away from politics.

I asked the instigator of the debate. "What do you think, Eddie? Will the Orioles take it all this year?"

"Who the hell cares about baseball. I'm more worried about that hypocritical actor making it to the White House. He'll destroy the unions, mark my words. I'll vote for a woman before I'd vote for that asshole."

George laughed. "Yeah, like a woman could win."

"Come on, guys, gimme a break," I said, "I came here to relax. It's been a tough week."

"Yeah, old Jimbo here had it so tough that he took a sweet little waitress home with him Sunday night."

"That's what I like about you, Stevie, you're getting to be like Big Sid; neither one of you knows how to keep a secret. You need to concentrate a little more on your drums and a little less on spreading gossip."

"How 'bout some details, man. The dirtier the better." Wayne said.

"What's wrong, Shorty, not getting enough at home?"

"My name's Wayne, not Shorty. Now you have everybody calling me that. Besides, you're not that much taller than me."

"I got at least four inches on you, short-stuff."

Stevie leaned over and rubbed Wayne's shoulder. "Wayne is so sensitive, Jimbo. He's not that short, he's just stands too close to the ground . . . and he's *sooo* much in touch with his feminine side." Then he kissed Wayne on the cheek and added, "That's why we love the little guy."

After Wayne elbowed Stevie, we laughed, raised our glasses, and drank together as if toasting a great victory. Funny, stupid camaraderie. While music at the club diverted my attention from the case, this therapeutic group session would numb Einstein's brain. All the immediate concerns about the Lakeview Manor faded—until Stevie brought them up.

"So, how's the case going?"

"What makes you think I'm working a case?"

"Come on Jimbo, we've been friends for as long as I can remember, and you know me as well as I know you. Besides, everybody at the club knew something was wrong as soon as you walked in the door. What can I do, Jimbo? You know I'm here for you."

"You're right, I should know better than to keep anything from you, but no, there's nothing you can do."

"Are you sure?" Stevie asked. "Nobody said anything, but we all noticed the bruises. A couple of the guys could make a visit."

I laughed. "Nah, they don't need to get involved. Just a couple dicey moments, but that's all over now."

"Then you wrapped it up?"

"Not yet, but almost."

"Well, let's drink to that."

We sipped our beers, then after a moment or two, Stevie changed the subject, "I know it's not your usual kind of case, but does it have anything to do with the jewel thefts that are happening around the old neighborhood?"

"No, it doesn't."

"Have you been up there?"

I took another sip of beer and shook my head.

Stevie leaned toward me, and in a close whisper said, "You

know now that Diane isn't blood and she never married. I always thought there was something special between you two."

I didn't respond. My beautiful cousin and I started our "affair" when we were both around ten, but something changed as we grew older when her kisses became more passionate. At first, I didn't mind, but when she placed her hand between my legs, I jumped up.

"Come on, Jimmy," she said, "we're only cousins." At the time neither of us knew my parents' secret. "It's not like you're my brother."

I didn't understand. Still thinking of us as kids crossing that improper, but harmless line, I never gave in though Diane kept trying. In any case, the make-out sessions continued, though not as often. Diane dated a lot of the guys in school, and I even heard rumors concerning her virtue, but refused to listen. I didn't look at her the night my mother's sister revealed the secret of my adoption, and I had no desire to go back to the home that Nora said was legally mine, the home and business she thought I should fight for.

"Jimbo, I know her mother's a bitch, but you and Diane—"

I interrupted Stevie before he could go any further, "Look, Stevie, Diane's an uncomfortable memory."

"Sorry, Jimbo, I shouldn't have brought it up."

"Not a problem," I said, "but since you did bring it up, why don't you give it a shot? You seem to know what's she's doing, and if I'm not mistaken, there was a time when Diane liked you quite a bit."

"She liked a lot of guys . . . have you forgotten that she acquired a taste for upscale living?"

"Then why the hell would she want a poor slob like me?"

"That special something you two had."

I smiled, "A long time ago. Now shut up and drink your

beer." That closed the subject.

I ate a ham sandwich and drank two beers, enough to give me sufficient courage to approach Ben. I left the boys to finish the rekindled political blitzkrieg that Eddie refused to surrender.

◆ ◆ ◆

By the time I got to the station, it was nearly two and Kathy was to meet me at three, so I ran up to the squad room where I found Ben typing on the keyboard with a hunt and peck method that made him look like a first grader learning to print.

"Are you sure you know what you're doing?"

"Hey, Jimbo, I'm just putting the finishing touches on the mess you made at the Manor. I smell beer on your breath. Been to the VFW chewing over love affairs and war stories?"

"Something like that." I paused, then slowly added, "Look, Sarge, about those finishing touches, I may have a couple changes for you."

"Jimbo, we've been over this a thousand—"

I interrupted Ben, telling him what I saw at the diner and all that Chris said, especially concerning the convenient time frame.

"So what? We all knew that somebody had to move in."

"I knew you'd say that, but Ben . . . Sellers? Think about it. Your new system revealed how far down the Manor's ownership goes and I remember Barlowe saying something about the cut from the escort service paying the lease. Freeport Warehousing probably doesn't know about the murders as long as they're being paid. None of the murders made front page news, Ben. Besides, the mob wouldn't need to frame Chris or anyone else because Hodges and Barlowe would have disappeared without a trace. Did either of the two guns used on Barlowe and his girl kill Hodges?"

Ben nodded. "Yes, the same gun that killed Barlowe also killed Hodges."

"So you're telling me that some gangster saved that gun knowing it would be needed to use on Barlowe? And then he brought a friend with another piece? Come on, Ben, it had to be that fat slob. Even you're not that gullible."

He leaned back in his chair and stared at me like he did back in Da Nang when I told him why I went after those two NCO's. He supported me after I told him what the two heartless dirtbags did and why they deserved a beating. But this was different. Would he support me now? With Chris Palmer free and the untouchable organization taking the blame, Ben's work was done; I could understand why it mattered little to him who took over the business at the Manor. But I also knew that Ben would never let a murderer get away with his, or her, crime.

"You know that you're screwing everything up."

"Ben, they can't get away with murder, and they will if we don't do something about it."

He straightened up and laughed, "Boy, your girlfriend is going to kill you. You won't get laid for a year. Oh, and her boss— all that bull he put out about fighting organized crime. He won't be happy, either."

"I can deal with them. So how much information can you get out of that contraption you're so proud of?"

"I can access criminal histories and property ownership like I found for the Manor, but I'm not sure how deep I can get into other areas."

"Well, if my hunch is right, that might be enough. Find out anything you can about Tony Sellers, Frank Barlowe, and Johnny Hodges. There has to be some kind of connection. I have reason to believe that Sellers may have served overseas with Hodges. Oh, yeah, and throw in Brewer. I don't know if that's his first or last name, but I'm convinced he has a hand in this, too."

"All right, Jimbo, I'll see what I can find, but it may take a while."

"Why? You said the world was at your fingertips. And by the way, the public will get a hold of this, you know."

"Come on, man, the government would never allow that. Besides, what do you do, commit everything I say to memory?"

"Just enough to keep you on your toes. Call me when you find something."

"Yes, boss."

❖ ❖ ❖

I rushed back to my office and sat at the desk where less than a week before I first met the mysterious Kathy Radney. It appeared that she, Sellers, and most likely Brewer, came hairline close to committing the perfect crime. As I stared at the names on the legal pad, some living, some dead, I recalled the false leads that Kathy so skillfully provided. Everything started to add up. Their plan began with the selection of Chris Palmer as the innocent target, and me as the naïve and inexperienced investigator who could be easily manipulated to help carry out their scheme to implicate the mob. Even the old man at the harbor who turned out to be a younger Vietnam veteran was given a minor role in the play, their meticulous research thorough enough to know that Chris's military service would motivate me that much more.

Kathy's knock on the door interrupted my thoughts. I let my guilty client in, then escorted her to the chair where she looked so perfect during our first meeting. Nothing had changed. Still flawless, she could have been framed and hung in a museum. Standing over her, I considered the effect of such a striking vision.

"Kathy, do you know just how perfect you are?"

She smiled without blushing, a gesture that pushed me over the edge. I grabbed her by the arms and lifted her from the chair until her face was inches from mine.

"So tell me this: If you're so fucking perfect, why the hell did you tell me about the diner?"

Her expression changed to fright, and she stammered, "Jim—"

I didn't give her time to finish.

"And why didn't you tell me how chummy you were with that fat son-of-a-bitch, Sellers?"

Kathy fell limp in my arms and started to cry; her dead weight convinced me to place her back in the chair. The pathetic outpouring of emotion stirred my sympathy, but I refused to allow her to manipulate me again.

"Answer me dammit! Do you think I'm that stupid?"

Then came the unexpected. Kathy stood and embraced me, not passionately, but thankfully, all at once, shaking, crying, and laughing.

"You did come to the diner. I knew you would."

"What the hell are you talking about?"

"I'm so glad they sent me here," she said through her tears.

"Who sent you here?"

"Tony and Brewer."

"Kathy, if this is some kind of—"

"No, Jim, I swear. It was them all along. They killed Johnny and the others, and they said that if I didn't do exactly what they said, that they'd kill me, too."

She began to fumble through her pocketbook for what I assumed would be a tissue. I gave her one from the box on my desk and thought about this latest surprise. Could it really be that simple? Though still doubting it, I gave in to the possibility that Sellers could put together such detailed manipulation, but not Brewer. He was too easily duped into shooting off his mouth. I mentioned that to Kathy.

"Brewer does whatever Tony tells him to do."

"Okay, Kathy, then start from the beginning . . . and no more games. I want the truth."

She took another tissue from my desk, blew her nose—gracefully of course—then sniffled in a childlike manner before finally continuing.

"I started working for Johnny over two years ago. He was a good manager because he kept the girls safe. All our clients are thoroughly vetted. Yes, Jim, it is true that some of the other girls sleep with their clients." She stopped and stared hard at me, "I don't . . . I swear."

Once again, she bowed her head and paused, but I didn't want her to get too comfortable.

"Don't stop now, Kathy, keep going."

"Okay, Jim. Those other girls liked the arrangement because Johnny took his usual commission without bickering over prices; he even let them decorate the lounge. The only condition was that the girls remain discreet because some of our clients hold sensitive positions. That's why we worked those girls from the diner. You'd be amazed at the names I could give you."

"Right now, nothing would surprise me, but you're not telling me anything that I haven't already guessed. Get to the part where Sellers moved in, because I got the impression that

Brewer had already been working at the Manor for some time."

"You're right about Brewer; he was already bartending there when I first started working for Johnny. I didn't see Tony until last spring when he showed up with the two Asian girls. It was obvious that he knew Johnny and Brewer from someplace—I think they were in the service together. Anyway, Johnny hired his girls even though he didn't want to, so I was a bit suspicious, but didn't think any more about it at the time." Kathy stopped there, then slowly shaking her head, she continued, "I never saw Tony again until after Johnny was killed. That's when he asked me if I wanted to help Chris. At the time, I thought he really cared, feeling guilty because he was the one who brought Chris to the Manor that night. I didn't know then that he had killed Johnny."

"So you came to me. Was that Sellers' idea?"

"Yes. He said that you had a reputation for helping veterans."

"But how did you meet Chris? It's too much of a coincidence that Sellers just happened to show up at the same time."

"After he sent me to you, I confronted Tony about his relationship with Johnny and how he met Chris. That was when he told me about his plan. He targeted Chris after he saw him with me, then he confessed to killing Johnny and said that he was taking over the business with or without my help, and that, if I didn't help, he would kill me, and Chris would spend the rest of his life in jail."

"Why didn't you tell me that, or go to the police?"

"He hit me, and he said that if I told anyone, he would hit me again. Jim, all I have is my looks. I know that men are attracted to me and, yes, I use that to make a living. When I was younger, I let the boys . . ." She paused, "I let them use me. I thought it was the only way to be popular. I know now that I was trash. And, Jim, I could do that anytime I wanted. Do you know how much money I could make if I worked like some of the other girls?"

"And you're telling me that Hodges never encouraged you to work like those other girls?"

"No, never. Johnny let me take care of my clients in my own way. But I knew that this kind of life wouldn't last forever, and that's why I went to the library hoping to find another career. I met Chris and he changed my world. I honestly believed that someday we could get married and raise a family."

"Then why haven't you called him? Why haven't you gone to see him?"

"How can I face him after all I put him through?"

"Okay, we'll get back to that later. What about Brewer? What's his part in all of this?"

"He's Tony's puppet. Tony gives the orders and Brewer follows."

"And the two bouncers?"

"Cliff and Pinkie aren't involved."

Her story seemed plausible enough, but suspicions concerning her relationship with the business still concerned me. And I didn't feel comfortable with the way she kept calling Sellers by his Christian name.

"You knew about Johnny's fiancée?"

"Yes. I knew everything about Johnny. I helped him run the business which is why Tony still needs me. I have all the contacts, and I know all the names."

"How do the Asian girls figure in this?"

"I think that's why Tony killed Johnny. Like I said, he didn't want any part of letting the girls in, but Tony insisted."

"Kathy, I still don't understand how Sellers could pressure

Hodges into doing something he objected to."

"Johnny changed when Tony showed up. The only thing I can think of is that he had something on Johnny, but I don't know what it was. Tony scares me, Jim. I suggested that we run the business from the diner, hoping that you might show up. Jim, if we can get rid of Tony and Brewer, won't that be the end of the whole mess?"

There it was. The hook. Suddenly there was a *"we."* She wanted me to do what she couldn't, which was to eliminate the competition. Even if she wasn't involved in the murders, their deaths presented the perfect opportunity for her to assume control of the girls. She admitted that she ran the business with Hodges—Sellers, especially with his disgusting personality, could only be a hindrance to its success.

Before I could attack Kathy for this latest attempt to manipulate me, the phone rang. It was Ben and, as it turned out, his timing was perfect.

"Jimbo, I'm putting you up for detective. You'll never believe what I dug up."

"I can only imagine, but try me anyway."

"In '69, Sellers was stationed in Thailand, not in the Army as he told Palmer, but in the Air Force attached to the Base Exchange. Then he got in trouble for—"

"Prostitution." I interrupted Ben with the not-so-wild guess.

"How did you . . . I guess that would make sense, but he was also working the black market, which means he had to have connections with the locals. It must have been a large operation, but Sellers was the only one to be court-martialed. Not only that, he served less than a year of a ten-year sentence before being released and dishonorably discharged. After that, nothing until last year when he was arrested in L.A. for—"

"Prostitution." The same reasoning prevailed.

176

"Of course. But get this: The charges were dropped."

"Sounds like Mr. Sellers has friends in high places," I said.

"I'll say. And I think they must be close by, which might explain why we never had cause to investigate the Manor."

"That makes sense. What about Hodges, Barlowe and Brewer?"

"I couldn't find anything on Barlowe. Other than he got an honorable discharge from the Marines in '70 after serving twelve years."

"Come on. I can see you smiling through the phone."

"I just wanted you to work for it. I thought you might guess it since you've been doing so well."

"Okay. I'd guess that Sellers served with Hodges, and probably Brewer, too."

"Right on, Jimbo. Hodges and Brewer served in the same unit with Sellers in Thailand. But get this: both were honorably discharged when they got back to the states, even though they had recently re-enlisted . . . Oh, and by the way, in case you're wondering, Brewer's first name is Horatio . . . no wonder he never mentions it, not that it matters."

"You're right . . . it doesn't matter. What were their ranks?"

"Hodges made it to first lieutenant and Brewer was a staff sergeant."

"That's not enough rank."

"What do you mean?"

"Look at the big picture, Ben. It's no coincidence that they all end up here together. Sellers obviously had something on Hodges, and that something had to be the black market they ran in Thailand. I'll take another guess that Sellers' business contacts in Thailand are still available. How else could the fat dirtbag get the Asian talent to the states? But, Ben, it doesn't add up that only Sellers took the rap in Thailand, a small rap at that, and then he gets out early? There's no way a first lieutenant has that kind of leverage to manipulate the system. Sellers' treatment only makes sense if some higher authority that was involved back in '69 is involved now, and that influence stretches all the way to the West Coast."

I looked over at Kathy, now mindlessly filing her nails. She had to hear my part of the conversation with Ben, but she paid no attention. That lack of interest bothered me, especially since a moment before her emotion flooded the room as the distraught victim of Sellers' plan.

"Ben, I can't explain now but get me a list of the officers attached to the BX when Sellers was there."

"Jimbo, I had to stretch this system to get as much as I did; I don't know how much more is available because I don't have access to federal programs. I'll have to—"

"Come on, Ben, you said you have friends with the FBI. Give them a call. I don't care how you do it, just do it," and I hung up the phone.

Seldom would I command Ben in that manner, but considering my unconcerned client sitting across from me, I had good reason. People owed Sellers. Hodges lost his life over this debt, and Brewer was either paying on that same contract or working as a willing participant. But there had to be someone else, someone with enough influence to pull the necessary strings that kept Sellers out of trouble as far away as California. Once again, the man who ran out when I confronted Barlowe came to mind—not only him, but what about the other influential clients of the service, some of whom came from out of town? Kathy said their names would surprise me. And even though Ben had enough to go after Sellers, that wouldn't uncover the person—or persons—of influence. Sellers didn't play the stoolie before, why change now?

Kathy cut into my thoughts with a clearing of her throat.

"I'm not accustomed to men ignoring me."

No longer intimidated, Kathy smiled pleasantly, her manner now relaxed. I stared back wondering if a stern look might dislodge her comfortable attitude, but it had no effect. The change troubled me, but not enough to push Kathy any further.

"I'm sure you're not. You can go home now. I'll take care of everything from here."

I could have pressed her more, especially since the possibility existed that she knew the identity of Mr. Big. Instead, I walked her to the door where she turned and hugged me.

"Be careful, Jim. Tony is dangerous."

◆ ◆ ◆

Kathy left me to review all that I knew, or at least what I thought I knew. The Lakeview Manor Escort Service, lately run by Johnny Hodges, a discreetly located, but profitable business, succeeded in large part due to that remote location in the county. This clandestine operation, patronized by a clientele with much to lose if discovered, was most likely supported by the patronage of an unknown party with enough influence to maintain the cozy arrangement that escaped the scrutiny of the law.

That is until Tony Sellers appeared.

It would be a safe bet that Hodges and his influential partner were in Sellers' debt. They either allowed or were coerced by the fat man to introduce the Asian girls into the operation until someone notified the feds by way of an anonymous tip. I had to assume that action to be an attempt to hinder the intruder's plan hoping he would just go away, but their strategy failed because Sellers' response was the elimination of Johnny Hodges as a statement of complete takeover. But the latest discovery indicated that the fat man's influence extended all the way to California. I wondered what names Ben might discover—that's if his new computer system, or that of his friends at the FBI, could dig them up.

And then there was the syndicate who, according to Ben's research, owned the Lakeview Manor. Could Sellers have some alliance with them? Unlikely, I thought, and yet the mob didn't scare him because their implication was a crucial part of his plan. Still, I just couldn't convince myself that Saturday night's visitors were anything but actors. After all, Freeport Warehousing was way down on the who-owns-what totem pole, so not only was it possible that Sellers didn't know about their connection, it was more than likely that the syndicate knew nothing about the murders, especially since either Brewer or Kathy could maintain the payment schedule in such a way that the ownership would be none the wiser.

My client's involvement became the troubling consideration. I wanted her to be the opportunist who planned to take over the business she knew so much about. But our latest conversation bothered me. How could she be so emotional while telling me about the connection between Sellers and Brewer along with their plans to take over, then as Ben and I talked, do a complete about-face, worried more about her manicure than our conversation? Something wasn't right.

There had to be someone else.

Naïve or not, I couldn't convince myself that Sellers, Brewer, or even Kathy had the brains to pull off such an intricate scheme. My suspicion of a remote playwright seemed to be the only likely conclusion. Someone with enough influence to keep the Lakeview Manor's questionable activities hidden from the scrutiny of Ben's department. The man who ran out of the Manor the night I confronted Barlowe became my number one suspect, even though I didn't recognize him as someone of influence in our area. Maybe he knows Mr. Big and contacted him along with the police that night. So, as long as those possibilities remained, Picasso's painting still appeared distorted.

I poured a Jack, and sat quietly for fifteen minutes before leaving to see if Ben squeezed anything more from his new computer. On the way, having little faith in modern technology, I tried to think of a different strategy that might expose the unknown party, but without success. Maybe we could put our heads together and come up with something.

◆ ◆ ◆

At the station, I found Ben in Captain Chandler's office. He waved me into the office where few were allowed.

"Ben, what did you do now?" I asked.

"It's not what I did, it's what you did."

"Me?" I tried to sound innocent without looking like a hypocrite as I looked over at Ben's captain seated behind his desk. "Captain Chandler, I don't know what this oversized cop-on-the-beat has been telling you, but whatever it is, I'm sure it's not true, and if it is, I'm just as sure that I have a perfectly legitimate explanation."

Like Santa, the captain laughed and shook like a bowl of jelly, but that was as far as the resemblance went. Even though his body type would welcome the cuddle of any small child at Christmas, his face revealed a rock-hard approach to law enforcement. The crooked nose and square jaw, along with his dark eyes and bushy eyebrows, were distinctive features of the man who delivered more beatings than he took. A force to be reckoned with, I was one of the few people who could persuade the captain to crack even the slightest smile.

"That's right, Jimbo, it's not something you did," the captain said, "but something you seem to have uncovered. Let me introduce FBI Special Agent Anderson."

The tall slender man leaning against the opposite wall had escaped my notice. He pushed himself forward and held out his hand. I accepted the gesture but, for some reason, disliked him from the beginning. His clammy grip reminded me of Ron Myers.

Captain Chandler continued in his usual slow and deliberate style, "I followed up with the FBI after Ben told me what they found. Of course, you understand that this matter can be—"

"Delicate to say the least."

The interruption came from the FBI special agent—and nobody interrupts Captain Chandler.

"Yes, very delicate, indeed," the intruder continued, "If State's Attorney Blake, and Congressman Hamilton in California, are not involved, any unfounded accusation could nonetheless severely damage their reputations, after all, they simply served on the board that court-martialed Sellers. We are aware of no other. . ."

My earlier assessment of this poster child for the FBI proved to be accurate. The agent was exactly like Ron Myers. But what the hell did he mean about the state's attorney and some congressman in California? I glanced at Ben and his boss, both obviously annoyed by Anderson's ill-advised interruption.

"Now, everyone knows about your reckless reputation, but you must. . ."

The agent continued talking, but I stopped listening even though the schoolmaster's stare from Ben told me to be quiet and pay attention.

". . .These sophomoric tactics are a liability in a case of this magnitude, the type of case in which you are obviously inexperienced. So, I suggest you step aside and let the professionals handle—"

Stern expressions be damned. I had to interrupt the overblown bureaucrat.

"Ben, is this joker for real?"

It was Captain Chandler who, uncharacteristically, played the diplomat, "Jimbo, calm down and try to understand—"

"No, Captain, he doesn't have to understand anything." The Myers clone spoke in anger, but for no good reason—he didn't know me well enough—yet. "If he doesn't cooperate, I'll serve him with—"

"Shut up, Anderson!" The captain emphatically cut off the fool in a manner more consistent with the precinct captain I knew. "No charges have been filed, and no reports have been made. I called you as a courtesy to Fred Hardesty who—in case you've forgotten—is your boss, and a personal friend of mine. He is also more than a little displeased with the way you handled the investigation of those people at the Lakeview Manor Motel where it seems that you missed a thing or two.

"Now, Mr. Smith is also a personal friend, and you're right, he can be a bit of a loose cannon every now and then." He glanced at me with a slight humorous grin, to which I sheepishly shrugged my shoulders in response. "But if it weren't for his stubborn nature, an innocent man would have been convicted, and the case would have been closed, no thanks to you. So, Agent Anderson, as of now, this is a preliminary investigation, and you will serve as an aide to Sergeant Quincannon and do nothing more until we ask."

What the bureaucratic boob didn't know was that I once helped Captain Chandler with a certain consumer issue, significant enough that I saved him a couple grand. Another example of taking care of others so they take care of you.

The captain continued after a meaningful glare at Special Agent Anderson, "Now, Jimbo, Michael Blake's position prevents us from using the usual—"

"Wait a minute."

I felt the interruption was justified, but the scowl from the captain prompted a quick explanation.

"I'm sorry, Captain, but before we go any further, someone has to explain how Blake and some congressman named Hamilton are involved."

"It was your idea," Ben said, "I called the Baltimore FBI office after I reached a dead end. Their system dug deeper into that BX operation where we found Blake's name, along with a congressman in California. Both were Air Force officers who had already served nine and ten years respectively, then resigned when they got stateside after leaving Thailand, but not before serving on the board that convicted Sellers, giving him that light sentence."

Ben's boss took it from there. "We'll let the FBI worry about Congressman Hamilton and his connection to Sellers' trouble in California after we finish with State's Attorney Blake whose position makes our job that much more difficult. He could hear of any action we may take, and even the simplest surveillance could get back to his office. Other than Fred Hardesty, the three of us, and now you, Jimbo, no one knows anything about Blake's possible involvement with those people from the Manor. What I had in mind was something of an undercover investigation confined to the two of you while Agent Anderson stands at the ready."

Captain Chandler cocked his head and squinted his eyes. Looking directly at me, he added: "This excludes any help from anyone who might know or work with Michael Blake."

Of course, he meant Nora. Like Ben, the captain knew of

our relationship.

"But what if I had a contact in Blake's office whose discretion I can count on."

"We can't take that chance, Jimbo. But if the time comes when we need your contact's help, it is definitely an option to consider."

Captain Chandler looked back at the scolded agent, now quiet as the proverbial church mouse. "In the meantime, Agent Anderson, your boss promised any help the Bureau can provide. Our resources are limited while your federal system is more accurate and detailed. Dig up all you can about that operation in Thailand and the charges against Sellers in California . . . Oh, and also anything you can find on the Lakeview Manor Motel, of course."

It seemed the captain was done until he added: "Oh, and by the way, Agent Anderson, when this is over, Fred also wants me to let him know how cooperative you were in our investigation. Do you understand?"

Anderson nodded, though I could tell he wasn't a happy guy.

"Specifically," the captain continued, "I want complete histories of the living and the dead that Ben gave you. I also want the names of any other parties associated with the BX in Thailand who might be in our area or in California while Sellers was there, and that includes anyone who participated in investigating Sellers, as well as all those on the board that convicted him. Make sure there isn't someone we missed. I'll expect the information on my desk at 8 a.m."

"I'll have to work all night."

"And I appreciate that, as I'm sure Fred Hardesty will."

FBI Agent Anderson left with his mouse tail stuck so firmly between his legs that I swear he was waddling.

With him out of the room, I could freely share my thoughts. Still, the captain had a plan, and rank does have its privileges, so I tried a little psycho-suggestion: "Okay, Captain, where do we go from here? How 'bout a trip to the Manor to lean on Brewer? I can get him to crack."

"No."

"Okay. You said that a search warrant might alert Blake; in the meantime, I can quietly check out Sellers' and Brewer's places. I'll bet there's some good stuff there that we can use. They won't even know I broke in."

"Ben, how do you slow this guy down?"

"I've been thinking about slipping him a mickey, or maybe a crack on the skull with my nightstick might possibly work."

"You already did that back in Nam . . . Come on, guys, we can't just sit around."

"Why not?" the captain asked.

"Because somebody could get killed," I said.

"Looks like the only people left are all part of the plot; who else could there be?"

"Well, me for one."

Ben laughed, "That would be no great loss."

"Yeah, and I love you, too. But how about Kathy? She told me that Sellers is the brains of the operation. Guilty or not, we might need her for a witness. And, hell, the way people are dying, Sellers, Brewer, and even Blake's head could be on the chopping block. We don't know who else could be involved."

Ben looked over at Captain Chandler. "I hate to admit it, but Jimbo could be right. With all the evidence pointing to the syndicate, Sellers or anyone behind this mess could clean house and never be implicated other than that connection from years ago."

The captain looked thoughtful, staring me down with an analyzing expression.

"Okay. Jimbo, go find the girl and sit on her. It does look like Miss Radney is the key to the whole mess. We'll meet back here tomorrow morning. Maybe Anderson can give us more evidence to connect Blake and anyone else involved. Who knows, the state's attorney could be an innocent victim who needs his political ass saved from a blackmailer . . . that's if his ass is worth saving at all."

Ben and I laughed. None of us had much use for the crafty politician.

"See you both tomorrow," I turned to leave.

"Wait a minute." Ben said. "You heard what the captain said. Don't do anything else."

"Hey, man, you know me."

"You're darn right I know you. That's why I'm telling you: You do anything stupid and I'll kick your butt."

I just smiled and answered, "You already did that back in Nam . . . Besides, I bet you still hit like a girl." Then I quickly left the room.

◆ ◆ ◆

It was just after five; I called Kathy's home from the station hoping she'd be there. She was and told me it would be okay to stop over. I didn't tell her why, especially since Kathy never mentioned Blake in her indictment of Sellers and Brewer. After all, the state's attorney's military connection might turn out to be a mere coincidence and that Kathy told the truth about her connection to Sellers. Naïve or not, I clung to the remote possibility that my client only wanted to take over the escort business.

I knew the section where Kathy lived. Upscale living in a section of Baltimore County designed to outprice the undesirables. I parked my car and walked up the brick path to the lobby door of her building. Colorful flowers, bushes, and a well-maintained assortment of trees shaded the complex in such a way that it seemed twenty degrees cooler. I knocked on the door of her top floor apartment and waited, but no one answered. Another knock produced the same result. I tried the door. It was unlocked. I went in.

The large apartment was immaculate, furnished in a similar style as my parents' bed and breakfast, not too ornate, but close to an elegant design that matched Kathy's charm. An impressive floral painting caught my eye, but my attention to the surroundings lost focus when the air conditioner turned off and I heard the faint sound of running water coming from a room at the far end.

Entering the hallway, I passed two relatively small bedrooms that shared a bath, but the sound came from farther down. Another door, not quite closed, and which I slowly opened, revealed a third bedroom. A king-sized brass bed, covered with a blue and white flowered spread centered the room, with two nightstands on either side. Only those pieces and a make-up table occupied space in the large room making it seem surprisingly, and somewhat unsuitably, barren. My attention wandered to the sound coming from the bathroom to my right. I quietly walked over to the partially open door and pushed it the rest of the way.

Kathy's silhouette outlined the lightly frosted glass of the shower partition. I gazed at her perfect shadow standing still as the water splashed on her face, then streamed down the curves of firm breasts, flat stomach, and narrow hips, all the way to those shapely legs. I backed out, silently closing the door.

Of course, I felt sinful. Temptation is not only a strong motivation, but an undeniable weakness. Ironically, I had surrendered to that same temptation years earlier when I spied on my cousin Diane as she showered during one of the few times she spent the night with us. I was just an experimental adolescent then, so my voyeurism can be excused, but as an adult I found it difficult to overlook that same guilt. Still, I couldn't shake the feeling that, on those two occasions, both Kathy and Diane knew I was there.

Suddenly, the door opened and Kathy stood in front of me, naked except for the towel wrapped around her head. I turned away, even though she didn't seem startled—or embarrassed.

"I'm sorry, Kathy, but you shouldn't leave your door open. Anybody could walk in."

"You called to say you'd be over, so I left it unlocked. You can turn around now."

A short terry robe did nothing to hide her figure and those beautiful legs, but still afflicted with guilt, I forced myself to maintain strict eye contact.

"I just left Sergeant Quincannon and his captain; we all agreed that your life is in danger. Get dressed and come with me to a motel on the other side of town that the police use for a safe house."

Kathy gave a subtle, almost comical grin when I said motel.

"Kathy, you have to know by now that you can trust me."

"I know, Jim, but that won't be necessary." She walked over and placed her hand on my cheek, "But you are such a dear."

"Kathy," I said more firmly, "You said it yourself; these men are extremely dangerous."

"Yes, I know."

She went over and sat down at the makeup table. I sat on

the bed across from her where we could see each other in the mirror.

"Sellers and Brewer have committed the near perfect crime," I said, "and you are the only person who can testify against them." Purposely, I left out the suspicion concerning Michael Blake.

"I know that, too."

"Then you must know the danger you're in. Once they eliminate you, the game is over."

She smiled at me through the mirror, "I can take care of myself," then nonchalantly continued with her makeup. Something didn't seem right in her manner, but, once again, I ignored the nagging suspicions.

"I'm sure you can, Kathy, but not in this case, and not with these people."

That quickly, she finished her work and turned to face me. She removed the towel from her head and shook her hair the way a model might for a photo shoot.

"How do I look?"

There was a slight, but noticeable difference. Though no makeup could be seen, her eyes were brighter, her skin more golden.

"Great. But Kathy, you must listen to—"

"Do you know the power that I have over men? I could make love to you in such a way that you'll never forget no matter how many lovers you have after me. In fact, it would be better if I show you."

She rose from the chair and dropped the robe on the floor, revealing the perfection. I struggled for a breath. Kneeling in front of me, Kathy undid every button, belt, and zipper as if she were a magician, and if I hadn't been so bewitched by her sensuous movements, I would have stopped her. But I couldn't . . . And I didn't.

"Make love to me like it's the last time you'll make love to any woman."

I experienced the power she mentioned, and she was right. To this day, I've never forgotten her and the surreal experience that ended much too quickly.

The breathtaking experience over, she kissed me, "I hired you to free Chris. You did a great job and I never lost faith in you, which reminds me . . ." She got up from the bed and went to the nightstand, opened the drawer and took out an envelope, "Here's the rest of the money I owe you." She didn't hand it to me but placed it on the bed beside me.

Can you imagine how I felt, sitting there naked with an envelope of money on the bed next to me? Shocked, overwhelmed, and confused describe just a few of my emotions. But more than that, uncontrolled anger struck me so hard that I felt sick to my stomach. Not long before, Kathy was the panic-stricken victim confessing all the sordid details of the events that had taken place at the Manor. It now seemed that she wouldn't have noticed if the building fell down around us.

"Kathy, what the hell is going on?"

"Jim, you must go. I have a date."

Ignoring my question, she disappeared into the walk-in closet.

A date! Was she kidding? I felt like yelling: *Next!*

I had to get away. I threw on my clothes and ran out the door, leaving Kathy's final payment on the bed. Speeding out of the parking lot, I nearly hit two parked cars and a Mercedes that was pulling in. Cursing the rich bastard, I noticed the light ahead turn to yellow, so I floored it, hit second, and fishtailed onto the main drag.

I had no idea where to go, or what to do. Anger controlled me. Never before had I compromised my profession as I had with Kathy.

I had become Ron Myers.

Speeding down the road to heaven knows where, I realized that Kathy's actions were an unspoken confession of guilt. In no uncertain terms, the beautiful question mark had revealed an involvement, or she surely would have recognized her need for protection. Instead, she calmly dressed for what she said was a date, and what I believed to be another night of business.

It was half past six, and there was no way that I could wait until morning, and no way that I could call Ben.

The taunting battleground and the skinny bartender beckoned.

◆ ◆ ◆

My Camaro once again had a mind of its own as it turned into the driveway and down to the empty parking lot of the Lakeview Manor Motel. Without thinking, I grabbed my gun from its hiding place. I was back in Vietnam in search of the enemy, advancing up the steps that I had been thrown down more than once, and into the familiar surroundings of the lounge where my demons would be faced yet again. The lounge was empty, too early for the hungry crowd. The door to Barlowe's office was open.

Not wanting anyone to approach from behind, I looked for the two bouncers. They were nowhere in sight. Cautiously, and with the gun hidden behind my back, I walked into the office to find Brewer sitting behind the desk where I had once threatened to kill his boss. He didn't notice that I had entered . . . or so I thought.

"Looks like you fell into a good thing."

Brewer looked up and calmly smiled as if he expected me, "Yeah, the company picked the man who knew the most about the operation."

"Convenient."

"No, not convenient, deserved. I've been putting up with Barlowe's shit for a long time. I worked hard for this chance, and after all that's happened, the company had no other choice than to pick me as that fat hog's successor. Anyone else would have created more questions, besides, they don't know about my part in any of this; more of the beauty in Tony's plan."

"Did you hate Barlowe that much?"

"Damn right. I hated that fat bastard more than life. Him and his fucking Marine Corps discipline."

"And I'll bet you hated him enough to kill him." I took a step toward the new manager.

Brewer's right hand, which was hidden under the desk when I entered, produced a gun. I stopped and tightened my grip on the .38 behind my back wondering who would be quicker, the foul-mouthed dirtbag or me, even though he did have the advantage with his weapon aimed and ready to fire.

"I'm not as dumb as you think, asshole," Brewer said. "In fact, I can't believe just how stupid you are. You followed every lead like a dog on a leash. We knew you'd be here tonight; it was just a matter of when. I only had to wait for the call. And I also knew that you'd have the gun you're hiding behind your back. Now I can kill you in self-defense."

Paranoia set in. Was this a trap? Did my client purposely

anger me, correctly anticipating that the Manor would be my next move, then call Brewer to warn him? I remembered her telling me to make love to her like it was my last time. Brewer said "we" knew that I'd be there. Who was included in the we? Everybody was happy and I refused to let it go. Did Kathy and Sellers count on that, too? How could they possibly know me well enough to predict my every move?

Blake. He no longer seemed like an innocent party. The state's attorney had to be the influential party who planned everything from Chris's frame to my involvement. He knew my reputation and he knew of my friendship with Nora, and I had personally witnessed his talent as an influential politician whose strength lies in the ability to manage any situation. But how could I be sure?

How much more did Brewer know? I took a chance.

"Okay, so you think you're an Einstein. Well, consider this: You're no better off than me. You're doing exactly what you're told and nothing more. How long do you think they'll keep you around? That's right, stupid, when all is said and done, Sellers and Blake will have no more use for you. Think about that."

"How did you know that Blake . . . Nobody's supposed . . ."

Brewer's stutter confirmed Blake's involvement.

More than that, there now seemed to be another manager with his mind running like a hamster on the wheel in its cage, but unlike Barlowe's lumbering rodent, Brewer's mental influence sprinted with no place to go. It was time to bargain.

"Brewer, listen to me. The cops know everything, including Blake's part in all of this, and because of that, the FBI is involved. You only have one way out and that's to give yourself up and make a deal. If not, you'll go down with the rest."

The hamster spun Brewer's caged wheel, now faster than ever.

"No. Blake's got everything under control. I don't know how, but he even knew you'd come back here again. I'll wait and see how things turn out before I start making deals. And besides, it's too late; I'm in too deep."

"Why because you committed murder?"

"Yeah, that and other stuff."

Slowly, Brewer stood and started toward me with his gun leveled at my chest. I needed to apply more pressure, more questions for him to think about or I was dead.

"You just don't get it, hot shot. You were dead the minute you shot Hodges."

"I didn't kill Johnny. I wanted him alive, but he wouldn't go along with Tony's plan to bring over the Thai girls, so he murdered Hodges and then Barlowe; he said they both had to be eliminated if his plan was going to work."

Brewer's determined expression revealed a commitment to complete his mission no matter what doubts he had about its success. The time had come. My hand squeezed the .38 preparing to make my move, but determined to eat away at that smug confidence, I kept pushing before taking that last, hopeless gamble.

"I can see Barlowe pissing you off, but what's not to like about Brittany? She seemed nice enough."

"Brittany was like that other bitch. So while Tony shot Barlowe, I had the pleasure of putting a bullet into that whore's head."

Before I had the chance to make what would probably be my last act on earth, I heard footsteps and a sniffling sound behind me. I turned to see Pinkie at the door with tears in his eyes.

"You killed Brith. You killed my thister!"

Brewer didn't respond because there wasn't enough time. With two giant decisive steps, Pinkie grabbed Brewer's gun hand with his left, bones snapping under the pressure from the big man's grasp. The scream that should have followed didn't because Pinkie's right hand seized Brewer's throat just as I had that first night, but the bouncer's grip proved to be more deadly than mine. I heard the sickening sound of more breaking bones and the fluid trying, but failing to make its way to Brewer's mouth which released his final breath of life. In a moment, it was over.

Brewer's head tilted to one side, eyes wide open, a slight trickle of blood emerging from his mouth and its swollen tongue, the lifeless body dangling from Pinkie's hand like a snake with a broken spine. I don't know how long he and I stood motionless until, placing my hand on his massive shoulder, I said, "It's over."

Pinkie released the corpse that crumbled to the ground. He dropped down to his knees next to Brewer's dead body and began to sob, slowly repeating Brittany's name without the slightest hint of a lisp. The big man's uncontrollable display of emotion affected me so deeply that I had to gather myself before calling Ben. He was there in ten minutes. I told him everything, beginning with my encounter with Kathy, and then I tried to leave.

"Wait a minute, Jimbo. Where do you think you're going?"

"I've got to find Kathy."

"Hey, man, you already blew that assignment."

"Look, Ben, she's all we got. Blake doesn't know that we're on to him and it's more than a good possibility that he has her. If she ends up as dead as the rest, I'll bet that shifty politician can get out of this even after what Brewer told me. Sellers took the fall before and he'll more than likely do it again."

"You're probably right about Sellers, but Kathy could be Blake's partner. Look at all she told you, everything implicated Sellers and Brewer. She didn't say a word about Blake. She could actually confirm his innocence. What makes you think she'll turn?"

Without an answer, I could only shrug.

"Well, wait for me and we'll find her together."

"No way, Sergeant Quincannon, you have too many legal handicaps. I'll do this alone."

Knowing it would be a waste of time, I raced to Kathy's apartment anyway, but unless her date began with a longer sexual treatment than she gave me, the two of them were most likely gone. Without bothering to park in a slot, my Camaro jumped to a stop when I popped the clutch while still in gear. Running into the foyer, I collided into a senior citizen who got in my way. He cursed at me as he fell against the wall. After a quick check on the old guy, and an even quicker apology, I ran up the stairs. Kathy's door was locked, so I burst through, recklessly running from room to room in a futile search for the client I knew wouldn't be there.

Furious with myself for being so gullible, I walked back out to the hallway wondering where Kathy might have gone. Meg's Diner would be the obvious place, but I doubted that Sellers was the date she mentioned. Still, thinking that a trip there might not be a total waste of time, I moved the broken molding, closed the door, and started for the stairs when an elderly lady standing at the door of the apartment across the hall called to me.

"Are you looking for Miss Radney?"

It occurred to me that the old girl must be approaching senility because she must have seen my struggle to close Kathy's door.

"Yes."

"She left about a half hour ago with a very nice-looking gentleman. I've seen him on the television many times; I think he has something to do with the government. I greeted her as always, but they seemed to be in such a hurry. Is everything all right?"

I assured Kathy's neighbor not to worry and that everything would be fine. She smiled and closed her door.

The man she described had to be Blake, and with that, my last hope for Kathy was gone. While true that the doubts about my client's honesty had harassed me ever since our first meeting, I still wanted it to be okay if two plus two equaled five. Now, like Dorothy from Kansas when she thought I was involved in her fiancé's death, I reassessed my math, accepted the obvious, and admitted defeat: My client deliberately participated in the plot to murder Hodges, Barlowe, and Brittany.

I was right, however, in my original judgment that Sellers wasn't the playwright of the murder drama. Brewer said that Blake had everything under control, so it wasn't the revolting fat man, but the skillful politician directing the operation. All of Kathy's actions, both in my office and later in her apartment, must have been orchestrated by the state's attorney.

But what about the fat man? The villain in the play. Sellers spoiled what was a pretty neat setup by bringing the Asian girls to Baltimore, apparently demanding payment for taking the rap in Thailand. But when Hodges fought back, Sellers immediately eliminated the opposition, making it clear to the foul-mouthed bartender and the state's attorney that he was taking over.

The image of Kathy sitting with Sellers in Meg's Diner crept into my mind and turned my stomach like the steak I almost ate that first night at the Manor. The Bogart/Astor film came to mind. Those two were even more incompatible than Kasper Gutman and Brigid O'Shaughnessy in *The Maltese Falcon*, the fat man and the bewildering beauty in the film noir classic involving the possession of a priceless bejeweled statue. Sound similar? In my case, the Lakeview Manor became the prize as Kathy took on the role of Brigid. Ironically, Brigid's guilt came to light in the end . . . Just like my client.

A sinister anxiety similar to the nightmares that torment me disturbed my thoughts. Breaking out in sweat, I tripped down the stairs, almost falling head first, and staggered to the parking lot like a drunken man. Leaning on the trunk of my car, my mind fought to make sense of all that had happened since the beginning of the case.

But rather than the beginning, the memory of the dead bartender hanging from Pinkie's grasp appeared in my mind's eye like some macabre painting. His death proved that my visit with Kathy wasn't as spontaneous as I thought. My client's seductive talent turned out to be a calculated part of Blake's plan to coax me into an appearance at the Manor and the confrontation with Brewer, all intended to bring about my final downfall. Act III of the play. Fortunately, Pinkie overheard Brewer's confession or that part of the plan would have most likely succeeded.

What would Blake do now that Brewer's assignment failed? And how would he deal with Sellers, the unwelcome catalyst? Not only that, but the plan to lay blame on the syndicate had also collapsed. What kind of new storyline could the playwright create?

And yet, when giving the last act of the play a second interpretation, I realized that Blake's reputation was not in immediate danger. Other than their military records, the state's attorney and his office had no connection to Sellers, Brewer, or anything else that happened at the Manor. Ben was right, seeing Sellers at the diner, working the business with Kathy proved nothing. More than that, no one else heard my conversation with Brewer; Pinkie only heard the last crucial seconds that saved my life. The fat man and Blake could still regroup, claiming that Brewer's testimony implicating the two of them was a desperate attempt to divert the guilt from himself, that he was the original blackmailer from the black-market operation, and that he alone was responsible for all three murders—two guns or not. Everyone would surely believe any explanation from the honorable public servant speaking at his next press conference:

*"Once again, we have been targeted by the evil forces that run rampant through our communities. Our fight must be resolute and ever vigilant. To meet this end, I am creating a task force led by my friend, Jim Smith. . ."*

But as the sun drifted beneath the evergreens surrounding the buildings, its intensity faded. A gentle breeze cooled the sweat on my shirt and calmed the anxiety that pushed me down the stairs. I focused my attention on the state's attorney's reaction to Brewer's death, which led to only one possible conclusion: Blake couldn't let me live, and with Brewer dead, he could no longer let Sellers live. After all, the repulsive gatecrasher's meddling forced Blake to come up with his plan in the first place, because had he not come to Baltimore, the escort business at the Lakeview Manor would have never been threatened. Now, the state's attorney's position in the community remained in jeopardy as long as Sellers conducted business at the Manor while holding the specter of blackmail over the crooked politician's head. I needed to find the fat man before it was too late.

I drove to a corner store where I called Ben to see if he had put out the call about Brewer. He had, but only as a one-eighty-seven—the police code for a homicide—without giving the name of the deceased. If Blake heard that call, he might assume that Brewer had succeeded, possibly giving me enough time to find Sellers. The state's attorney couldn't follow up because that might cause suspicion as to his involvement.

I recalled my first thought when I closed Kathy's door just before meeting her neighbor. The diner. If my timing was right, Sellers might still be there satisfying his enormous appetite while conducting business.

Assuming that Sellers also might have heard about a death at the Manor, I sped to Meg's Diner praying that the fat pig believed that Brewer had carried out Blake's plan and that he was now free to assume control of the business with the new manager's help. I entered the parking lot from the far corner where my car would less likely be seen from inside. Luck was on my side. The Lincoln was parked in the front row. I drove to the back of the building and grabbed my gun.

Cautiously snaking my way through the crowded lot, I approached the expensive town car, and opened the back door. Fortunately, it was unlocked. I slid in and positioned myself on the floor behind the driver's side. Before long, the door opened, and Sellers got in.

The car dipped when the fat man fell into the driver's seat. Until that time, I entertained the possibility that Blake dropped Kathy off, and that she would be working the operation that one last night—but the single door closed, and the car pulled away.

I counted the few turns that led to the familiar drive until Sellers wheeled the Lincoln toward the Manor. He drove at a snail's pace, which was far too slow for me because the adrenaline pumping through my system wanted me to jump on the fat man and beat the crap out of him right there. But I had to wait for the right time. Finally, the town car came to a stop. I guessed that Sellers saw the police cars and assumed that Blake's plan worked. I pictured a satisfied grin on his beefy cheeks. He shifted into reverse and started to back out when I jumped up and shoved my gun into Sellers' right ear until it broke the skin and drew blood.

"Now, scumbag, let's go talk to a friend of mine."

"You're hurting me, man."

"God, I hope so. Drive, but nice and slow."

Sellers shifted into forward and followed my directions, slowly driving toward the Manor. Ben, standing on the porch at the entrance to the lounge, smiled and shook his head when he saw me. I smiled back and relaxed my grip just enough that the muzzle dropped from Sellers' ear. Sensing my overconfidence, and quicker than I thought possible for the fat man, he hit my wrist with the back of his right hand, forcing the gun away from his head and into my face. I was lucky it didn't go off or I'd have lost my damn nose.

The fat son-of-a-bitch then slammed on the brakes, jerking both the car and me, giving him enough time to get out before I could recover my balance. Like my adrenaline rush a minute before, having the barrel of a gun shoved half an inch into his ear must have accelerated his system even more than mine because I couldn't believe my eyes when I saw him sprinting into the woods, carrying what looked like a .357 Magnum. How could the fat man move so fast?

I opened the door, fell out of the Lincoln, and rolled on the ground away from the car now drifting toward the Manor without a driver. Then, without bothering to look for Ben or any of the other cops, I chased after Sellers.

Once inside the woods, I stopped and listened for a sound of any kind. Sellers could have gone in a couple different directions, but the busy highway would be his only chance of escape. Pushing aside the thick shrubbery, I hurried down the overgrown path that led to the sound of the rush hour traffic. Sellers had a good head start after my lapse of concentration; if I didn't catch him, Ben would never let me hear the end of it.

The dense forest filtered the light from the late afternoon sun creating a ghostly and dreamlike mist. Blistering heat radiated from the ground reminiscent of a faraway jungle slowing me down. The hair on the back of my neck bristled as my breathing strained. The trees stirred as if men were climbing on their limbs while the ground shook with explosions from rockets and mortars that seemed to be getting closer and closer. Sweat dripped from my forehead, burning my eyes. My heart pounded as the memories of hidden snipers, booby traps, and landmines became real. They were there. Somewhere out there the enemy was hiding. My right hand pressed against the grip of my pistol, while my left searched for the barrel of the M-16 that wasn't there. I was no longer looking for Sellers. A different enemy was closing in on me.

*He's here. Somewhere he's here. He knows where to hide. This is his country. I've got to kill him before he kills me.*

Dizzy and weak, caught in the nightmare of another place and time, I heard what sounded like foreign voices, but too far away to be sure. Then came a tap on my shoulder. Still lost in a dream from years past, I turned and faced the .357 pointing at my head. The figure holding the gun said something, but I couldn't understand the words. He spoke again. Words that sounded like an echo from another room.

"You're alone, Smith, your buddy isn't here to save you this time, so drop the gun."

I stared at the enemy in front of me, slowly beginning to understand who he was. Then something in my manner gave the impression of an ill-advised move because the fat man pushed the enormous gun against my forehead and said more forcefully, "I said drop it. I don't want to kill you . . . not yet anyway."

His command and the pressure from the .357 against my head delivered me from the past. I dropped the gun.

"Thank you, Mr. Smith."

"How the hell did you move that fast?"

"Looks are deceiving; I'm in better shape than you might think. And I've learned to use the terrain around me."

I stared at the fat man and his Magnum. So this was it. Many times in Vietnam I tempted death, ready to find out if justice waited on the other side. Now the grim reaper teased me, first when Brewer had his chance, and now with another gun in position to kill. Pinkie saved my life before, but he wasn't around now, and neither was Ben.

"Come on," Sellers said, giving me no more time to think, "Let's go for a walk; you lead the way."

"Where to?"

"Back to my car. I'd get nowhere on foot; my only chance is for you to help me. You're my ticket out of here."

"The police will never allow that, but assuming you do get away, what comes next? And what are you going to do with me?"

"You? Oh, I'll let you go, so you can get married, raise a family, and live happily ever after in a house with a white picket fence."

Okay, so it was a dumb question with an unspoken obvious answer, but I had already decided that if I were to die, the fat man was going with me. Ben and his men had to be closing in, so as we walked toward the driveway with Sellers' gun pressed against the right side of my spine, I challenged his arrogant confidence while waiting for the opportunity to take some desperate action that might not result in a trip to the morgue.

"By the way, in case you're interested, Brewer's dead; Pinkie broke his neck. Apparently, nobody knew it, but Brittany was his sister; the big man overheard Brewer telling me that he shot her at the same time you killed Barlowe. I still don't get their murders, Sellers. Why did they have to die? Was it because you needed more evidence against the syndicate? And is that why you sent those actors to my place."

"I killed Barlowe for two reasons: first, he was a nosy son-of-a-bitch who would never let me take over the business, and second, yes, their deaths were intended to look like a mob hit. All part of the plan, but I don't know anything about any actors."

"Well, Brewer told me everything, and I've already told the cops all that he said, especially concerning your import business with the girls from Thailand. That'll bring back the feds and there's no hiding from them. Oh, and by the way, he also told me about Blake's involvement."

"So what, Blake can take care of himself. He's one of the reasons I've been running for the last ten years. He owes me after I took the fall for him and the others back in Thailand."

"That includes the congressman who got you out of trouble in California?"

"That's right. I don't care what happens to either of them. That idiot in California thought I'd be happy after he set me up with a nine-to-five job, but that's not my style. I want my girls back in business, and the Manor would have been a sweet operation if only Hodges had agreed. So, when he didn't go along, he had to be eliminated. And then there was you . . . you just wouldn't stop meddling after I spent so much time and effort blaming the mob. Anyway, I still have contacts and I know how to stay alive. So now that you've managed to screw everything up, I'll use you to get away, dump your body, and live off the land until the smoke clears. It'll be easy in the mountains of Maryland or West Virginia. Eventually, I'll move on and set up my operation in some other place. It's a big country."

"Why do that? Make a deal. Give up Blake and—"

"Bullshit, man, I'm guilty of murder and human trafficking. My only deal would be life. I go crazy when I'm locked up. You can't imagine what it's like for me; that one year in the brig was hell. I'd rather take my chances in the mountains. Now I've had enough of your—"

Ben jumped from the bushes, "Give it up, Sellers!"

"Smith goes first!" Sellers yelled, putting his left hand on my shoulder and shoving the gun against my back.

"Don't worry about me, Ben. Shoot the bastard."

"Yeah, Ben, don't worry about your buddy here. But listen, all you have to do is let me go and you'll get him back, safe and sound. I promise. Believe it or not, I've come to like this annoying idiot, and I only kill those who deserve it."

Ben knew, as I did, that Sellers only wanted to stall long enough to make it to his car with a hostage, but I chose to use the empty promise to kill some time. My hands gestured away from my body as I spoke to Ben, slightly moving my arms the way people do when they use their hands to emphasize their words.

"Ben, maybe this piece of crap isn't worth dying for. Let him go; I'll go with him, and we can still get Blake, after all he's the reason for . . ."

With each arm gesture I turned just slightly toward Sellers, nodding my head in his direction, and acting like I was pleading his case. Then, as mine did in his Lincoln, the gun's pressure eased, drifting farther to my right just enough until I thought there might not be a better opportunity to strike. There would be no second chance.

Finally, the time seemed right. Mid-sentence, I spun around, knocking the gun from his hand with my left arm, but not before it fired, luckily only grazing me above the belt line.

Ben fired the second shot. Sellers fell to the ground, the corpulent mass of flesh collapsing like a mound of gelatin, dying more gracefully than he lived, and getting better than he deserved. I stared at the lifeless body, blood flowing from his head. I felt compassion for Barlowe and especially Brittany, but the death of the two murderers stirred no emotion at all, only that justice had been served.

But now what? I looked at Ben, "Why did you have to kill him?"

"What! Talk about gratitude. Next time I'll let him shoot you."

"There won't be a next time . . . he's dead."

"Dammit, Jimbo, I should have left you back in the mud at Da Nang."

"It's too late for that, too."

The coroner, already there for Brewer, came to take Sellers' body out of the woods. I met Ben at his car.

"You know I didn't mean what I said back there. Thanks, buddy."

Ben smiled, "Being your guardian angel is part of my job description."

"Well, you almost lost your job this time."

"Hopefully, that'll be the last, but I doubt it."

"I'll do my best . . . Any chance I can catch a ride back to the diner to get my car?"

"Not a problem." Ben called over to one of the officers

standing with the coroner. "Hey, Dundee, can you give Jimbo a ride over to Meg's Diner?"

"Sure thing, Sarge . . . Wait a minute, Jimbo, I can't have you bleeding all over my cruiser."

"Come on, man," I said, "It's just a scratch."

He smiled. "All right, I'll get you a towel to put on the seat anyway. Let's go."

"See ya, Ben."

"Wait a minute, Jimbo. What are you going to do? We don't have enough to arrest Blake unless Anderson can dig up some concrete evidence."

"To be honest, I doubt there's anything for Anderson to dig up. Blake wouldn't be that careless. No, Sarge, our only chance is to find my client and get her to testify against him."

"Okay, let's say you do find her. What makes you think she'll turn on him? I hate to be the one to disappoint you, buddy, but from all you've told me, she's in it with Blake."

"But what if Blake's using her, Ben? He had to be the man who picked her up from her apartment, and other than seeing Blake on television, Kathy's neighbor didn't say anything about seeing him with her before."

"Come on, Jimbo, don't be so naïve. Why are you so intent on believing that this girl is innocent?"

The fictional character of the guilty Brigid O'Shaughnessy came to mind once again. "I don't know, Ben. I gotta wonder how she got involved with Blake in the first place. He must have recruited her after Sellers came to town. There's no way the state's attorney would have been caught dead hanging around the Manor, let alone dating one of its employees—"

"You mean with one of its hookers."

"Okay, even if she is, I've maintained from the beginning that her sole objective is to take over the business. Maybe that's the deal they made."

"You're amazing; you have an answer for everything."

"Not an answer, Ben, a possibility."

Officer Dundee's cruiser pulled up next to us. "You coming, Jimbo?"

"And how do you intend, first finding her, and then getting her to give him up?"

I smiled. "I'll let you know later."

My right side, burning from Sellers' deadly intention, needed a little attention before searching for my client. After getting my car, I headed home for a quick shower, peroxide cleanse, and clean shirt, all of which would take less than ten minutes. I needed to find Kathy as soon as possible, but if her death was part of Blake's plan, my client may have already met her fate. On the other hand, it seemed possible that his plans for Kathy weren't urgent because he would have to find a way of killing her without implicating himself after making the mistake of being seen with her by Kathy's neighbor.

So, where did that leave me? If I had walked away after Barlowe's and Brittany's murders, life at the Lakeview Manor would have continued with only a slight interruption. Everyone would have been happy, or so the saying goes. Now, after two more deaths, the future of the business and my client's life hung in the balance. What would the Manor's ownership think of that?

I parked and walked up to my office hoping there still may be time to find Kathy, all the while wondering that, if it wasn't too late, what incentive could possibly convince her to testify against Michael Blake? Not only that, but assuming that Blake had picked her up, where would he take her?

I climbed the stairs to my office, opened the door, and headed for the bottle of Jack on my desk when it suddenly became apparent that Kathy's whereabouts no longer mattered . . . another part of the play, probably the last act, was about to begin.

Comfortably seated at my desk chair, the honorable state's attorney grinned, "Hello, Jimbo."

I turned and closed my door, shaking my head at the part of the play that I never saw coming.

The playwright's grin broadened into an arrogant smile, "Don't be shy, my friend, come on over and have a seat."

I walked over to my desk, but didn't sit down like Blake wanted. After pouring two fingers of whiskey, I held the bottle of Jack out to my guest who looked very much at ease with his hands resting on the arms of my chair in just about the same position as Brewer sitting at Barlowe's desk. My inner voice told me to be cautious.

"Want a hit? I can get you a clean glass."

I hoped he would reach across the desk giving me an opportunity to jump him, but he sat still, like he knew what I had in mind.

"No thank you, I don't drink; it's bad for the image."

"So's murder."

"Right to the point. That's one of the many things I admire

about you, Jimbo."

"Where's Kathy?" I asked.

Blake showed off his perfect white teeth, answering only with a patronizing snicker.

I expected the worst, "You killed her, didn't you."

"No, and why should I kill the girl who loves me unconditionally?"

*His lover? What else did I miss?*

"Because she's the only person who can upset all your plans."

"My plans? It may look like that to you, but very little of this awkward situation was my plan, though because I know you so well, I assumed the role of advisor. It was Sellers who served as the mastermind, or so he thought. He wanted all the manufactured evidence to implicate the organization so he could take control of the escort business after the authorities finished their investigation. I only found it necessary to fine-tune the proceedings a bit here and there, first by using you and Kathy—my suggestion—and then, by having her deliver certain ideas to you that Sellers didn't know about."

"And I suppose there's still more fine-tuning to come?"

"Nothing that I haven't already anticipated."

"And I guess I'm involved?"

"Of course, Jimbo. You've been one of the major components since the very beginning. I assume Brewer and that pain-in-the-ass Sellers are dead?" When I didn't answer, Blake nodded. "You wouldn't be here if they weren't. You do good work, Jimbo, I counted on your celebrated stubborn nature, and you haven't let me down for a minute."

I took a sip of the Jack, "So you think you know me that

well?"

"The proof is there for anyone with an ounce of perception to see. You followed every one of Kathy's leads whether you trusted her or not, all meant to confuse you, to keep you guessing so you couldn't get a firm hold on Sellers' scheme." He snickered again. "I bet that missing legal pad bothered you."

"That was you?"

"Yes, I thought it might rattle you. Taking your notes was actually an ad lib that I thought of when I checked out your place. You should lock your door, Jimbo; you never know who might wander in. Anyway, I did have one serious concern—"

"Really?" I interrupted. "But you had everything thought out so perfectly."

"Only one small uncertainty, Jimbo. While I believed that your temper would cause you to act rashly—as it did—I worried that your inexperience and moral character would interfere."

"How could my morals be a problem?"

"That you might not kill the others. There was always the possibility that you would adopt some quixotic notion of bringing them to justice. That's why Chris Palmer became the perfect candidate for the frame because his service record would motivate you to do anything possible to free him. All good planning. Every detail worked against you. Even the old guy at the inner harbor—"

"Hey! He's not old."

Blake laughed, "It doesn't matter, does it. Nora told me about the old guy—or whatever he is—after the two of you spent time at the harbor. I told Kathy to take Chris down there and point him out. Then she told Palmer she'd meet him at the old guy's bench the night Sellers killed Johnny. Sellers didn't know about that because he put all his faith in his implication of the mob." Blake shook his head and chuckled, "My fine-tuning there almost backfired when Palmer pulled his zombie act. I thought I'd have to think of something else, but providence took control and Palmer spoke up—"

"Providence has nothing to do with any of your plans, Blake."

I kept interrupting Blake, hoping to upset his comfort level, but he continued, sounding more like the narrator of a documentary than a cunning politician.

"That doesn't matter, Jimbo, because one way or another, the old guy told you that he saw Palmer that night, then Nora gave you the bad news concerning his shortcomings as a reliable witness. I knew the disappointment would anger you even more. Your temper is well-documented, Jimbo. I've seen it for myself, and I gambled on your emotional instability throughout the last few days, hoping you'd lose control. You didn't let me down, Jimbo, especially after your last meeting with Kathy."

*Jimbo. Jimbo. Jimbo. Stop calling me Jimbo, you bastard.*

"Nice thinking, Mr. Blake, but Brewer told me about your involvement, and the cops know about your relationship with Hodges, Brewer and Sellers, along with some congressman in California named Hamilton."

"Brewer never could keep his mouth shut, and none of this would have happened if I had taken care of Sellers when I should have back in Thailand. Everyone involved knew he'd be trouble, but I didn't want to take the chance of getting further involved by exterminating that fat scumbag. In any case, Barton Hamilton and I managed to maneuver our way onto that board because we'd also have been facing charges of misconduct if any one of the three revealed that we took kickbacks from their black-market operation. So, while relatively simple to arrange an off the record deal for Hodges and Brewer, Sellers' case posed a problem. He needed to be convicted and sentenced after he got caught running his little prostitution enterprise on the side. Johnny and Brewer knew they had no choice in the matter, but Sellers objected."

Blake leaned back in my worn swivel chair, then laughed.

"Can you imagine? Sellers actually thought we could give him the same deal as the other two. It took quite some time to convince the dummy that he had no choice. Anyway, to make this long story short, after I left the Air Force, Johnny and Brewer followed me here where I brokered the deal with Barlowe to give Brewer the bartender's job—he was too stupid to do anything else. Then I set up the escort business for Hodges. It's ironic that Johnny's legit business became Sellers' specialty."

"So Hodges didn't initiate the prostitution?"

"No. He was as strait-laced as they come; I don't even know how he got mixed up in the black-market operation. Anyway, after catching the girls adjusting their job description so to speak, he decided to let them work that action on their own while taking his normal percentage. In the meantime, Hamilton negotiated an early release for Sellers, then set him up with a job in California thinking that would be enough to make him happy, but I suspected it wouldn't. Sellers is . . . Excuse me, I mean Sellers *was* a special kind of man, never satisfied. It's Johnny I feel sorry for; he was the best of the bunch.

"Nevertheless, none of that matters. Hamilton and I served in Thailand the same time they did, so it's reasonable that we sat on the board that sent Sellers to the brig while the other two negotiated their honorable discharges. The Air Force agreed to Johnny's and Brewer's compromises because they didn't want any bad publicity, especially with public opinion being as it was against the war. On the other hand, that fat slob's hearing is a documented military record which will prove that his implications concerning me were nothing more than a desperate attempt to exact revenge. As far as Brewer goes, his military history is easily linked to Sellers, so their alliance is understandable. And, even if it does come out that I found Hodges and Brewer work, everyone knows what a kind soul I am, so finding work for my brother veterans won't come as a surprise. In addition to all that, I purposely steered away from the murders at the Manor. Your girlfriend handled the entire investigation, so there's no evidence that I was ever aware of Sellers' presence, a man I barely knew other than that military hearing. When all the facts are revealed, Jimbo, I'm just an innocent bystander implicated by coincidence and vengeance."

"And what about me and Kathy?"

"You won't be a problem for long."

I didn't like the way that sounded.

"And you're sure Kathy loves you so much that she won't turn you in?"

Rather than answer, Blake flashed the vacant smile of a man who held a secret.

Controlling my temper became more and more of a struggle that Blake efficiently manipulated while he sat silently stoic, aggravating me that much more. Not a muscle moved, not so much as a twitch or slight spasm from his perfect features. It became exceedingly difficult to restrain myself.

I stood still, staring at the enemy who smiled back at me while I sipped on my drink. Why was he there? My death along with that of my client had to be part of the last act. A valid assumption at the time, but why all this drama? Why all the explanation and wasting of time? The decisive state's attorney apparently believed he had everything under control. Could we be waiting for Kathy? It made sense that we would die together. Was he going to kill both of us in my office, making it look like something it wasn't?

I was thinking too much. Wasting too much time of my

own. The heat was getting to me and the fans did nothing to cool off the scrambling hamster running around in my brain. There had to be a way to upset his egotistical confidence. Keep interrupting. Keep asking questions. That might bring out part of the plan.

"But what if Sellers and Brewer didn't die? What if I quit after Chris was free? Wasn't placing the blame on the mob Sellers' intention from the beginning?"

"That was the advantage of the mafia story, and you're right, blaming the organization was Sellers' plan once he told me that it would be necessary to eliminate Johnny. He expected you to throw doubt on the state's case against Palmer—as you did— then back off after Barlowe's and his girlfriend's murders looked like a syndicate execution. After that, with the manager out of the way, he and Brewer could step right in. The fool did all this without knowing that the syndicate indirectly owns the Manor. I learned of the distant connection when I first approached Barlowe about Johnny and Brewer. He told me that the motel and restaurant weren't doing very well because of its remote location, and that his lease agreement with the syndicate was in jeopardy. Because of the precarious financial status, he agreed to the introduction of an escort service. Then, after I sent some influential clients Johnny's way, Barlowe's money worries were no longer an issue."

Blake stopped and let out a belly laugh, "Of course, the company doesn't make visits like those Kathy described to you, but knowing your addiction to late night movies, I thought that the suggestion of such an overly dramatic scene might strengthen your doubt concerning their involvement. In any case, if Sellers' plan worked, he and Brewer would run the business, and I would take my usual cut while they dealt with the boys from out of town . . . That's if the owners did support the takeover, and you know how that would end up if they didn't. So now that those two idiots are dead, I may be out a little money, but I'll get by."

"All very true. Looks like you've thought of just about everything, except for one small item. What about me? I know you have to kill me, but you can't kill me here . . . How could you possibly explain that? In fact, I may start screaming bloody murder right now."

"Oh, come on, Jimbo, that's not your style. A big tough guy like you crying for help. No, my friend, you're probably coming up with all kinds of ideas as we speak. Besides, you don't think I'd eliminate you without doing something fantastically diabolical, especially after all we've been through together."

He was right and he was wrong: I wouldn't scream bloody murder, but not because of toughness, but due to curiosity. I had to see the play through to the end and how Kathy, most likely alive for the moment, fit into the finale, all the while hoping that there still may be a chance to save her.

Blake chuckled like he was sitting at a bar drinking with his buddies, "Believe it or not, there was a time when I entertained the possibility of letting you go, convincing you and the police that Sellers' and Brewer's explanations were a last-ditch effort to implicate me after ruining their military careers. Once again, I could proclaim you a public hero and thank you for saving my political future, but like I said before, I knew you would never give up. Now, since the police know what Brewer told you, I'll attach a little more blame on the Manor's ownership and clean up the best I can."

"Which includes?"

Blake answered with that intolerable smile.

I hoped our conversation and my questions might give Blake reason to relax as both Sellers and I had back at the Manor. Still standing, only a few feet away from the enemy, with only the desk in my way, I kept talking, acting as cool as possible in the heat of my office, waiting for the right moment to throw my drink in his face and jump. I looked down at my shoes, making the same casual gestures with my hands and arms as I had in the woods before Ben shot Sellers, occasionally turning away from eye contact. I let a little of the Jack slip down my chin then wiped it off, doing anything that might make Blake relax. I wouldn't have to yell for help; Blake would be the one screaming bloody murder.

The time had come. I took a slow breath in . . .

I must have flinched too early. Blake didn't relax as Sellers had; from his lap he grabbed the gun that I didn't see—my .38— and aimed it at my heart.

"No, my friend, it won't be that easy; I found your gun when I took the pad." He shook it at me, "Come on, taped under a drawer, who wouldn't guess that. You know, this is funny in a way. When Sellers showed up and started all the trouble, I remembered how you almost ended my career. I considered your personality and the way you approach your business—tenacity and an astonishing knack for self-preservation—a tough combination to beat. Just for a moment, a very brief moment, I entertained the idea that your ambition might be strong enough for us to join forces. It's sad that you're so damned honest. I could never trust you."

This time I laughed, "You can't trust me because I'm too honest. Mr. State's Attorney, you are definitely in the right line of work."

The corrupt state's attorney's smile disappeared as he let out a sorrowful exhale, "Jimbo, I do hate for our time here to end, but we must take a ride. We have a date with a beautiful girl. Now, change your shirt. I can't have you looking like a bloody victim."

◆ ◆ ◆

After watching me change my blood-stained shirt, Blake led me to his car while maintaining a safe distance behind, obviously aware of my intention to wring his crooked neck if given the chance. As it turned out, his car was the same Mercedes I almost hit leaving Kathy's apartment.

"Nice car. How can you afford such luxury on your salary?"

"I live on a tight budget."

Blake told me to drive while keeping a safe distance away on the passenger's side. At that time, I didn't look for a chance to overpower him because the state's attorney's planning still fascinated me. Even more than that, I wanted to find Kathy, praying that she was still alive so I could somehow persuade her to testify against her boyfriend. Surely Blake's replacement would offer my client a deal if she turned state's evidence.

Blake's flawless final act lay in wait. The cunning state's attorney taught me a lesson about intensive research that I could use in the future—if I had a future. He knew, as I did, that my only chance to stay alive would involve getting close enough to wrestle the gun away. Physically, I had the advantage; more accustomed to tennis and golf, the politician wouldn't have a prayer against a down and dirty street fighter like me. So, how could I outsmart the man who had made no mistakes up to that time? Yet, even as I drove his luxurious car and considered my strategy, he intently stared at me and grinned, "You don't think there's a way in this world that I'm going to let you get near me, do you?"

Blake directed me to the county office building complex, then pointed to a street three blocks away. "Park over there."

"On the street? Why not in the garage?"

"Just do as you're told."

I followed his directions as Sellers had followed mine but slamming on the brakes didn't seem like a practical option. I parked the Mercedes with Blake braced with his back against the passenger side door, all the while taking deadly aim with my .38.

Bide my time. Wait and pray for that opening, that one mistake he hasn't made. But as we walked toward the county complex, still accurately reading my thoughts, Blake kept a safe distance behind until we reached the courtyard.

"Wait a minute," he said.

I stopped and turned to face him. He took an extra step back and smiled.

"Now listen very carefully. Your gun is in my pocket, I want you to walk beside me like we're the best of friends. But if you try anything at all, I will blow you and anyone who happens to be in the lobby to kingdom come. Do you understand?"

I nodded, but not honestly. At that time of the early evening, only an armed desk sergeant would be on duty, so the first chance I had . . .

When we entered the lobby, I realized that any action on my part presented more of a gamble than I was willing to take. Sergeant Polhaus, still recovering from his injury, must have rotated from his desk duty at the jail to Blake's building which by itself would have been good. The complication, as bad luck would have it, was that his wife and young son were with him, most likely waiting for his shift to end.

"Good evening, Sergeant."

"Hello, Mr. Blake. And hello, Jimbo. Are you two joining forces?"

If Blake was surprised that the sergeant knew me, it didn't show. Susan greeted me by name and Lucas ran over to hug me. I helped coach a soccer league that the boy played on at the time.

Jumping Blake would end in disaster, so the play continued.

"That's right, Sergeant, there have been new developments in the syndicate's connection to the Lakeview Manor case. We'll get things straight now that we have Jimbo's help."

"Well, Jim Smith is a man you can depend on, that's for sure."

"And I, too, am sure of that, Sergeant Polhaus." Blake said, "So come on, Jimbo, let's see if we can't put some of these criminals away."

Blake used his left hand to sign the register, then stepped back for me to do the same. I thought of penning the word "help," but didn't want to take any chances with the safety of the Polhaus family.

Once again, I followed Blake's instructions, strolling to the elevator just like he said, as if we were the best of friends. My escort did seem to relax after noticing my friendship with the sergeant and his family, but as soon as the elevator doors opened and we entered, Blake jumped to the corner, pulled out the gun and, once again, aimed it at my heart.

"You know what floor, push the button."

I pressed the button for the seventh floor.

"Your office? Isn't that just a bit risky?"

"Overthinking a situation is one of your few faults, Jimbo. You need to relax and enjoy the ride."

"You politicians sure are good at handing out advice."

"I'm not a politician; I'm a public servant doing my best to make the world a better place in which to live."

"If that means handing out morsels while keeping the big bites for yourself, like that nice German-engineered Mercedes, then you're doing a great job. Shouldn't you buy American? I would think that—as the public servant you claim to be—you'd want to flaunt the appearance of the working man's hero."

"Keep trying, Jimbo; you'll never get under my skin."

The elevator stopped. Blake motioned with the gun for me to go first. He stayed four feet behind as we made our way to his office where a major part of Act III was revealed.

As soon as we walked through the door, Kathy Radney ran over to Blake, hugged, and kissed him, "Where have you been; I didn't think you'd be gone so long. I was scared, Michael."

"Now, now, Kathy," Blake said, never taking his eyes off me, "I keep telling you not to worry. Go over there and sit on the sofa while I take care of our friend here."

"But what are you going to do with him? You haven't told me."

I laughed before Blake could answer.

"What's so funny, Jimbo?"

"Sellers said he was going to let me go so I could get married and raise a family."

Blake shook his head, "What an idiot." Then he kissed Kathy on the cheek, "Go on, baby, sit over there."

Kathy kissed Blake again, turned and smiled at me on her way to the sofa. I had finally met the real Kathy.

"She's something, isn't she, Jimbo?"

Embarrassed that my beautiful client had so easily

exploited me, there was little I could say. Kathy Radney was the actress I suspected but refused to accept her to be.

"I have to admit that I wasn't sure my sweetheart could pull it off, but she came through like a pro."

Kathy blushed as if her part in the play was worthy of a Tony Award for best supporting actress. It became clear that I had little chance of getting her to turn on Blake.

"Now, Mr. Smith, go over there and sit down next to my girl."

"What if I don't?"

"No one is working this late, and the cleaning crew doesn't start until nine. The shot won't be heard."

"What about the blood stain on your carpet?"

Not a problem, as you will soon see. Now sit down." Blake turned and locked the door, his eyes still focused on me. "We don't want to be interrupted, do we."

I chuckled to hide my concern, "Come on, Mr. State's Attorney, let's see what you got."

I sat next to Kathy as Blake commanded and made a quick appraisal of the room. The furnishings were sparse befitting the image of the dedicated public servant Blake pretended to be. Two straight back chairs placed in front of a large wooden desk occupied the center of the room, while against the wall behind the desk, stood two metal file cabinets, and beside them, a second door that led to his secretary's office and a possible means of escape. The sofa where Kathy and I sat was only four feet away from the two chairs which were five feet away from Blake standing beside his desk in front of the second door.

Blake had made his first mistake. Until then, Blake had been very careful to play keep-away so I couldn't get my hands on him. But in this small room that was at most fifteen by twenty, I could jump those four feet, throw one of the two chairs at him, and make a desperate charge. If quick enough, that action could knock the gun from his hand before he fired, or if he did hold on, possibly make it to the second door—hopefully unlocked—before he could get a decent shot at me.

The do-or-die strategy could have worked . . . if there was more time . . . Blake had already made his way behind the desk, "No, Jimbo, I wouldn't try it."

The state's attorney running around in my head annoyed me, but I smiled anyway.

"I gotta hand it to you, man, you are good. Yes, I would give anything to get my hands on you, but you have to tell me . . . how are you going to explain my body? After all the work I've done this past week, you owe me that much."

Blake laughed, "Jimbo, since you'll already be dead, I guess you'll never know."

"Then it shouldn't hurt to tell me how you think you're going to get away with killing me. Come on, Blake, satisfy my curiosity. You can't just leave my body here."

"Of course not, your murder must follow through on Sellers' plan by incriminating the mob in such a way that it will be impossible to doubt their responsibility."

He glanced at, and then I noticed, the large package beside his desk marked: CAMERA EQUIPMENT: DO NOT XRAY! Blake leaned over and laid his hand on the parcel, "Yes, Jimbo, this harmless looking box is very important to your future, and mine. I mailed it to myself from New York."

He paused and stroked the box as if it were a beloved Labrador Retriever.

"In this inconspicuous parcel, rests a particularly interesting incendiary device, one that will not only annihilate most of the seventh floor, and a good bit of the one above, but its detonation will trigger an extremely destructive conflagration, destroying any evidence of my involvement in this regrettable mess that Sellers created. This ingenious piece of handiwork is a credit to intense research, and one that did take some time to assemble. With all the earmarks of a mafia hit, its effect will be so catastrophic that after I'm forced to shoot you—which I'm sure you'll insist upon—no autopsy in the world would find the bullet hole. Ashes to ashes; dust to dust."

"Forensics have come a long way. How can you be so sure they won't come up with something?"

"Not after this explosion and fire; it will effectively cremate you. I doubt that they'll find enough of you to fill a teaspoon, that's if they even bother after I tell them about the death threats I've received."

"I guess you have thought of everything."

"Yes, I do believe I have. So, very soon, I will excuse myself, have Sergeant Polhaus witness my departure, telling him that you stayed behind to keep an eye on Kathy—"

"Keep an eye on me!" Kathy jumped up and shouted. "You can't leave me here with a bomb!"

"Kathy," Blake said calmly, "I told you not to worry; I'll show you how to get out in just a minute. Now please sit down."

Slowly this time, but without the confident smile, Kathy obeyed her lover.

Blake turned his attention back to me, "I'll tell Sergeant Polhaus not to let anyone enter the building until my return because a reliable source told me that the mafia is planning to eliminate Kathy, the last witness whose testimony could hurt them. So, while you're supposedly guarding Kathy, I am going to meet the anonymous informant whose identity is too sensitive to compromise. In a short while, the bomb will detonate, killing the two innocent citizens who willingly risked their lives by challenging the mob—"

"Two!" Kathy shrieked.

"Kathy, stop!" Blake quickly responded to his lover's interruption, "You won't be here. I'm going to hide you where no one will ever find you. Now, I've told you not to worry; I'll tell you about your escape in a minute."

"But how will you account for an assassination attempt so late in the day?" I asked.

"I always work late on Tuesday; it's a matter of public knowledge. Oh, and by the way," Blake continued, "I had the foresight to have the package delivered early this morning, so not only did my secretary sign for it, but anyone who came in my office today saw it sitting there, even your girlfriend. So you see, Jimbo, I have considered every contingency. That is, unless you have something to add."

"Yeah, this is all well and good, but what about the organization taking the blame? Don't you think they'll come after you?"

"I have to tell you, Jimbo, at first I didn't like Sellers' plan to implicate the syndicate, especially since there is that monetary connection to the Manor. But now that their probable guilt is exposed, I can make efficient use of the three murders and this attempt on my life. Think of the national exposure I'm about to get. The FBI will provide me with a bodyguard while I run for the Senate on the platform to eradicate organized crime. Of course, I won't make that much of an effort—just enough to impress the voters, and little enough to pose any threat to the syndicate. Once in the Senate, I'll find other ways to impress the public."

"And what about Brewer's and Sellers' stories that implicate you? I told the police all that they said. Doesn't that contradict your syndicate implication?"

"Remember what I said in your office: those two dimwits were grasping at straws by trying to incriminate me. They wanted revenge. Not far from the truth as far as Sellers is concerned. Then, as for the mafia, this attempt on my life is retaliation after my public promise to expose them. Remember, Jimbo, you attended my little press conference after Palmer's release. Besides, like I said before; do you really think they'll bother after today? Any investigation into today's explosion would uncover absolutely nothing because there's nothing to uncover. Time will pass and the motel along with its escort business at the Manor will either resume or shut down completely. Any further attempts on my life will only attract more attention to their operations. No syndicate wants that kind of exposure."

Out of ideas, but still waiting for the right moment to attack, I said nothing. There must be some way to frustrate the state's attorney's plan, but what? Then I noticed the sofa shaking. It appeared that Kathy wasn't comfortable with her lover's plan.

"Okay," I nodded toward Kathy, now noticeably apprehensive, "How do you know your girlfriend will stand by you? Are you positive that she's the love who would never betray you?"

He looked at Kathy and smiled, "I don't believe she would."

I turned to face my deceitful client. "Kathy, what makes you think your boyfriend won't get rid of you after he takes care of me? How's he going to hide you where no one can find you? And with all his ambition, do you really think he'll keep a prostitute around?"

"I'm no prostitute."

"You screwed me quick enough."

"I did that because Michael told me to." Her voice began to

quiver. "Don't you see, everything I did, I did because that's what Michael wanted me to do."

"That's my point, Kathy. Your reputation—"

"That's enough, Jimbo," Blake snapped.

"No, it's not enough. Kathy, listen to me—"

"I said shut up, Smith!"

"He's wrong, isn't he, darling," Kathy said as she squirmed in her seat. "You know I'll do anything for you. You said my job at the Manor can be explained. Please tell him he's wrong."

The state's attorney opened the center drawer of his desk. "Hold on, sweetheart. I'll show you how I'm going to silence our friend here."

Blake put my .38 in his pocket then pulled out another gun from the drawer, this one with a silencer attached. "Just in case," he said, then pointed the deadly weapon at my head.

I looked at Kathy who looked at me and snickered, "See. I knew he wouldn't hurt me."

My last thought would have been *"What a cold-hearted bitch"* until I heard the silenced muffle of the shot that passed through Kathy's skull.

I jumped up and grabbed one of the two chairs from the front of his desk; but before I could throw it, Blake aimed at my heart, "No, no, Jimbo."

I'll never understand why Blake hesitated. He should have pulled the trigger as soon as he turned his aim my way and I would have been as dead as my client. Instead, he gave me an arrogant smile as if pleased with himself for the murder he had just committed. He even took a moment to glance at Kathy's lifeless body like an artist admiring his work. Then he smiled even more broadly at me and slowly raised the gun.

In the brief moment that seemed like an eternity, time stood still like a freeze-frame from a broken movie reel. My adrenaline boiled, igniting the blood that raced through my veins. My hands tightened on the chair that I was about to hurl in desperation as I prayed that the bullet would only wound me when . . .

A crash at the door, followed by a roar from Ben.

*"God Dammit!"*

Ben's attempt to break in the door failed but provided enough distraction that I had time to throw the chair before Blake got off the shot that flew past my head, hitting the picture of him and President Carter on the wall behind me. Ben's second attempt turned out to be more successful as he burst through the door, knocking it off the remaining hinges.

"Police, Blake. Drop the gun."

No longer did time seem like an eternity, but the speeding blur of a split-second. Blake fell back when the chair hit him but nimbly jumped up and pointed his gun at Ben standing by the door. I shoved the heavy desk against him as he fired, but Blake's shot hit Ben before he could shoot back. Cursing at both of us, Blake escaped into the adjacent office through the second door.

"Dammit," Ben swore again.

I jumped up and ran over to the man who had just saved my life, nervously searching for the wound, "Man you have no will power at all. What did Mrs. Quincannon tell you about that potty mouth?"

"Well, dammit, how the hell did I let him get that shot off?"

"You said we were getting slow; maybe you should retire."

Ben reached for his right side where he and I felt the warm

texture of blood.

"Dammit to hell," he said.

"Dammit is right. Ben, you big baby, he barely nicked you." More than I told him, the wound bled quite a bit, but like so many similar wounds I'd seen before, it didn't look life-threatening. "It would have been worse if I didn't shove the desk against him. He was aiming at your heart."

"Yeah, you're a real hero; now go after the son-of-a-bitch."

"No way. I'm getting you out of here; that package by the desk is a bomb."

"No, I'm all right," Ben looked at Kathy's lifeless body, "I'll get her and call the bomb squad from downstairs."

"Okay, but leave her, just get yourself out."

Ben smiled, "You know I never leave evidence at a crime scene. Now get your ass out of here. But Jimbo, be careful, dammit."

"There you go again. I can't wait to see Louise."

Ben handed me his gun.

"You expect me to use this heavy son-of-a-bitch?"

"It's better than that toy you have. Now stop wasting time."

I ran down the corridor and from there to the exit for the stairs. Blake had to be aware that the police would have taken over the lobby by then, so he most likely made his way to the roof and a possible means of escape to another building.

Following Ben's advice, I cautiously opened the door to the stairs. The corrupt state's attorney could be waiting for me and no way did I want to play the hostage role again. I stepped into the stairwell, my head on a swivel, looking for any sign of movement while listening for even the slightest sound. Nothing. I climbed the steps and looked down the hall of the eighth floor, but doubting that he would stop there, I started up the last staircase.

Suddenly, like my experience in the woods at the Manor, anxiety and confusion from the past struck. The same labored breathing, my heart racing. A knot squeezed my guts as the silence pounded in my ears. It was bad this time. Worse than before, the shadow of the jungle attacked again, but with more intensity. I collapsed on the step, struggling to catch my breath and trying to convince myself that I wasn't chasing a Vietnamese soldier, but another kind of enemy.

Still gasping for air, I staggered up the stairs to the roof like climbing a hill in Nam. I pushed the bar on the door. It wasn't locked. Too easy. The last few days proved that, like the firefights in the jungle, desperate men take desperate action. Blake had only two options available: give himself up, or escape by jumping onto the roof of one of the adjacent buildings in the county complex before the police closed in.

Of course, there was one other alternative: murder me, the nemesis who destroyed his future. Desperate men. Desperate actions. Didn't Thoreau say something about desperation?

*Not now, concentrate on now.*

My focus responded to another adrenaline rush. I caught my breath and burst through the door onto the hot roof that felt like thick jungle grass, rolling until a vent stopped me. Lying there motionless for what seemed like another eternity, still intently listening for a noise of any kind, I heard only my labored breathing.

After repeating a short prayer, a petition for help, the gravel on the roof slowly replaced the jungle floor that wasn't there . . . but the odor remained, that toxic sense of danger that foreshadows the imminent threat of death.

With my breathing finally under control, silence returned. Not even the whisper of a breeze. The early evening business lights from the street below created faint eerie shadows. Indistinct voices I assumed to be policemen echoed from the other buildings, but nothing else. Could Blake have escaped before they took position? Anyone could make the jump to either of the two buildings that were only feet away.

"Blake," I called.

No response.

"I know you're there, Blake. The cops are all around. You can't get away."

Nothing. Maybe he did make that jump.

"Answer me, dammit. There's no escape. Give it up."

The voices from the other roof paused. Had they seen something, or did they stop because they heard my voice?

"Blake, I'm going back and lock the door behind me. Sooner or later the cops will close in. You shot one of their own. What are the odds they won't blow your sorry ass to kingdom come. Giving up is the only thing that will keep you off the coroner's table. You've used up all your contingencies, man. There's no way you can dream up some other trick that'll get you out of this mess. Give it up, Blake. Give it up now!"

Finally, a voice drifted out of the shadows, "Okay . . . Wait a minute."

In the dim light, next to a large air conditioner, I saw a hazy figure moving, then Blake's full body as he stood. He threw out the silenced gun and raised his hands, "I guess you win."

"It's not a win with all the dead bodies you left behind."

"Well, think about it, Jimbo, if it weren't for you, Barlowe and his girlfriend would have been the last. That damn stubborn nature of yours gummed up the works from the beginning. Maybe I was wrong choosing you."

I stood and slowly walked toward him, "I guess that's one way of looking at it."

I didn't expect what happened next. Like the strategy I used on Sellers at the Manor and tried to use on the state's attorney in my office, Blake must have thought our banter would relax me, taking my mind off the danger. He was almost right.

Barely visible in the dim light, on the air conditioner unit next to him, about waist high, lay my gun. His body jerked as he grabbed it, aimed, and fired. Blake got off two shots. I felt a stinging burn on my forehead as I dropped to the ground, firing back in a wild pattern three or four times. I never knew for sure, but at least two rounds from Ben's pistol hit the crooked politician as their impact drove him backward and off the roof. State's Attorney Michael Blake screamed as he fell until silenced with the dull thud of his body hitting the pavement nine stories below.

I got up, walked over to the ledge, and looked down at the corpse illuminated in the streetlights when that part of Thoreau's quote came to mind: *Why should we be in such desperate haste to succeed, and in such desperate enterprises?*

The sickening sight of the deceased and the burning on the right side of my head made me a bit woozy, so I turned away from the roof's edge. I touched the insignificant wound that, if his aim had been better, would have fulfilled Blake's climax for the last act of his drama.

*Ben! I've got to find Ben.*

I ran toward the stairs where Sergeant Polhaus met me.

"Not this way; the bomb squad's still working."

"I've got to get to Ben."

233

"Don't worry about him; he's more concerned about you, and he won't leave until he knows you're safe."

We crossed over to the justice building, a short jump—one of the two Blake could have used for an escape—then down the elevator to the lobby and outside to the courtyard. Over by the road, at the back of an ambulance, Ben was lying on a stretcher with an IV in his arm. I started to run over but had to stop for the body bag that most likely contained Kathy Radney to pass. To this day, I wonder if she were devil or angel, opportunist or pawn. Sam Spade sent Brigid O'Shaughnessy to the gallows; because she loved Blake that much, Kathy would have only gone to jail. It hurts to think that if she had only trusted me from the beginning . . .

I turned away and sprinted over to Ben.

"How goes it, big guy?"

"How do you think? I took a bullet for you."

"Like hell you did. Blake was aiming at you. I saved your sorry ass when I shoved the desk. Besides, if you'd been strong enough to break in the door the first time, I could have jumped him."

"No way, Jimbo. You'd have been dead by then, and anyway —"

The medic interrupted our debate, "Look, I hate to break up this emotional reunion, but if we don't get Sergeant Quincannon to the hospital, he might bleed to death." Then, turning my head, "And I'll fix your wound on the way."

"What happened to you?" Ben said.

"I got this doing your job."

"That's enough, gentlemen." The medic wanted no more bickering.

I followed Ben's stretcher into the ambulance where, true to his word, the medic bandaged my wound on the way to the hospital. Ben stopped arguing and lost consciousness which worried me until I realized that it was the painkillers taking effect. When I looked at the medic, he smiled, "It was the only way to shut him up."

At the hospital, a team rushed Ben to surgery while a nurse escorted me to an exam room where she removed the medic's bandage and reexamined my head wound.

"Do you have any other injuries?" Forgetting about Sellers' near miss, I told her no.

She applied a clean bandage and gave me a shot. No longer able to control my emotions, my shoulders shook as I began to cry.

"He'll be all right," she said, placing a consoling arm around my shoulder, "I'll take you to a place where you can wait. Mrs. Quincannon is already there."

I pulled myself together and followed her to the waiting room where Louise sat silently praying, the prayers obvious to me because Ben's wife has a particular glow whenever she talks to God. She sensed my presence before I could speak and rushed over to greet me with a hug.

"Shouldn't this be the other way around?"

"James, we are all in the hands of the Lord. Ben will be fine."

We sat together on a couch where Louise recited prayers that were more biblical than conversational while I quietly whispered my usual spontaneous dialogue that contained more questions than appeals. Less than an hour later, the doctor came in.

"Sergeant Quincannon is in recovery and doing fine. Your

husband is a lucky man, Mrs. Quincannon, the bullet missed all the vital organs. He'll sleep through the night, but you'll be able to see him in a little bit."

Louise looked at me and smiled, "God's will."

Not long after that, Ben was taken from recovery to his room. A nurse came to get Louise who immediately held out her hand to me. I broke down again when I saw him lying in bed, blaming myself. Sensing the guilt, Louise put her arm around me, "Don't punish yourself; Providence has a hand in all that happens."

"You know this is typical for me . . . a Quincannon always coming to the rescue."

"My Lord, James, please don't refer to me by that darn name. I almost didn't marry Ben because of that darn name."

We both laughed because "darn" is the closest you'll ever hear Louise Quincannon come to any kind of inappropriate language.

A nurse came in and noticed the bloodstain on my shirt that reappeared from the first bullet I dodged that day.

"Let me look at that, Mr. Smith."

"Not necessary, nurse." I looked at Louise, "Thanks to Providence, it's only a scratch. I'll go home and put some peroxide on it."

I kissed Louise and left for home. On the way out of the hospital, I met Nora running down the hall toward me.

"Where have you been? I've been looking all over for you." Hugging me tightly, she pulled away far enough to touch the bandage on my head, "Are you all right?"

"Yes, I was with Ben and Louise."

Nora began to cry. "I heard someone was shot. I was afraid

you were killed."

"Mine is barely a scratch, Ben's was worse, but he's out of danger. We can come back tomorrow. Let's go home."

I spent the night with Nora at her place. Not only did I sleep without waking that night, but it was the first time Nora and I had ever laid together without making love.

# WEDNESDAY

## August 22, 1979

It was after seven in the evening as I sat at my desk recording the previous week's events in my journal. Nora and I spent the better part of the day visiting Ben and Louise at the hospital. The doctor said that Ben could go home in a week and back to work on limited duty in about a month, but it would be a little longer before he could work out or play golf. Ben immediately warned me not to touch a club until he was back in shape. Louise whispered "meatloaf" in my ear, and I got the message. Ben would win as long as she fed me. Some of my ethics are so easily compromised.

At the end of the day, I was pleased with the outcome of the case, but the death of so many troubled me, nonetheless. If Ben hadn't burst through the door when he did, if I hadn't been fast enough to turn away from Sellers' gun in the woods, or if Blake had been quicker with his shot on the roof, I might have been included in the body count.

Sergeant Polhaus was responsible for Ben's timely appearance. Not long after I left the Manor, Ben became worried that I might do something typically irrational, so to keep track of my movements, he put out an APB for Lloyd Thursby known to frequent the Muddy Water Inn. Thursby was a drug pusher and pimp I traced to the infamous tavern and sent to jail. Blake and I had just entered the elevator when Sergeant Polhaus heard and understood the cryptic message, so he contacted Ben who told him to keep an eye on things until he arrived. Whether their actions were the hand of Providence, as Louise believed, or just good police work, didn't concern me.

As a side note, I heard that Barton Hamilton used Blake's planned excuse citing revenge as Sellers' motive to implicate him—only in his case, it worked. The congressman claimed that Blake persuaded him to find work for Sellers in California as a benevolent gesture for the man they sent to the brig. He denied having any involvement in the black-market operation in Thailand or in Sellers' prostitution business. The congressman also denied having any knowledge of Blake's illegal involvement with Hodges, the foul-mouthed bartender, or the fat scumbag, Tony Sellers. Ironically, a couple years later, Hamilton would be indicted for tampering with federal contracts but received a light sentence after he ratted on a couple of his co-conspirators. Three weeks after his imprisonment, Hamilton was found dead in his cell. Like Mr. Joe said: "What goes around, comes around."

As I finished polishing my journal, the room darkened with the approach of a late summer storm heralding the arrival of a welcome cold front. The wind kicked up, blowing hard and violent through my office, banging the blinds on the sills of the windows I didn't want to close. The breeze, though furious at times, felt good considering the oppressive heat of the last few weeks. An occasional lightning bolt illuminated the room. The wind calmed, and the rain began to pour. I closed my journal, turned off the fan on my desk, then leaned back and relaxed as the summer storm raged outside.

Much too drained to accept another case, I chose to ignore the knock on the door, even though I could have used the money after leaving the envelope with Kathy's final payment on her bed. I closed my eyes, but quickly opened them when I heard the door slowly open. Three men stood in the doorway, all too similar to those from the previous Saturday night.

*When will I ever learn to lock that damn door?*

My instincts, and the lessons learned in the last few days, told me to grab my gun. I reached under the drawer but came up empty because that was the .38 that Blake had taken, and which now occupied a space in the police evidence locker. Could this really be happening, and could they be . . .

"May I come in?"

"Looks like you're halfway there."

The familiar figure walked over while the other two again waited by the door. He sat down in the worn chair that Kathy Radney occupied when the Lakeview Manor case began.

"We met the other night, but I neglected to introduce myself. My name is Robert Hogan, I represent Freeport Warehousing."

*Good God. These aren't actors; Blake didn't send them either. They're real, and now the gangster owners of the Manor are going to take care of their final piece of business. What the hell am I going to do?*

"Mr. Smith, I'm sure that you are quite tired, so I will immediately address the reason for my visit."

He set his briefcase on my desk and slowly opened it. I looked at the two men in the doorway who hadn't moved and decided that, if I had any chance at all, I could casually stand, then sprint to the open window next to my desk where I could break through the screen and jump down to the bushes one story below hoping they would cushion my fall giving me enough time to get away. That's if I didn't break any bones from my desperate attempt. But before I had the chance to rise from my seat, Mr. Hogan took a small piece of paper from the briefcase.

"My clients are very pleased with the manner in which you conducted yourself throughout the investigation of the Lakeview Manor. As I told you, Mr. Barlowe was innocent, and if the matter had been closed with his unfortunate death, my clients would have endured unwanted and undeserved scrutiny. Because of your refusal to accept the obvious frame, the company will be spared that inconvenience. Please accept this check as payment for your services."

He handed me the check that I read with the aid of a lighting flash.

"I don't mean to sound ungrateful, but five thousand dollars is entirely too generous."

"On the contrary, my clients have paid twice that amount with less successful results. Thanks to you, we will now replace the management at the Manor with no further interference from the authorities."

Thanking Mr. Hogan, I put the check in my desk. We stood together and shook hands.

"Here is my card. Call if there is ever a need. Oh, and by the way, your next dinner at the Manor is on the house."

I smiled at his generosity and was left alone to enjoy the majesty of the summer storm that brought welcome relief from the heat.

# ACKNOWLEDGEMENT

To My wife, Mary, the Harford Writers Group,
and a special thank you to Katie Sank, without whose skill
and guidance Lakeview would have never made it to print.

# ABOUT THE AUTHOR

## Jim Wheeler

Jim Wheeler is from Baltimore, Maryland, has a BS in English from Towson University and an MLA from The College of Notre Dame University. After spending four years in the Air Force, Jim wrote human-interest articles for local papers while working thirty-eight years on the Baltimore waterfront. Jim retired to devote his time to writing and unintentionally driving his wife insane. He and his wife live in Jarrettsville, Maryland and enjoy spending time with their son and his family.